The Button Boy

The Button Boy

Lawrence Kadow

To order additional copies of this book, contact:
Xlibris Corporation
1-888-795-4274
www.Xlibris.com
Orders@Xlibris.com
86684

To My Friends That Inspired and Helped

Roni Fisher

Alaine Borgias

Marshall Seaman

Peter Smith

Jason Stoane

Jack

Shaun

Reivers

&

Lara

Skylers Map of Ferndale

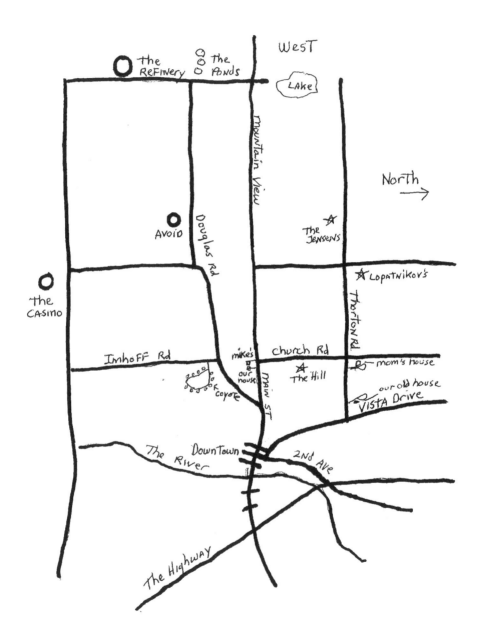

Chapter 1

Mid-September 2030

Without taking his eyes off the two shadows, James reached down and quietly picked up an arrow. By touch, he fit the nock onto the string of his compound bow. The intruders were not totally visible, but he could see their shapes within the nearby stand of dead alders. If they were to step out from the trees, their moon shadows would be visible against the late summer grass. They had remained still long enough for the frogs to begin croaking again. It would have been so easy just to reach down and pick up his night vision monocular, if only to confirm what he thought he was seeing—the batteries were rechargeable and he did have a solar charger, so that wasn't the problem. His fear was that the reflection of moonlight from the lens would give his position away. The same moonlight that could expose them could expose his location.

He stayed focused on where he thought the two figures were. The frogs went silent once again; the pair was on the move. Finally he saw them step into the field at the edge of the trees. They were coming close to the forty-yard range. James was accurate at this distance—he had hunted extensively with a bow and this was no different. His heart raced. He knew that he had the advantage over them. But it was what he didn't know that made him nervous.

Simultaneously, the two visitors froze in their tracks. They had to have felt him watching them, or maybe they were just inexperienced at raiding and too scared to move forward. Though he couldn't discern their clothing, from their close proximity to one another, it was obvious to James that they weren't the military raiders. More than likely they were two really hungry survivors that needed to feed their families. Besides, James thought, the military guys didn't need to sneak about at night. They had enough firepower to take what they wanted in broad daylight; no one dared challenge them.

James was hoping that these men would reconsider their quest. He didn't have a clue as to their identity and he didn't care; he just wanted them to leave his house alone. Since the change, James had been able to avoid killing or even wounding anyone. In fact, he avoided any human contact as much as possible. It was just safer that way. And he felt more secure by keeping a constant watch.

He wasn't sure of the exact date, but he knew that the first day of fall was close at hand. It would also be his thirty-ninth birthday. James cursed himself for not keeping better track of the days. Calendars were rare and he hadn't seen one since before last winter's storm. Considering the conditions, keeping track of time wasn't a necessary part of survival.

Only a few weeks earlier, the midnight hours had been warm enough that he hadn't needed a coat during his watch. The smells had also changed as the dryness of the summer gave way to autumn rains. Now, most of the nights were overcast and damp, the field a sea of blackness, so it was fortunate for James that these two had chosen tonight, one of the coldest, clearest nights since he'd started regular watches to protect his place. He wouldn't have been able to spot them otherwise. The chill didn't bother him much; at least there was no wind. He had huddled outside his home, even in the wind and rain for most of the last four months. Anymore, it was careless not to keep a constant watch through the nights. Most nights were uneventful, and sometimes Lara would sit with him, though they were cautious to keep their talk to a minimum. Mostly James stood his watch alone, since Lara was his relief every morning: the nights were her time to rest and the mornings his.

A shadow moved. They were inching closer once again and looked to be headed toward the garden in his back yard. Maybe they just wanted some vegetables, James thought, or maybe they had more in mind and were there to kill him and rape Lara. Either way, they weren't welcome. Using a bow in the dark gave James the advantage: if he took out one of the raiders, he would have plenty of time to draw and shoot another arrow before the second raider even knew which direction he was being attacked from.

James swallowed hard. Thinking about killing someone was entirely different than really doing it and it was difficult for him to attack someone that hadn't yet caused him any harm. He also knew that killing a person meant he was likely killing someone responsible for feeding others. Even wounding someone could have a dire result. There was nowhere to get treated or buy the drugs necessary to fight infection. After so many months protecting what little he had, James still wasn't ready to have another's death on his conscience. His first thought was to shout a warning, give the two the opportunity to walk away unharmed. But James knew this wouldn't be strong enough; they could try a different route on another night. Hunger can make you do things you normally wouldn't. If he was going to let them live, he needed to instill some fear in them.

He quietly set the bow on the deck and pulled out his .22 caliber pistol. Since long before the change, he had stockpiled plenty of ammunition for this gun, but rarely did he use it. Tonight he would make an exception. He lifted the weapon and aimed it not toward the two men, but towards their path. Their silhouettes didn't move gracefully; they were probably weak from hunger. When they continued a little closer, he fired two quick rounds into the ground. After what seemed like a full second of pandemonium, James watched as both raiders retreated in an all-out run back to the stand of dead wood; their shadows eventually disappearing in the darkness. He breathed a sigh of relief, a moment of calm, and then jolted back to alertness. He clicked on his portable Hasbro G.I. Joe two-way radio and listened.

After about fifteen seconds, he heard, "Neighbor eight to Neighbor twelve, are you secure?" blurt through his radio.

James pressed a button and replied, "All is clear" before turning the power back off. The voice on the radio was his neighbor, Mike. James had tried to broach a friendship with him, but soon realized the two of them were from different worlds. In fact, James relationship with Mike had become strained shortly after moving in. Despite their differences, he found a sense of security knowing that the west side of his house was guarded. He never doubted Mike's ability to do his job. If those two raiders had wandered towards Mike's house, James thought to himself, he probably would have shot them and bragged about it afterwards.

Mike was the only other person connected with James' G.I Joe radio system. In fact, he was the only one besides Lara that James communicated with. Even then, their interactions were few and far between. That was the way both men wanted it. There were no other neighbors, but Mike had insisted that they use 'Neighbor eight' and 'Neighbor twelve' as their call signals. If some bad guys were listening in on their broadcasts, Mike had said, they would think that there was a whole network of armed neighbors ready to defend what is theirs. James looked at the now-silent radio and shook his head. Bad guys. That was Mike's term for all others. James didn't agree with this. Not everyone was bad. And being hungry didn't make you a bad guy.

A few seconds after James clicked off his radio, Lara appeared in the open window to his left. The shots had obviously woken her. James gave her a thumbs-up signal. She nodded sleepily and stood there just long enough to verify that the world was not coming to an abrupt end before returning to her bed. He felt a twinge of guilt for interrupting her sleep. She didn't look too alarmed, so James didn't go inside to calm her. Lara's stability was a priority to him; she'd helped him get through a very tough time. He hoped that she would soon fall asleep and forget what happened.

Come morning, watching the house would be her responsibility. But just watch. She had instructions that should anyone come too close, she was to wake him with three shots from the pistol, but not attempt to shoot anyone. Although they had been together since the previous winter, and they'd been through a lot since they first met, they weren't lovers. Like James, Lara was a survivor, and surviving was easier together. They each filled a void in the other's life. At times, their lives seemed to be balanced on the head of a pin. If one of them was to die or otherwise leave, the remaining partner would have a much greater difficulty surviving. Like them, others had joined together for survival purposes. James couldn't remember how long it had been since he had seen a lone wanderer out on the main road. It just wasn't practical in these new times. He was fortunate and content to have paired up with Lara.

Time passed slowly on the nights he sat outside guarding their shelter. It would have been easier if he could read a book or use the time constructively—they had a headlamp and rechargeable batteries— but he couldn't risk wearing it; he'd be seen on the deck from several hundred yards. Books, the only luxury left for them, were saved for those times when he and Lara sat out together in the evening sun—even on the brisker autumn evenings. He smiled to himself; she always became so absorbed as he read aloud. It was the only way that she could escape the fear, and James took pride in this therapy, an escape for both of them. There was no shortage of books; they were plentiful if you searched the damaged houses.

As the dark sky became enhanced with the hint of dawn, James could view the fields much easier. The landscape looked like a tornado had passed through. None of the trees were standing anymore, and debris from vacant houses was strewn everywhere. On rainy days it looked worse. When he wasn't guarding his and Lara's place, or taking his few hours rest, he spent his time cutting firewood, hunting, and preparing the house for winter. Firewood was plentiful for now, but without any living trees, there'd come a winter without fuel. James didn't like to think about it, especially after the last, nearly unbearable winter, when nothing was intended to survive but somehow a handful of people did. Instead he focused his energies on putting up as much firewood and food as possible for what was ahead. He was determined to be better prepared.

Despite last winter's hit to the surviving population in his corner of the Pacific Northwest, James still found it was necessary to keep his guard high to protect what was his. Money and gold and other things that used to indicate wealth no longer had any value. Not that he had any of those things. The only things that could keep you in the game were food and weapons. He included shelter in that list, but not everyone did. James found that there were two types of survivors: those that established a place to live, and those that wandered through looking. The wandering ones were the most dangerous. The house he now considered his and Lara's wasn't really his, and it didn't matter anymore that he wasn't the owner. When he'd come upon it, it wasn't occupied, no one left alive that cared, so he'd acquired it. It was far safer than his previous house, too, with three sides open to the fields beyond, and the fourth side backed by another house—Mike's. When James found the place, the doors and windows had already been boarded up. He kept the lower half of the house sealed. If an intruder wanted in, he would be forced to ascend the outside stairs to the second floor.

As the dawn was fully underway James took one last look around. He stood and stretched his back and legs, then headed through the back door and into the bedroom to wake Lara for her turn as the sentry. Without speaking, he knew that she'd had difficulty going back to sleep; she appeared more tired than usual.

"Sorry about the shots."

"What did you see?"

"Just two guys working their way toward our garden. I needed to scare them away and I didn't want them coming any closer."

Her short blonde hair looked like it had been through a battle. She kept it cropped intentionally, and she only wore men's clothes. With her thin frame, it was easy to mistake her as a male from a distance. That was intentional too. There were few women left alive in the northwest and Lara did not want to bring attention to herself. Like James, she avoided human contact as much as possible.

James waited outside the bathroom, listening as Lara poured water into the toilet to flush it. She handed the empty bucket out to him, which he carried into the kitchen to place back under the sink; he'd removed the drain pipes so that their wash water would flow into the bucket instead; this 'gray water' was handy for flushing their only working toilet. They counted themselves lucky: their last house didn't even have a functioning toilet. Instead they had used a bucket with a toilet seat resting on it. James thought about the foul smell that constantly lingered in that house. This new house was a big improvement.

On the counter stood a five-gallon gas can that held their fresh water. James lifted it and gave it a shake: it needed to be refilled, so he headed with it to the back door. There, he grabbed the small crossbow he'd modified for bird hunting and set out down the hill towards a narrow trail that snaked through the same stand of dead alders the intruders had passed through. Once he was clear of the small dead trees, the narrow path led into an open field with tall grass in its terminal phase before winter. Seeing the grass for the first time had given him hope; it meant that not *everything* had died. It was in this field that he'd discovered the drainage pond. It was almost impossible to see since it was surrounded by a dirt berm that concealed it from all sides, and James had literally stumbled upon it in his search for water. It was obvious to him that the pond had been made for a housing development that had never gotten off the ground. Over the last decade, he recalled a lot of construction projects had been started but never finished; a futile attempt to rescue the economy. He soon learned that some migratory waterfowl had also survived. They would land there only to rest on its waters through the night and usually left shortly after dawn. Other than grass, there was nothing there worth staying for.

On most mornings, with his crossbow in hand, he would walk down to the nearest berm and creep up over its edge. He stayed hidden behind a barricade that he'd built. Sometimes there would be ducks, but not all the time. This morning he counted four Mallards, more than he had seen at one time in weeks, and hoped it was a sign that the fall migration was underway. Almost instantly he felt the nervousness of a gambler. He briefly paused to sum up the situation—experience dictated that if you took your time, you'd lose your chance—before rising and shooting the bolt in the direction of the nearest drake. The crossbow was incredibly accurate at this short range, and the bolt he shot had been modified with a three-pronged frog gig that stuck to its target like Velcro. The notched end of the bolt was attached to a long string of fishing line that exited from beneath the crossbow, ideal for retrieving a bird if it ended up very far from shore. No sooner had he shot the crossbow, he stood up to scare the surviving ducks into fleeing away from him. The pond was long and narrow, so naturally the ducks would leave the water in a direction that was easiest; they almost ran across the surface towards the opposite end of the pond. As quickly as James stood up, he kicked a block of wood that he'd wedged behind the barricade. As engineered, a large rock about the size of a human head dropped from a pole at the other end of the pond. Suddenly, a fine nylon fish net sprang up right in the path of the fleeing ducks. While the drake managed to escape, the two hens didn't have enough height to clear the net and became entangled. James ran over and without hesitation twisted their necks. Three ducks in one morning made for a very good day, considering that his weekly average was only two.

James was grateful for the pond. It had been his and Lara's main source of meat since moving here, and he hunted as often as possible since he didn't have a way to keep meat more than a few days. Stores no longer existed, groceries were a thing of the past, but he had stockpiled, and carefully rationed, some staples like oatmeal, rice, flour, and sugar. The pond was also a source of drinking water for the rare times when rainwater wouldn't meet their needs. He didn't like the pond water; it had to be boiled and it never tasted clean. Sunshine was nice but rain was their lifeblood. After resetting the net for the next morning and filling the gas can with water, James picked up his ducks and headed back towards the house, his mind on ways to improve the trap. One duck had escaped today. One duck too many.

The trip between the pond and house always made him a little nervous. The daylight and the open field left him exposed, plus he was awfully far from the house. So while he left the smaller .22 caliber with Lara every day, he kept a large caliber pistol with him just in case something unexpected happened. Most anyone left alive had guns and knew how to use them. He climbed the small rise that both his and Mike's houses sat upon and quietly stepped up onto his neighbor's rear deck. It was obvious that Mike had a full view of the field and the trail leading to the pond, and had he wanted to terminate James—it would have been easy. For that reason alone, James occasionally shared his bounty with Mike. He tapped gently on the back door. Cindy, Mike's housemate, pulled open the door and stepped out; making it obvious that Mike was probably already asleep. James handed her one of the hens.

"I got lucky this morning," was all that he needed to say.

Cindy only smiled back. She was somewhere in her early sixties. James didn't understand—or even care—how the two had come together or shared the same house. She was unique in that she did nothing to engage in or stimulate conversation. However, Cindy could grow vegetables like she was born to do it, with numerous small gardens spread out in the half acre behind the house, well-concealed from the road. James had come to expect that whenever he dropped a duck off with Mike and Cindy, Cindy would return the favor in a day or two with a small basket of vegetables. James came to the conclusion that Mike needed Cindy's vegetables and Cindy needed Mike's protection, and that was as far as that relationship was going to grow. It was in a way how things were between James and Mike—distant but symbiotic. James knew Mike never hunted and suspected that he had hoarded a supply of canned meats; he'd once caught Mike burying some empty tins.

With his morning tasks done, James walked the remaining fifty feet to the back of his place. He was tired. The all-night vigil always left him that way. Once he reached the deck, he laid the two ducks on a table where Lara would find them, and turned to scan the area. He spotted her out in their garden looking for ripe tomatoes. Recently, this had become an obsession of hers. The summer's growing season had been so short that the tomatoes weren't turning red, and the first frost would probably arrive within two weeks. Maybe next summer's crop would turn red. Their beets and carrots were doing fine and were almost ready to harvest. Any food was better than nothing. His worry, one he didn't share with Lara, pertained to the soldiers.

Skyler had returned for a day just three days prior. He told James of reports that the military were harvesting whatever they could get their hands on for the upcoming winter—and their type of harvesting didn't involve gardening or any friendly trading. Each encounter with the soldiers terrified James. Once, he had shared some beans with them without letting on that he had more. They also didn't know that Lara existed and he intended to keep it that way. But with the garden harvest underway, it would be difficult to hide their stores. If he lied and they found out, losing their stores would be only half the punishment.

He hefted the gas can up on the kitchen counter and picked up a nearby pencil. Searching about briefly he found an old blank strip of paper and jotted down a message for Lara. It gave instructions that if Skyler showed up, she should wake him right away. His long night and short morning completed, James headed into the bedroom to get some sleep before the sun set once again.

Chapter 2

Almost ten months earlier, on the last day of November in 2029, a woman walked through the streets of Ferndale. She carried a shopping bag in each hand. The sky was overcast, without the threat of rain, and the air was much colder than it should have been. Her attire, a bright red coat— formal and clearly not intended to protect someone from the elements— made her look out of place in the small town. She was tall and attractive. Yet, despite what she projected, she was scared. She didn't want to be here. Occasionally, she turned her head to make sure that she wasn't being stalked. Over the last few months, she had grown to fear the downtown. The types of people it drew were not to her liking; she saw them as uncaring. The only reason she was here was because she was looking for a food vendor. Only a few weeks earlier, you couldn't cross the road without being accosted by one looking to "sell" what they had. So much had changed in such a short span of time.

Each of the two bags she carried concealed a Wal-Mart brand gallon of gasoline, sealed and ready to use as a commodity. They had cost her almost twenty-five dollars apiece two years earlier. Last spring she'd begun using her stockpile of gas to trade for food; it was the only thing of value that she could barter with. After she traded these, she'd only have two more left and then she'd be without anything to pay for food—which had become so scarce and expensive. Only two weeks earlier, a gallon of gas was worth ten pounds of food in a fair trade. There was always someone that needed the gas since it was no longer available. All the pumping stations were closed up.

Today, though, she was willing to accept ten pounds of food for *both* gallons of gas just so she could get off the street and back home. She was very cold and the little town was uncomfortably deserted, almost as if something had chased everyone away; there were no traders. Her son had been waiting for her since morning, waiting for her promised return before dark with something to eat. She thought of the hopeful look on his face. Neither of them had eaten in three days. Shivering, as she felt the coldness penetrate her coat, she realized that if she didn't find someone to trade with soon, she would be forced to return home empty handed.

She left First Avenue and walked down Main to Second Avenue without seeing a soul. There was simply no one around. Businesses had long ago closed up, the buildings exoskeletons of a once thriving culture, but usually there would be some people around buying and selling food and other necessities. Where were they, she thought. Finally, she made her way to Third Avenue. In a line of abandoned cars, she spotted an SUV with someone in the driver's seat. She walked closer. The license plate caught her eye. It was from British Columbia. She was aware that many Canadians were leaving Canada for warmer climates, especially now that the border was no longer manned by guards and traveling south was undeterred. She quickened her pace, knowing this was an opportunity. Spotting her, the man in the driver's seat leaned out the open door, almost falling into the street with his haste.

"Do you have gas to trade?"

She nodded. He fully exited the vehicle then, as he looked around nervously. She noted that he was dirty, like he had been sleeping on the ground instead of in his car, and his odor caught her off guard. She was tempted to move on but knew that this might be her only chance to barter. The man held up a gold bar. Crestfallen, she shook her head. What good was gold to her, she thought, as she turned to walk away in despair. Then she heard the man say, "I have some potatoes."

This caught her attention. She turned and waited for him to continue. When he didn't elaborate, she simply asked, "How much?"

The man reached in the front seat and held up a dirty plastic bag of potatoes. They'd probably been dug from someone's garden more than a month earlier; probably not from his garden. They were small, but they didn't appear to be shriveled or have blight. The bag could not have contained more than eight pounds. The woman held one of the gallons out toward the man.

He shook his head and said, "I need both gallons or it's no deal."

That small sack might last her and her son four days, maybe five. But she didn't have any other options; it was going to be dark in less than two hours, and it was getting colder by the minute. She reluctantly handed over both bags and took the potatoes in exchange. The man quickly stowed them behind the front seat. It wasn't safe to empty them into his tank in the daylight. The woman watched the man climb back into the SUV and slouch down in the seat, out of site.

She turned to leave for the hour walk home. At least, she thought, her boy would have some food tonight. Suddenly, she heard a heavy rumble come from behind her. She quickened her pace but kept turning her head to see what it was; the noise was so out of place and it alarmed her. When a Humvee came into view, she watched it slowly roll past the SUV and saw the men peer inside, but the vehicle did not stop. Instead it kept cruising up the street toward her.

Chapter 3

The man in the Explorer SUV prayed that the Humvee would just keep moving—and was relieved when it did so. But he thought about the woman in the red coat. She must still be on the street; there wasn't enough time for her to make it to safety. She had seemed nice enough, in a desperate way, and if she would have not accepted his offer, he would have gone ahead and given her the potatoes for just one of the gallons. He wanted to get away from Ferndale that bad—one gallon would have done that.

Now as he peered through the top of his steering wheel, he could see the brake lights of the Humvee turn bright. The personnel carrier came to a halt next to the woman. He had to ask himself why anyone these days would walk around dressed in something bound to attract attention. Maybe she wasn't aware of the new threat. One of the soldiers stepped from the passenger door. He was a big man; his size alone would have been intimidating, but he was made more so by his Kevlar-clad uniform and his dominate stance. The man in the SUV watched the whole scenario. The soldier reached his large hand out like he was expecting something. The woman stepped back and appeared to be pleading, clutching the sack of potatoes to her chest. She turned to run, but the soldier moved too quickly. His hand caught the tail of her coat, pulling her to the ground and dragging her to the vehicle. She made an effort to roll away, but the soldier, looking annoyed, placed his boot firmly on her chest. He grabbed the bag from her, tossing it through the open door before making to step back into his vehicle.

As the man in the SUV watched all this, he whispered, "Please don't move." Against his wishes, the woman reached out and grabbed one of the cargo pockets on the soldier's pant leg. Without hesitation, the soldier turned and brought his foot down on the woman's throat. Her body went limp. The soldier didn't even look back as he climbed into his seat. The brake lights on the Humvee dimmed once again just before it pulled away from the woman's lifeless body.

The man watching was compelled by fear to wait until dark. It pained him to see the woman lying there; her bright red coat acting as a beacon. He prayed for movement but there was none. He felt like a coward for not drawing the soldiers' attention from her. He hated the soldiers for what they had done, both to her and to him. He didn't deserve this. She didn't deserve this—he'd known when he met her that she was one of the good people. Everyone left living could be categorized as either good or bad. The soldiers were bad. Surviving was hard enough. The soldiers only made it worse.

The man shivered; the temperature was dropping. It was already colder than he'd ever remembered, and it wasn't yet December. He'd slept in the Explorer since leaving his home, and his wife, in BC. Unable to convince his wife that they would be better off in the States, he'd left Canada without her. He'd told her that he would return for her, but they both knew that this wasn't going to happen.

Some nights the cold was almost unbearable. Tonight would test that unbearable mark, but he was heartened. Combined with the little gas that he already had, the two gallons would get him out of Ferndale and maybe another seventy miles to the south. For now, he just wanted to get away from the soldiers. He had only been in Ferndale a couple of weeks, and had actually thought of staying, but in that short span, he'd witnessed how they'd changed the culture of the remaining population, turning it into one dominated by fear. He knew he could not stay, afraid in his own right that he'd soon cross paths with them. He'd heard rumors that there were towns in California and Oregon that still thrived. At least it would be warmer there, he figured, if he could get that far. Like him, people came to town with their bags and boxes of vegetables, expecting to drive away with enough gas to get them to the next town. Instead, most were left empty handed. The soldiers took what they wanted without offering anything in return.

As dusk fell, the man became anxious to leave, his decision all the more imperative by what happened to the woman, now dead in the road. The same body that made him fear leaving at the same time inspired him to flee. He was also motivated by the fact that he hadn't seen the soldiers in almost two hours. He started the engine and, without waiting for it to warm, shifted the transmission into drive. He made an immediate U-turn to avoid driving past the woman's body and headed toward the interstate. He'd wait until he was nearer the freeway to pour the gas into his vehicle, so he drove slowly to conserve what was remaining in his tank until he reached the overpass, where he pulled off. There was no one else in sight. Five minutes later, the Explorer was venturing south on Interstate Five. With the additional gas, the man thought he might just make it to Seattle.

For the next hour, the man didn't see any occupied vehicles or people on the highway. Maybe going south had been the right choice, he told himself with confidence. But the drive along the freeway was agonizingly slow; there were just too many abandoned vehicles to navigate round. Even though he convinced himself that the slower pace would improve his mileage, he was still a long ways from Seattle. As he neared the outskirts of Everett, the needle on the fuel gauge finally came even with the capital E. He would need to pull off and look for another source of gasoline before much longer.

Suddenly, his way ahead was fully blocked and he slammed on the brakes. The SUV skidded within inches of an abandoned car. He knew the freeway went further south, but it came to an abrupt end as it disappeared beneath a sea of parked vehicles.

He turned off the engine, and sat in the seat not knowing what to do. The freeway was solidly blocked with cars, bumper to bumper and door to door, as if it was a long parking lot. He looked around. He didn't feel safe about leaving his vehicle to investigate so decided to sleep there, cold though it was, and make a plan when daylight returned. There was enough moonlight filtering through the night's overcast to allow him to see the cars ahead of him. As his eyes adjusted to the darkness, he saw that many of the vehicles had broken windows. He became suddenly alert and no longer felt that staying was such a good idea.

He restarted the engine and quickly shifted into reverse. Suddenly, something slammed into his vehicle from behind. His SUV was being pushed forward into the car ahead. He began to panic and pressed on the accelerator. The tires smoked as they spun in reverse but the SUV continued forward until it was shoved into another car. Before the man could reach for his door handle, his window exploded into the left side of his head. All sights and sounds abruptly disappeared.

The man awoke. He felt movement and realized he was being carried. He kept silent as he tried to evaluate his situation, evaluate his injuries. Two men held his arms as two more carried his legs. He could feel warm blood escaping his scalp between his left ear and eye, and his head hurt more than he could have imagined. The motion stopped briefly before he felt himself being thrown up into the bed of a truck. He landed on something soft. Then he felt the cold softness. Flesh. The right side of his head was lying on someone's abdomen. He heard the tail end of a remark, " . . . another stupid Canadian." And then a laugh. Suddenly the man wanted so badly to see his wife again, if only just to tell her that she was right about everything. Blood ran over both eyes. He could no longer hear his captors. He reached up with his left hand to slow the flow of blood when he heard a voice above him. All sights and sounds abruptly disappeared, this time forever.

Chapter 4

Except for a small amount of light peeking from the vents of the wood stove, darkness surrounded him. It was December first of 2029. Since yesterday, the weather had deteriorated exponentially. James wasn't prepared for the extreme change; nobody was. His small house sat shoulder-to-shoulder within a row of almost identical houses, thin, poorly insulated shells for the low income built some sixty years earlier. It was cheap rent and it had a wood stove—two things he valued. Beyond that, it wasn't much, but James didn't require much. Since the collapse, he kept only a week's worth of food with him; most of his staples were in storage not too far away. It was safer that way. Having any quantity of food on hand could make you a target of the have-nots. There were plenty of them around.

Through that first afternoon, James watched the conditions deteriorate. The wind velocity had increased until the windows in some neighboring houses had shattered. James finally bundled up and weathered the elements just long enough to nail plywood over his windows. He narrowly escaped frostbite in the process. This storm was so outside the norm. He hoped that the conditions would subside soon; his provisions would soon be gone.

Even with the wood stove burning twenty-four hours a day, the house barely stayed above freezing. On the first night after the intense weather shift, he closed off the bedrooms and slept on the couch. The winds and the colder temperatures did not abate. Snow kept falling, horizontal most of the time; he could hear it as it pressed against the back of his house. He could also hear the sounds of nearby houses being pulled apart by the hurricane force winds. This continued day after day. Finally, his wood stove could no longer keep ahead of the sinking temperature. The temperature inside his home often dipped below freezing.

James was weary from the cold. This inability to leave his home was something new and unwelcome. The solitude beyond anything he had experienced before and overall making things harder to bear. The days were lonely but the nights were even lonelier, dark now that the winds had arrived and wiped out the electricity. He left the light switches on just in case. The heavy pounding of the wind also kept him from sleeping fully. Each morning when he woke, still tired, he dreaded the hours ahead, just waiting, confined, little to eat. There was nothing he could do until the weather warmed enough to allow him to step outside again.

James' senses became accustomed to the odors and the lack of daylight; much like a homeless man is used to his smell and doesn't realize how he offends others. His supply of firewood sat stacked out near the rear property line, but it might as well have been a mile away for all it was worth. After James made a couple of futile attempts to reach it through the snow and wind, the two cords of wood remained untouched, engulfed in the snowy landscape. Actually getting to the wood and digging it out would have called for a Herculean effort, and he didn't have that in him. Instead, he had to improvise. While he had stacked about ten days worth of wood in the garage before the storm arrived, it lasted only the first six days. So in an effort to keep warm, he burned all of the interior wood trim in the house, door trim, baseboards, and even the doors from the kitchen cabinets. Finally, he even burned the dining room set and the small end tables that bookended his only remaining piece of furniture, an old couch. One solace James had was books; he spent much of the daylight hours reading. There was nothing else to do, and as yet he had not resorted to burning his books. Through the large sheet of plywood that covered the living room window he had drilled several holes. These allowed daylight to come through during the brief part of the day that the sun was over the horizon, and a short time when he could read, huddled on the couch. Otherwise, his home was as dark as a cave. This far north and this time of year, the days were very short. His home was a prison whenever the sun went beyond the horizon of the western coast.

Watching his calendar, James saw Christmas come and go. While he had been diligent with rationing what he had when the storm arrived, he was nearing the end of his meager food supply. Ignoring the hunger had become his biggest task next to keeping warm. The first week was the hardest. His weight loss was obvious without the use of a mirror. And a trek to one of the storage lockers where his surplus of food was stored was out of the question in such conditions. His mind and body were stressed, worsened by his worry about the house. How much more could it handle with the wind constantly buffeting it? What would he do should the house fold under the constant hurricane-speed blasts? He felt trapped, but while it stood, the house was the trap that kept him alive, a thin barrier between him and the deadly sub-zero temperatures. His garage, on the other hand, was not so crucial to his survival, and shortly after Christmas, James decided to disassemble it from the inside for fuel. There was little left to burn from within the house.

He was used to storms in this corner of the country. They usually would last a couple of days at the most and follow with better weather. Not this time. His thoughts returned to his need for body fuel; it was clear that if he was going to live through this, he needed to get food while he still had some strength. He was running out of options.

James had considered taking from another, even if it meant kicking in a door at a neighboring house. The problem was that if people still occupied that house, just by kicking the door in, he was inadvertently killing them. Even if they had food, they wouldn't hand it over—and what then? On the other hand, if he kicked in the door of someone prepared for an intrusion, he could be killed. In his deprived state, James didn't know what to do. He wasn't even sure if he still had any neighbors. There had been no sign of anyone in over a month, but then, like him, if anyone was still around, they'd be sequestered inside, out of the elements. The lack of food and firewood, combined with the fear that his house might cave in—it had all became a huge psychological burden. He questioned his religious beliefs, or rather the lack of. He even wondered if he was being punished. In a moment of clarity, the answer to that question came easily. He was still alive and so many others were not.

The winds and temperatures were so extreme that James wondered if this might be the beginning of a new Ice Age. He quickly doused that idea, humoring himself that he was being affected by 'cabin fever' or paranoia. James reminded himself to remain logical and focused. Spring would surely arrive in another three months, as it normally should. And until then, his primary concern was food, and finding a source within a short distance of his home.

Back in mid-November, James recalled, he had hunted Canadian geese behind a nearby farm. The farm had appeared abandoned—at least no one had shown themselves when he'd fired his shotgun. He knew that the geese couldn't survive this cold; maybe they weren't able to escape from it either. Maybe the winds had come up before they were able to continue their southern migration. He knew that they didn't like to fly in heavy snow storms. The thought got him excited: their carcasses might be preserved in the snow. He thought of the slight difference in today's morning; the wind had briefly abated, just a couple of hours. If the wind quit again the following morning, he thought, he could use that window of opportunity. The farm was a little less than a mile to the north and James estimated that a trip there and back might not be fatal if he dressed heavily and worked fast. The respite from the wind, that brief stillness, gave him hope. The great weight on his soul seemed a touch lighter.

Pre-dawn the next day brought the anticipated break in the wind, yet James held off on the hike to the farm out of fear. He did take advantage of the lull to retrieve some of the firewood that was buried in the snow out back, and found that he was able to handle the cold as long as the wind was still, as long as he was back inside before the wind returned. James noticed a pattern in the last few days; sometime before dawn, the wind would vanish, then, once the sun was well over the horizon, the wind would appear once again. That gave him a small window of opportunity, maybe two hours, maybe more. Even though it had only been a few days, a pattern was forming. He knew that it was almost ten days past the solstice. The days were starting to get longer. There was hope.

The following morning James awoke early; the expected silence was there once again. It was still well below zero degrees Fahrenheit, but the lack of a sixty-plus mile per hour wind could make travel on foot possible. By 7:30 am, he was dressed and waiting for just a bit more daylight. What day was it? Probably New Years, he thought. Hopefully 2030 would be an improvement of 2029, it couldn't be much worse. He had on every piece of warm clothing he owned—a combination of hunting and skiing garb that made him look almost comical, especially with his camouflaged face mask. Both hands were layered with wool gloves covered with nylon mittens. He figured he could travel in the current conditions, a couple hours possibly, but when the wind returned, he'd better be within a few minutes of shelter. Yesterday, as the sun rose higher over the edge of the horizon, it triggered something that brought the wind back to full force; sometimes just a slight rise in temperature was enough to start the cycle all over again.

James took his .22 caliber rifle and wrapped some rags around the muzzle and magazine to keep it from getting iced up. This, along with two candles, a one-liter bottle of kerosene, an old compact mountaineering stove, and a small aluminum shovel went inside a game bag. Contemplating the bag of supplies, James made a sudden decision and tossed in the last of his food: a half stick of margarine and a small container with about a quarter cup of sugar. If he didn't make it back, he would need the food, little as there was. Would he need his sleeping bag? He already had more weight than he wanted to carry. James decided to leave it behind. If he didn't find any geese, he told himself, he would start looking in houses for something to eat. He remembered seeing a child's plastic sled hanging in the rafters of the garage; probably left by the previous tenant. It would come in handy if he did find the waterfowl. He retrieved it and set the bag of supplies on it. With a big sigh, he opened the front door and plunged into the cold white world.

The neighborhood was like a ghost town. There were no footprints in the snow, no smoke coming from any chimneys, and no signs of life at all. The sky was gray but it wasn't snowing; a thin layer of clouds that might disappear when the sun rose. The houses on his side of the street looked mostly intact, while those on the far side had obviously suffered irreparable wind damage—missing roofs, shattered windows, snow filling the rooms where once people gathered. Debris from the destruction was scattered about, embedded into the drifted snow banks. Should he stay and search for food here? He thought not; his instinct told him his odds were better if he could reach the farm. He kept moving.

Pulling the sled down the center of the street where the snow had not drifted, James didn't stop at any of these empty houses but kept his momentum and focus on the farm and the potential for meat. Still, he couldn't take his eyes off the homes, the pervasive destruction all around him. While he hoped there were others still alive besides himself, it was a thin hope. The homes were destroyed, and the vehicles, some that he knew at one time served as sleeping quarters for the homeless, were buried under snow. The desperate chose vehicles over abandoned houses because it was easier to keep the inside of a car or truck warm than it was a house. James shuddered at the thought of what was inside the buried cars and kept moving up the street.

At first, his progress was easier than he'd anticipated because the snow had been blown away from the center of the street. He skirted the edge so his feet were on asphalt while his sled rode silently on a thin carpet of snow. But when he reached the intersection, a line of cars had formed a wind barrier that caused the drifting snow to pile up several feet. James tried to climb this drift but sank in up to his crotch. He looked for another way around, but there was no easier way to get past. Finally, he slung the rifle over his back, laid his game bag on the sled, and then lowered himself over that, his lower legs hanging off the back of the sled. Using his hands and feet, he propelled himself up the grade without sinking. He was pleased with himself, especially when he was rewarded with a ride down the backside onto the road that led to the farm. From there, he was able to walk most of the distance, only having to stop twice along the way to sled himself over another sizeable drift. Along the entire way, power poles and trees crossed the road making it impassable by anything other than on foot.

Traversing the hundred-yard driveway that led up to the farm, though, was a different matter. It was lined on its northern side by a row of broken, jagged poplar tree trunks, large and small limbs strewn everywhere. The snow had drifted on the leeward side of the trees making the driveway impassable. James moved further down the road until he found an area on the windward side of the trees that had been blown clean of snow. He passed the sled under the barbed wire before climbing over. As he towed his sled towards the barn, he looked again at the poplars and paused, realizing that since he had left his house that morning, he had not seen one single tree still standing; each appeared to have frozen and then snapped like a dry twig. Even the largest of conifers was not spared. His toes started feeling the cold through his thick boots and he regained his objective. He needed to keep moving.

The last time he had hunted the geese that wintered in the region, they were on the far side of the barn by the irrigation pond. If they had been pounded by the extreme weather, he hoped they would have tried to get shelter by bunching up against the outside wall of the barn. As James made his way around the back he could see the two-story farmhouse come into view. The wind damage to the structure was the worst he had seen yet. The roof had been completely torn off and scattered across the field to the south. Only two exterior walls on the second floor remained, every door and window destroyed. If someone had tried to ride out the storm in that house, they weren't around anymore to talk about it.

Against the barn's outer back wall, as suspected, he found a large snowdrift. He pulled out his shovel and started digging. It was slow going because the drift began some fifteen feet away from the barn. After ten minutes of digging and scraping, his shovel hit a hard lump. Feathers. He widened the area—more feathered lumps. He was elated and struck hard with his shovel to lift one of the birds. But it was solidly frozen to the ground. James thought for a moment. He needed something stronger that would give him more leverage. This was a farm, there would be tools. Then he remembered seeing a garage next to the house. Its single large door still intact, still closed.

Motivated only by getting those birds free and back to his house, James moved quickly and jogged around the corner of the barn to the path between it and the garage. Just before reaching the building, he felt a puff of wind from the northeast. He was cutting it close. With a jerk of the handle, he managed to break the garage door free from the frozen concrete and push the double door up. Reality sank in at the sight of a car in front of him: there probably was at least one person, maybe more, dead inside the house. Putting the thought out of his head, James moved to a rack of garden tools and found a five-foot-long pry bar and ran with it back to the barn.

James was able to ram the chiseled end under a bird, put all his weight to it, and pop the frozen body off the ground. Within two minutes he had four geese loose. Suddenly the wind kicked up in earnest and lifted the sled off the ground. James grabbed it, threw the four birds and the game bag on top, and headed for the garage. He was breathing heavily and had even generated some warmth with his efforts. Still, there would not be enough warmth or time to return home safely. He'd for sure get caught in the full-on wind and freeze, dead like the birds on his sled. He wasn't about to let that happen and figured if he could ride out the day and the night inside the car in the garage, he could return home during the calm of the following morning. But as he reached the garage, he looked at the old house not twenty feet away, and a thought crept into his mind. Old places like that—it could have a cellar that might offer better protection than the garage. And it might still have some food stored within.

James took a chance and ran up the back steps into what was left of the kitchen. Every cabinet door was open; there wasn't any food to be found in here. The countertops and sink were encrusted with snow, and the snow that had come in through the open windows and door was banked up three feet high against one wall, a wall that had a door, a closet, James thought at first. When he saw a flashlight hung on a hook next to the door, he realized: this wasn't a closet. He ran back out to grab his shovel from the sled outside and was grateful when he stepped back into the kitchen for what little protection the room gave, as the wind had kicked up another notch, the bitter cold growing worse. He had only minutes left to work.

Shoveling in a near frenzy, James moved enough snow away from the door to pry it open. He shoved his face mask down to his neck to dry the sweat he'd generated and peered down into the darkness. He could not see anything. The lack of light meant that there were no windows. Then a stench wafted up to his nostrils. It was pure sewage and he turned his head away from the unexpected assault to his senses. He wasn't about to go down there; the garage would be the better choice. He was at the kitchen door when he heard a faint noise from the cellar, a rustling. He stopped, stopped his breathing too, and listened. He only heard the wind whistling behind him. Then for some reason he stepped back to the basement door and said, "Is anyone there?"

Only silence answered him and again he turned to leave for the garage. Then he heard a faint voice cry out, "Help me."

Chapter 5

James knew he had only seconds in which to make a decision. He had no idea what he would be getting into if he stepped into that basement, but he'd have trouble living with himself if he didn't. He knew the score: rescuing someone may prove to be more of a burden than a blessing. The wind had increased to a constant hard buffet—maybe thirty miles-per-hour, and he felt its affects through his insulated clothing. His toes were already numb. He bolted out the back door and ran back to the garage. From the sled he grabbed the bag with the geese and pulled three geese out. One goose was left in the bag with the last of his food supply, the stove and the fuel. If the winds exceeded seventy mph once again today, the wind would enter through the large door and tear the roof off this building. It might still be necessary to use it as a shelter. He pulled the door down and bolted for the house. His heart raced as he made calculated moves. With his bag in one hand, he stood at the threshold of the basement. On a whim, he grabbed the flashlight from the wall and pushed the switch; as expected, the cold had sapped all the energy from the batteries. He tossed it aside. Grateful for his mask over his mouth and nose, James took a deep breath and stepped onto the top landing of the basement before closing the door behind him.

Even with his mask, the smell of the air with the door closed was nearly overwhelming, a combination of human waste and garbage. James stood there in total darkness and resisted the urge to flee. Reaching into his bag, he felt around until he found a candle, then reached into his upper coat pocket for his small oblong tin. He pulled out a single match before carefully closing the tin and placing it back into his pocket. Striking the match against the door, he lit the candle and waited a few seconds for the flame to grow to full height before he blew out the match. James surveyed the scene below him. A set of wooden stairs led down to a box-shaped room. Shelves covered the visible walls; they were cluttered and he imagined the history they held of the house's former occupants. Garbage covered the entire floor and a five-gallon plastic bucket stood in the far corner. He could not see anyone and wondered if he had imagined the voice. In the center of the room was an elevated rectangle of garbage and blankets and James figured there had to be a mattress under that debris, judging by the shape. The pile shifted slightly revealing the source of the voice.

His first action was to remove his mask, not wanting to frighten this person. Taking a deep breath, but without moving any closer, he said, "My name is James. Are you okay? I'm not going to hurt you." The candle light was just enough to see movement as a face appeared from under a wad of blanket.

The face was so dirty that he couldn't be sure whether it was a woman or man until she spoke. "Do you have water?" Her voice was thin, raspy.

James descended several steps and looked at the woman, with only her face showing, he guessed her to be about middle-age, maybe younger. "I don't have any now but I'll get some." The last time he'd had anything to drink himself was early that morning and without much food, he also needed water. His small stove would come in handy to melt some snow. But first, if he was going to have to ride out the wind in this room, he'd have to remove that bucket. The stench was even more overpowering now that he was at the bottom of the stairs. He had to find a container for the snow, get the waste bucket out the door, and fill up the new container with snow in one fast trip. The wind was probably at a deadly speed considering the sub-zero temperature.

Scanning the many shelves, James spotted a large tin, a Christmas container of some kind. He estimated it would hold between two or three gallons of snow, enough to melt down to maybe one or two quarts of water at the most. James grabbed the tin and shook the dust out before stepping around the mattress to get the waste bucket. He fought for control of his gag reflex as he lifted the bucket. It was heavy, and managing the stairs in near darkness with both hands full was cumbersome. At the top of the stairs, James had to set the heavier bucket down to turn the door knob. When he pushed the door open with his shoulder, he felt resistance from fresh snow blown against it. Using his boot, it took five kicks to get it open wide enough to fit the waste bucket through without spilling. Noting how fast the snow built up behind the door as the wind increased to a deadly speed, James understood why this woman had been trapped; he'd have to prevent getting trapped himself once he was closed up behind the door for the rest of the day and night—up to twenty hours, maybe more. For the moment, though, he set his mind to the immediate tasks. The waste bucket he placed in the furthest corner of the kitchen—with the wind and cold, he was certain it would freeze solid. Then he began scooping snow into the empty tin as fast as he could. The cold was more than unbearable; it was beyond description. And James knew that every second in this wind tunnel was probably another second closer to frostbite, or death. Finally with the tin mostly filled, James could not tolerate any more and retreated to the basement. He pulled the door behind him until he heard the latch click into place.

The basement had been cold when he first opened the door, but now that the wind had exchanged the air, it was well below freezing. The woman under the blankets remained motionless as James worked the fuel bottle onto the stove's fuel line. His fingers were so numb that he needed his vision to guide him. With a quick twist of the valve, he released just enough kerosene to start the stove. Fortunately the wind had not extinguished the candle he'd left at the base of the stairs, and using its flame, he was able to bring the stove up to its full potential before balancing the tin of snow upon its three spindly supports. For the next thirty minutes, James watched as the flames curled up the bottom of the tin and slowly melted the ice. Not to waste anything, he held his finger tips near the glowing flame to warm them. The one liter of kerosene could burn for only about six hours. He would need to be conservative until he was sure that he could return to his own home. As the stove burned, James could smell a change in the air; the flames helped subdue the overriding stench. The woman remained motionless throughout all this. He sat quietly as he waited.

As the last of the snow melted, James dipped a bare finger into the water to test the temperature; he wanted it to be warm enough so that it didn't exacerbate her weakness. When it was slightly above body temperature, he turned off the valve that controlled the kerosene. Using a rag as a pot holder, he lifted the tin from the stove. He poured about a third of the water into a smaller can. Into this, he poured in about half of his sugar and swirled it around until it was dissolved. He paused for a moment, unsure how to rouse the woman. Finally, he just reached down and shook the bulge that he guessed was her shoulder. The woman was startled at first, as if she had fallen asleep, but she quickly recovered and turned to face him.

"Drink some of this," he said, reaching the cup out to her.

She freed a hand from under the blankets, and James helped her guide the small can to her mouth. As soon as she tasted the sweetened water, she started gulping it. James took control of the can and would only allow her to sip. She finished off the water and asked, "Is there more?"

"Yes, but let's see if you can keep this down first," he replied, giving her a faint smile.

She relaxed on the mattress once again and briefly closed her eyes before asking "What was your name again?"

James knew that the more they spoke, the harder it would be to leave her if she proved to be beyond help. He remembered an old saying, *In for a penny, in for a pound*, and decided that it was a little

few mornings. That's why I even ventured out yesterday. So if we are to go, we need to leave here at daybreak." He looked at her thin layer of clothes and jacket before adding, "And we'll need to find more clothing for you. I'll take a look upstairs at first light and see what I can find." Even though the roof and some of the second story walls had been torn away, he hoped that maybe there was an interior closet that was still intact with some warm garments inside.

The woman nodded, then curled up once again under the mound of blankets, and within minutes she was snoring lightly. With the nourishment in her, her condition didn't seem as bad as James had feared. But he wasn't sure if she was able to walk: she hadn't left the mattress since he'd first encountered her. Still, he was optimistic that he could get her back to his home before the winds returned. He periodically looked at his watch. It was almost five-thirty. First light would be after seven. He would need to secure some extra clothing and have her at the top of the stairs by seven-thirty. He curled up behind her and waited.

An hour later, James picked up his small shovel and quietly ascended the stairs. A firm nudge to the door opened it. Without the wind, the path of the door had stayed clear. Yet he instantly felt the bitter cold that always seemed to be the worst in the pre-dawn hours. As he stepped into the kitchen, the glow from the impending dawn cast just enough light for him to see. James climbed over the snow drift that ran through the kitchen and stepped through a doorway that led to a dining room. Snow had built up on the dining table and chairs as well. A hutch filled with fine dishes peeked out from another snow drift. The scene was surreal. Like something out of a Dickens novel. He continued on into the living room and spotted a coat closet near the front entry. The contents of the closet weren't quite what he was looking for; it mostly contained light jackets and umbrellas. "Surely these people must have dealt with winter before now," he uttered to himself, frustrated, before continuing his search. Since there wasn't a clothes washer or dryer in the basement, there must be another room where they shed their farm clothes or stored other coats. Moving back through the living room, he headed towards another hallway that had closed doors on each side. The first door he opened was a bathroom. The toilet tank and bowl had both split from the frozen water. The second door was the laundry room with no outerwear to be found in there. He'd have to venture upstairs. It made him shudder to think about the dead couple above him. The missing roof and walls didn't appeal to him either.

The steps upstairs were completely covered with snow, and climbing them was difficult. As he worked his way to the second floor landing, he saw the extreme damage from the relentless heavy winds; it was astounding. Besides the roof being gone, most of the walls were missing. James could still see where the bathroom had been; its pipes protruded up out of the snow, the fixtures blown clear of the platform without the walls to protect them. And in the largest room was a big mound of snow—most likely the bed with the old couple. He shuddered to think he was standing only a few feet from two frozen lifeless bodies. A partial section of a wall was the only thing that had kept the bed from blowing away. The scene with the open roof and absence of walls was beyond description. Even more strange was a quadrant of standing walls in the center of the destruction, seemingly defiant against the wind. A set of double doors was held shut by two feet of snow piled up against them. James started shoveling a path for the door to swing open and within minutes was looking into a closet. Success. He grabbed an adult-sized snow suit, a down-filled hooded parka, mittens, and a pair of hiking boots. Before descending the stairs, he glanced once more at the pile of snow that served as a tomb to the elderly couple.

Chapter 6

Thankfully the snow suit fit her well and the large, puffy down coat plus the too-large boots gave her a masculine appearance. The early morning brightness, though, was almost too much for their eyes to handle. They stopped at the garage where James found a pair of sunglasses stuck above the visor in the car. He gave them to her. Even with the glasses, the glare still pained her eyes; they watered heavily. But she, like James, wanted to move on, and without exchanging any words, they left the farm.

James had her start out walking as he pulled the sled with his game bag alongside. He figured at some point she would need to ride the sled, but until then he encouraged her to keep moving. The way she had to deliberately place one foot in front of the other was almost like watching a drunk come out of a bar. However, the further they traveled, the steadier she became. She didn't complain about her eyes any longer, either, but kept the glasses on. About halfway back to his house, James was no longer nervous about getting caught in another wind storm. He suddenly stopped and looked straight at the woman.

"What is your name?"

"Lara, my name's Lara Cooper," she replied, and gave him a wan smile.

"Well, Lara, we should be there in about twenty minutes."

They reached the fringe of his neighborhood, and the same large snow drift anchored by the abandoned vehicles. James told Lara to stay put as he climbed onto the sled and pushed his way up and over the drift. He returned in the same fashion minus the cargo. He then had her kneel on the front of the sled as he pushed with his legs until they rose over the peak and were able to slide back down to street level. As he loaded the gear back onto the sled for the short walk up to the house, he caught Lara staring at the houses on the far side of the street. She was in awe as she took in all the damage caused by the wind.

"I didn't realize how much had happened while I was trapped in that cellar," she whispered. James was silent, not sure how to respond. So much had happened in so short a time, and more than houses had been destroyed. The destruction extended to living things—trees, animals, and people.

As they neared his house, James dropped the rope and reached into his bag for the rifle. He fumbled with the safety, and then pulled off his mitten to gain better purchase. The door hung inward teetering on a single hinge. James entered with the barrel pointed ahead. He made a sweep through the house before determining that no one was inside. The door hadn't come off its hinges by itself. James appeared at the doorway and motioned for Lara to come inside. No words were exchanged. As she stepped towards the door, the wind whipped up with enough force to lift the plastic sled and spill its contents onto the ground. The sled took flight and skittered down the street.

Once they were both inside, James focused on getting the door shut. The shattered frame left nothing for the door to latch onto. He set Lara to lean her weight onto the door to keep it closed, and went down the hall where she couldn't see him. He returned, maneuvering a tall bi-fold door and set it against the living room wall, then hurried back into the hall, returning a moment later with a canvas bag.

Lara watched all this, knowing only that if she moved, the front door would blow open. The cold had numbed her toes and she realized that this room was much colder than the cellar had been, and almost as dark. She could smell wood smoke, mixed with other odors she couldn't identify. Through the dimness, she saw that the carpet was littered with garbage and bits of wood. Another surge of anxiety struck her. This place was no better than where she'd been. And then the door pushed against her as a big gust of wind rocked the small house. She turned towards James, wanting to say something. The words stuck in her throat. He seemed not to notice her, but she watched as he worked on the doors hinges. Just focusing on his actions seemed to calm her nerves. She ignored the wind with its hushed roar and kept her mind on what he was doing. Her anxieties retreated as she watched him. She wasn't alone in this dark and musty cave.

Unaware of the battle within Lara's thoughts, James took Lara by the shoulders and moved her aside as he took her position at the front door. He placed one of the new doors crosswise against the front door and hammered it in to the door frame with the blunt end of a hatchet. After he put in a fourth nail he stepped back as if inviting the wind to test his handy work. In answer to his challenge, the wind hit hard enough that they felt the force through their whole bodies. The door held tight.

James turned to Lara and stood silently, searching for the right words. Finally, he said, "We need to get a fire going before we freeze to death."

As James broke up the other half of the bi-fold door with the hatchet, Lara watched. He looked up at her and saw her eyes go to the front door, then to the room, then back to him, a confused expression on her face. He set the hatchet down and said, "Someone broke into my house while I was gone."

They could now hear the wind reach near its full force and a large gust shook the structure. She digested what he had said before asking, "Do you know who?"

"No," he said. "Hell, I haven't seen another human besides you since November. I didn't even think there was anyone left around but me."

"Did they take anything?" She looked about the room. The only things that were moveable were the couch and the stove.

"I checked first thing. They got some stuff. Some matches, a candle and a book. Nothing critical."

"When I moved in here, I built a trap door in a closet floor just in case someone did break in while I was out. I kept my waste bucket on top of it. Whoever it was didn't bother lifting the bucket." He had been careful about storing what possessions he had in the crawl space. The few items that he owned could not be replaced.

James poured a few drops of kerosene on some small pieces of wood and threw them inside the stove. A candle appeared. He lit this before setting the match to the wood inside the stove. The added light in the room was a relief. James left the stove's door slightly ajar so he could watch the flames grow. As he stared at the flame, he continued, "Someone must have seen me leave yesterday morning. I suppose it could have been someone passing through. But I'm guessing it means I probably have a neighbor getting desperate. I just don't know where they live."

By now, the fire had enough volume to add a larger piece of firewood. Lara watched as he shut the door and adjusted the dampers. He went down the hall and closed the bedroom doors to conserve what little heat the stove produced. He returned carrying a cooking pot filled with a solid chunk of ice and placed it on the top of the stove.

Even though the room was still below freezing, Lara could feel that the temperature was rising and significantly warmer than when they first got there. She noted how all the windows had been boarded up to protect the glass from the wind, but the plywood had small holes to provide just enough light that she could see her surroundings. Her eyes quickly acclimated to the low light. The living room opened up into a dining room, but there were no table and chairs. In fact, the only furniture was an old beat up couch. She looked at James and said, "There was only one."

"Only one what?"

"Only one neighbor, or thief, or whatever," she replied. "If there had been two or more, don't you think they would have taken more?"

James pondered this for a second before answering, "Maybe. Still, this means that I need to sleep with a gun and the next time I go out for food, I need you to go with me."

"You make it sound like I'm a burden," she said as she sat down on the couch. Determined to convince James that she was not the weakling he'd encountered in the cellar, she said, "If you leave me a gun, I'll make sure that no one gets through that door."

James smiled at her. Having this woman around might actually make his life easier.

The next three days proved to be identical to the last five in that the wind would die down during the night and then rise up sometime around ten o'clock the following morning. James spent their first morning repairing the front door so that it would stay shut and locked without boards nailed into the frame. Even with the repair, the door leaked cold air around the edges whenever the wind gusted. Otherwise, Lara and James got into a routine of venturing out early enough to collect snow for melting and to discard the contents of their waste bucket. They would then spend the rest of the morning salvaging wood to feed the stove. At the first sign that the wind was returning, they would retreat back inside. Each day, it felt like the wind returned a few minutes later than it had the day before, much like the sun would appear a couple of minutes earlier each day since the solstice, and set a little later. The lengthening days gave them hope that spring, and maybe some normal weather, might actually return. As extreme as the winter had been, however, a normal spring was hard to imagine.

On their first night together, James had pulled a mattress from one of the closed-up bedrooms and set up his bed at the far end of the living room, letting Lara have the couch since it was close to the stove. The next morning as Lara handed James a cup of tea, she asked, "Why did you sleep so far from the fire?"

The directness of her question startled James. "I guess I wanted to give you some space."

"That's silly; it's much colder over by the wall. And, well, I don't want any space. I would sleep better if you were closer."

The next night, James moved the mattress over next to the couch and fire. In the morning, he was surprised to feel her warm body at his back; she must have joined him sometime in the night. Neither made comment as they went about their morning tasks. The next night, it happened again. Just before it was time to sleep on the fourth night, Lara took her blankets from the couch and laid them out on half of the mattress. As she lay down with her back towards James and pulled her blankets up to her chin, she answered his question before he could ask. "I don't like sleeping alone anymore."

So far there had not been any sign that anyone else was even alive in the neighborhood. Even though maybe ten of the almost thirty houses dispersed through the area were still inhabitable, there was no smoke from the chimneys, no fresh footprints in the snow, and no sounds of any kind other than the wind howling. Yet James couldn't shake the feeling that they were being watched as they went out each morning. Once, James returned with a solid wood door from one of the houses that had lost its roof. With it, he replaced his damaged hollow door. Lara watched him as he struggled to remove the old frame

"It'll help keep the heat in," James said, seeing her unspoken question. "Plus, it'll help me sleep better."

"Even though the neighborhood is empty, you still feel someone's out there? Someone dangerous?"

James shrugged his shoulders and didn't answer, because he didn't know the answer. He worked fast to get the job done before the wind picked up again. Once the new door was in, he swung it closed, tried the deadbolt, and was content. The heavier door seemed to lighten his burden.

Afternoons and evenings, when the wind made staying outside unbearable, Lara and James got to know one another. Lara was dumbfounded by James' proclamation that he knew all along that civilization was going to unravel. But when he laid out the chain of events and his interpretation of them, she understood his thinking and was impressed with his foresight instead of thinking him paranoid. It made her feel stupid that she hadn't seen it all coming. The harsh winter they were finally coming out of was not one of his predictions, but the end result would be about the same.

Lara opened up about her past and told James that she had been a licensed nurse and had worked in a home for the elderly. She'd felt her work important, and even when the funds quit coming in and the facility's manager was having trouble buying food or medication for its residents, or paying the staff, Lara had kept showing up. Sometimes she would bring in canned fruit she'd put up the summer before, or a loaf of homemade bread when there was enough electricity to bake. But one morning in the middle of June, she had arrived to start her shift and found her favorite patient dead in his bed. She checked the next room, and the next—all the residents were dead, all still in their beds. Her first thought was that some insane, horrible person had gone on a killing spree and might still be around, but when she rushed to the office and found the manager dead at her desk, blood all over, a gunshot wound to the temple, Lara understood what had happened. The manager's hand was still holding the pistol. A handwritten note splattered with blood explained her actions and asked God for forgiveness. Lara had no one to call, or any way to call anyone for that matter, so she turned and walked away without looking back. A few days later, there was a gun fight over food at the apartments where she lived. The next day she moved in with her friends on the farm; they had been begging her to leave town and join them for several weeks. She felt safe there, sharing in the farm work through the summer and fall, until the attack by the soldiers.

James listened intently to Lara's story. The despair and overall sense of things falling apart were common to everyone. His experiences of late had been much like hers, and he'd witnessed his share of atrocities, but he'd been lucky to not have suffered such traumatic events as she.

Even with his worries, Lara's presence had a positive effect on James. Having someone to be concerned for, to share with, made circumstances endurable. Though there were mornings when Lara preferred to stay inside while James went out (James kept these times as brief as possible), mostly they went out together to scrounge for what they could from a vacant house—a new one each day. Their primary reason was to search for food, but they never did find anything to eat. They also looked for necessities, like candles and matches, and James found that if they searched for Christmas decorations, they could often find a large candle or two.

One morning, they came across some suitcases packed with clean clothes, all men's. Even so, some garments looked like they'd fit Lara, and she held pieces against her body and asked James how she looked. The "shopping spree" bordered on silliness and Lara smiled for the first time since he'd found her huddled, awaiting death, in the cellar. They ran back to their house, each with a small armload of clothes. By the heat of the stove, they stripped the soiled clothes off their bodies and tried on different pants, shirts, and undergarments. They ignored each other's nakedness as they traded their old clothes for newer ones. When they finished, James fed their old clothes into the plastic bag. Lara wanted him to burn them. He looked at her apologetically, "We don't have that luxury. We might need them again someday, or maybe someone else will."

Lara was so grateful to have a place to stay, and someone to be with. She knew she didn't have much to offer James, but to do her part in making circumstances more comfortable, she cleaned the place up a bit, especially all the refuse on the floor. She helped him with the chores of keeping the fire going at night, waste disposal, and preparing a meal each day from the goose meat they so carefully rationed.

But chores only took up so much of their time, and James and Lara spent much of their afternoons reading, or discussing politics and beliefs. James was quick to let her know that he didn't believe in God or Jesus or Satan or anything else that couldn't be seen or touched. He also declared that he trusted no one. This made Lara raise an internal eyebrow, since clearly James had grown to trust her, a complete stranger. But she didn't challenge him. Instead she had countered with the fact that it was unlikely that humans could trace their roots to a tiny micro-organism, and that some sort of higher power *must* exist. She even postulated that maybe the storm and global collapse were God's way of cleaning out his garage. Their exchange of completely polar beliefs didn't cause any strain; each had grown appreciative of the other's presence and had resolved that it was necessary to respect different opinions.

For all his worries, Lara wasn't the burden that James feared she would be. He had grown accustomed to living alone, but now his life held new value as he shared it with her. Every night when it would turn too dark for anything else, James would group three candles together and read aloud to Lara, it became a sort of therapy for them. She absorbed what he read without interruption, received it as a gift. And James was grateful to be able to give to her.

But the chore of survival was never far from James' mind. And on a night after Lara had been with him almost a week, he watched as she scraped meat off a wing bone of the last goose. "There is a storage park on the other side of town. I keep some supplies there. I need to go there while I have the opportunity."

"Are you going for food? Can I go with you?"

"I *am* going for food and I *don't* want you to go with me."

"Why not?"

"It's just—I don't know what I'll encounter, and I think it would be safer for both of us if you stayed here. I'll be able to travel faster, too"

Lara paused in her meal preparations for a minute. James could see that she was weighing the options. He added, "I need you stay and guard this place."

"How long would you be gone?"

"I'll leave before daylight. I'm pretty sure that I can do it in less than three hours. I might get caught by some wind, but I should be all right, and I'll be as fast as possible."

Lara knew they needed the food, and she was apprehensive about being left alone, out of contact with him, but there was no alternative. That night, Lara asked James if they could pass the time by playing cards instead of him reading to her. This way they could talk. She asked about his plan, what problems he might encounter, what back-up measures he'd take if something went wrong. She fed him every scenario she could think of, and James had an answer for each. Since the sled had blown away with the wind, he would use a backpack; he'd anticipate a longer time getting back because of the weight of a full pack. But he'd take his collapsible trekking poles to help him get through snowdrifts and to overall make the burden easier. He'd bring some matches and a candle, but leave the small kerosene stove with Lara. If the wind returned sooner than expected, he'd seek the nearest shelter and return the following morning. He'd take his hunting bow and a small quiver of arrows and his hatchet, and collect the handgun he kept in storage, leaving the small rifle with her. They didn't verbalize why she might need the gun, but they both knew the possibility. Thankfully he'd already taught Lara how to load, aim and shoot it, and that just firing a gun near an intruder might be all that was needed.

When every possible scenario was covered and recovered, Lara laid her blankets out on the mattress as if to say that she accepted that he knew what he was getting into. With their backs pressed together, they were lulled to sleep by a mixture of sounds created by the wind and the crackling fire.

Chapter 7

In the dark of pre-dawn, Lara boiled water while James packed. They didn't talk. Lara watched him as she sipped her tea, clearly apprehensive.

By seven, there was just enough light to see up and down the street. The air was still. James stepped out onto the front step dressed in a neoprene ski mask, ski goggles, and an old insulated coverall. His pack was securely strapped on. His eyes swept the neighborhood. Nothing had changed. Though it was unnecessary, he reminded Lara to stay inside and to keep the door locked, then matter of factly, even lightly, said, "I'll see you in a few hours." Until he returned with the supplies, Lara would be without food.

As he walked away, James glanced up at the clear blue sky. He bent down and picked up a long two-by-six plank that he'd scavenged the day before. Dragging the plank with one hand, he headed down the street towards the large drift, scanning each house and yard for any sign of movement. As usual, no smoke from the other chimneys, no footprints in the snow. But also as usual, James couldn't shake the feeling that he was being watched.

When he reached the snowdrift, James placed the two-by-six vertically on the slope so that it came close to the crest. Balancing himself with his trekking poles, he carefully stepped up the plank, then reversed his method to get down the other side, leaving the board at the base of the snowdrift.

One of the scenarios that he avoided mentioning to Lara was that his storage locker could have been broken into. If this was the case, he was prepared to make a detour for another locker that he had, one he'd not told Lara about, some twenty minutes further south. He had done the math and knew for certain that if he had to make a run for the second locker, there wouldn't be enough time to get back to the house the same day. But they were out of food and he'd have to chance the longer trip. James reminded himself that this trip was no different than any other. You dealt with every obstacle as you came to it and don't worry about what you can't control. Still, some fears traveled with him.

The road that James walked on was named Vista Drive, a wide river of asphalt covered with wind-packed snow, but with a clearing in the center that made progress easier. The view below him made it plain to see why they had chosen this name. The road led downhill into the town of Ferndale, the occasional fallen power pole or abandoned car creating the only obstacles. He just needed to get through the neighborhoods lining the road, and to the other side of town. James stopped and sniffed the cold air. Though many of the homes were damaged beyond repair, the scent of wood smoke was coming from one of them; it was barely detectable to him and he couldn't identify its source. All he wanted to do was to pass through without being noticed, and now the possibility of someone tracking his movements concerned him. What you don't know can be dangerous, plus, this would be the only way back when he returned, and anyone watching might realize that. One of the houses on his right was boarded up, but it didn't have any boards over the front door. Most of the snow had been removed from its concrete steps, too—obvious indication of inhabitants. He saw another house a few doors down that had just the faint whisper of smoke escaping from its chimney. He hoped people in these houses were no different than him, doing what they could to make it through this horrid winter, but not bad people. No matter what, James reminded himself, he needed to focus on one thing and that was to get the food and bring it back. He thought about Lara. She would be fine as long as she kept the door locked. He continued following the almost two-mile road downhill before it abruptly ended at the edge of town. By the time he'd made the turn onto Main Street, he'd passed no less than eight houses that he estimated could be inhabited.

Ferndale's downtown was really only three blocks of store fronts. About half were banks or restaurants—or at least they once were. It was a typical layout for a small town that supported a refinery. As James walked down the center of the street, he observed that every large window had been blown out; snow had partially filled the hollow structures. Every light pole was down, creating obstacles along the street. There were large chunks of roofs, doors, walls—and broken glass everywhere. Abandoned cars added to the maze. The desolation of downtown was worse than the nearby neighborhoods, so much more debris from the size of the buildings alone, but the large signs that normally sat above the entrances to these businesses were now spread all across the street creating further obstacles for anyone trying to pass through, even on foot, to the bridge over the river. It amazed him that this town had stood for over a century and now it was reduced to this.

As James climbed over and around the wreckage, he checked his watch. He'd been traveling for forty minutes. There was still another mile to go once he crossed the river. How long was it going to take him when he was walking back uphill with fifty pounds of food? He needed to pick up the pace.

Finally, as James reached the bridge, the sea of debris disappeared and the road was clean of everything, including the snow and ice. The river, completely frozen now, ran in a northeast to southwest direction, the same path as the wind: anything close to the river banks had been cleared away by the fierce winds. As he crossed the bridge, he could remember only two times in the last twenty years that the river had frozen over from bank to bank. James looked upstream. He was able see all the way to the other bridge that crossed a mile upstream; only the loss of several hundred trees, frozen and snapped off near their trunks, could create such a scene.

He'd never considered having a storage unit on the far side of the river would be an issue for him. The river, just naturally separated the residential districts and the commercial zones. He remembered how each July the residents would celebrate the founding of the town with a carnival, pancake feeds, and a grand parade. They called it Pioneer Days. James tried to remember the last Pioneer Days celebration. It seemed like so long ago, maybe as many as ten years had passed since the last celebration. Each year, even James would get caught up in the festivities. After all, he worked at the local refinery, as did most of the breadwinners in that community and something about the town had gotten under his skin. He'd felt like he belonged, even though some considered him a loner since he'd never married. But he did have his friends, knew many of the town's inhabitants, and people were always warm towards him. Friendly and warm to everyone. Now most of them were gone.

What separated him from most others was that they hadn't seen the same dark cloud on the horizon that he had. He couldn't understand how it wasn't obvious to everyone. Yet most were lulled by a false sense of security: Keep living like you always have and the world won't change. They were so wrong. Sometimes he wished he'd followed a one-time notion to become an environmentalist and help steer humanity towards a more sustainable future. However, deep down he knew that mankind had already crossed a line in the sand: the world's population couldn't exist without cheap oil, and that dependency would cause the end of things. The sad part was that even while the oil was still plentiful, the environment was dying. Instead of environmentalism, he chose engineering, so he could make enough money and prepare for the worst. James didn't harbor regrets. Besides, nobody would've listened. Nobody **did** listen even the ATV, he knew he might not have time to reach the closest shelter before he would freeze to death.

James made another pull on the starter without results. Out of pure anger and frustration, he pulled again and again, rapidly, crazily, until on the eighth pull, the motor coughed. As insignificant as it was, there was hope. He paused briefly, catching his breath, before pulling again. It sputtered and chugged. One more pull and both cylinders fired.

A sense of relief swept over James as he turned the key on the ATV. The gauges lit up. Without letting hope overcome him, he quickly turned the key off and stepped around to the front end to look at the winch; it was driven by a small electrical motor. Walking to the back, he lifted the charger and placed it in the rear box. The running generator also fit in beside it. After kicking the transmission into neutral, he pushed the ATV over to the front of his own locker, then put the transmission back into gear to lock the wheels. He then pushed the winch toggle into reverse and watched as it started spitting out cable attached to a hook. It was working, but he felt the seconds ticking, almost a full minute before there was enough cable for the hook to reach the pile of debris. After clipping the hook onto a solid section of fencing, James pushed the switch, and the winch started pulling in the cable. In disbelief at the delays, James heard the motor grind to a halt. The battery charger couldn't supply enough flow for the electric motor. James left the charger attached to the battery, but plugged the winch directly into the generator's second outlet.

It worked. As the slack lessened, the fencing started to shift toward the ATV. Then, as the resistance increased, the ATV slid on the icy ground towards its load. James waited until the front tires butted up against the pile before climbing onto the seat to add his weight to the vehicle. With that, the fence was once again moving and so was all the debris on top of it. When the cable had fully retracted, he pushed the switch back into neutral. The generator droned steadily as it fed the vehicle's battery. Climbing over the fencing, he looked down onto what remained of his locker.

At first there was nothing discernible. His eyes searched the tangle of wood and metal. Then he spotted the top of one of his three metal drums under a sheet of aluminum; and he quickly pulled that and the other debris off. The barrels, which he had picked up when he worked at the oil refinery, were waterproof with locking lids, perfect for storing food and supplies. Before stowing them away here, James had stenciled WEED KILLER on the front of each in hopes that the warning would be a deterrent to others.

He glanced at his watch: two hours and ten minutes had elapsed. There was definitely not enough time to get the supplies packed up and back home. He had maybe fifty minutes to find shelter from the cold and increasing wind. James looked at the ATV and the still-running generator for a moment, then with a determined set to his lips, formulated a new plan. He pulled off a mitten and pushed his hand into the right front pocket of his ski pants, pulling out a small ring of keys. Fumbling for a moment, he found the right key and unlocked a small padlock on one of the barrels. The lid came off easily. He pulled out two large plastic bags. Each bag contained several smaller plastic bags, with rice, oatmeal, sugar, and flour, and underneath the dried goods were tins of cooking oil, soy sauce, tea and coffee. Each food bag was supposed to last him a month. Unlocking the next barrel, he pulled out a nine millimeter semi-automatic pistol, a box of cartridges, and a book. James loaded the pistol and shoved it inside his coat pocket. Unshouldering his pack, he filled it with the two food bags and threw in the book and cartridges before tying his trekking poles, bow and quiver onto the outside. With the pack back on his back, he climbed over the debris and to the ATV.

James calculated that the ATV's battery had been charging for maybe twenty minutes. Whether it was long enough or not, he had to risk it. The ATV was the only way he could get back in time. Attempting to hurry on foot through the debris-strewn downtown would be laborious and ultimately futile—it would just take too long. He'd noticed that the bridge on the east side of town appeared to be intact. It connected to face up in the street. James' gut dropped, but he had no choice but to pass near the corpse. He slowed to a stop, even though he had no time to lose, captured by the sight. Her face was ashen gray and she had clearly been there for some time. The snow had drifted around her body, but the incessant wind had kept her face and parts of her torso snow-free. The lapels of her bright red coat protruded from the snow. He was mesmerized by her hair, like long tentacles, moving in the wind. Shaking himself alert, James released the clutch and steered around her supine figure. He had to get home.

The freezing wind was now lifting ice crystals into the air creating a look of fog, a hazy white smoke. Subdued by the haze, a corner of his mind suggested he find instant shelter, to get out of the unbearable cold; there was no way he could handle the cold even for a few more minutes. But then he jolted to reality: he would die if he didn't get back.

Gunning the engine, he released the clutch and sped up the long hill. He dodged downed trees and slowed only enough to climb over the utility poles in his path. The cold bit his face and his extremities grew numb. When the wind gusted hardest, the tires lost traction and the ATV slid sideways. To counter this, James released the throttle until the tires grabbed the road again. His earlier fear had been that someone desperate for food would see him and come after or follow him. But he realized now that no one would dare venture out in these worst conditions. With home just a half-mile away, so close he could see it clearly in his mind's eye, James heard the engine cough. The rhythm of the cylinders was interrupted. Was he almost out of fuel? Was the fuel-line or gasoline freezing? The engine coughed again, and again—every four or five seconds. Holding his breath, as if it would help, James willed the engine to keep going. Reaching home was his only chance for survival.

At the top of the hill, the road leveled out and the engine settled. James made the last turn before his street and at that point desperation took hold of him, every part of his body and soul so frozen that he was sure he wouldn't make it if he had to run even just the last short distance to his door. Visibility had deteriorated so completely he could no longer differentiate the top of the drifts and covered mounds of abandoned vehicles from the white wind. Amazingly, he spotted his two-by-six plank, the only break in the sea of white. "In for a penny, in for a pound," he whispered as he sped up the slope of the drift, speed and momentum keeping the tires from sinking. Before he reached the peak, the engine coughed again, then twice more, nearly stalling. His forward motion slowed and the rear tires broke through the crust of the drift. He was sinking. But in that same instant, the vehicle leveled out, the engine caught, and James gently increased the throttle to coax the ATV out of the small craters created by tires and down the opposite slope.

At the final uphill grade towards his house, the engine sputtered again and, without a lingering cough, died completely. James was only twenty feet from his front door, but it seemed a mile. He tried to jump off, but his legs and arms were so frozen, so stiff, so utterly numb that he dropped onto the hard frozen ground, his heavy pack acting as an anchor. He tried to stand and couldn't feel his feet, yet he somehow staggered for the front door. He grabbed the door handle and threw open the door, for a split second wondering why it was unlocked, then slammed it shut and turned around.

Lara stood directly across from him with her back against the wall, the rifle pointed at his chest. He could see that she was in tears, but before he could say anything or step any closer, she swung the gun towards the couch. Confused, and ripping off his goggles, James looked to where she aimed and saw a small man with his knees drawn up to his chest.

Chapter 8

The warm smoke-filled room was illuminated by three sets of fluorescent lights spaced evenly across the ceiling, ballasts humming. A gas-powered generator rumbled in the adjacent room. Yet the seven men didn't notice the sounds. Not anymore. The constant noise enveloped them like the chirp of crickets on a warm summer night. Only it wasn't summer. The ferocity of the wind and cold reminded them of that each time they tried to go out. According to their calendar, tomorrow would be Christmas day. A date that now held little meaning to them.

Sergeant Lyons got up from the couch and stretched his arms. The air reeked of cigarettes and sweat. He sniffed the sleeve of his fatigues then drew his face away with a sneer. The ventilation system in this place sucks, he thought. He glanced at the men sitting around the large table playing cards, some sort of poker no doubt; they didn't play much else. He was a big man, six and a half feet tall and at least forty pounds heavier than any of the other men, yet no one acknowledged him standing there. Two empty wine bottles stood on the floor at the base of the couch. He accidentally kicked one over as he turned towards the small kitchen. Still no one looked up from the game. His head was pounding. He wanted to blame the stifling air, but he knew it was the wine. He looked at the small sink; faucets dry since the day the wind arrived. He reached for a pot on the two-burner stove; it still had a bit of water in it. He popped three aspirin into his mouth and washed them down with a swig from the pot, draining it. Let someone else fill it with snow, he thought.

Lyons shuffled over to the desk in the corner. He scanned the monitors. It was the same snowy scenes that had been playing for the last three and a half weeks. The only clue that they were live images came whenever the wind rocked the cameras. It amazed him that the cameras still worked. The radio sat silent. Ever since being trapped by the storm, Lyons embraced selective listening. There wasn't much to hear. He looked about the messy desk for his cigarettes. When he found them, he counted them out. Lyons always made a habit of counting them in front of the others; he didn't trust anyone, but this time he couldn't remember how many had been in the pack before he'd passed out, so it didn't matter. He decided he wasn't ready for a smoke and looked over at the crates of Mason jars, tossing the crumpled pack back on the desk. Nothing but canned fruits and vegetables. What he wouldn't do for some meat.

The windowless room they occupied wasn't designed as an all-inclusive living quarters for seven men, but it was all they had. Of the four doors, one was a weapons closet, another the bathroom (used only as a place to toss garbage ever since the pipes froze); the two heavier doors led to the attached garage and directly outside. It was a lot like being in jail, only they were the guards. The building was within throwing distance of a large gasoline storage tank, and it was their job to guard the tank and its precious contents. That single tank's capacity when full was 1.5 million gallons and it was still mostly filled to capacity, the gas having never been distributed because the army thought that they might have need for it. As of now, the army was the only government.

This refinery was about five miles west of Ferndale, right near the waters of North Puget Sound, intentionally situated in close proximity to a deep water channel. Once there had been two refineries poised along the shoreline, until one of them had taken a rocket in a gasoline storage tank and its roughly four million gallons of gasoline went up in flames. Most of the employees and the guards on site, specifically there to prevent such a disaster, were killed in the explosion. The terrorist that fired the rocket didn't seek credit for the explosion and was never identified. However, whoever it was had inadvertently succeeded in delivering a deadly blow to an already weakened government and economy. Security was immediately increased at the remaining refinery, with military-assigned guards on duty at all times. It was hardly an exaggeration that a crow couldn't fly within 500 yards of the storage tanks without getting its feathers singed. That is, if there were any crows left. Lyons was one of the first soldiers stationed here, and he hated the duty. He was a soldier, not a security guard.

On the northeast corner of the remaining refinery sat five very large storage tanks. These once held the gasoline reserves for the northwest corner of the United States. Gasoline and jet fuel were dispensed by truck throughout Washington, Idaho and northern Oregon. As gasoline prices soared and sales declined, four of the tanks were left empty. With the rapid increase in unemployment, most people could no longer afford the cost. The tanks sat in a pattern much like the five on a die, with four surrounding the fifth in the center. The outside storage tanks were connected by heavy-duty chain-link fencing as high as the top of the tanks and looking much like a spider's web. It was security net the Army Corps of Engineers had come up with based on a system that worked at refineries in the Middle East. Should a rocket impact any of the four outside tanks, the result would have been anticlimactic; they held nothing but air. And as long as the soldiers were on duty, the only way the center tank could be reached would be by air.

Through the previous summer, there had been eighteen men assigned to guard "the tank," as they affectionately called it. In August of 2029, their numbers were reduced to eight when the government folded and most enlisted personnel were ordered to return to base. Going from eighteen to eight meant that each man worked sixteen hours every day. With no days off at all, stress levels instantly increased, especially since they knew that with their reduced number they could no way thwart an all-out assault, if and when it happened. Plus, what little sleep each man could snatch was usually interrupted, either by radio chatter, doors banging as men returned from patrols, or the conversation of those not on duty. Long hours with minimal sleep did little for morale.

Morale was reduced even further as they listened to reports of supply flights going out to other sites closer to Fort Lewis, their command center. Their station in Ferndale was furthest away and supplies simply quit arriving in early November. There was only about two weeks of packaged meals and bottled water left, and they would be out of cigarettes before that. Lieutenant Alvorez, a seasoned veteran officer who was in charge, kept a close eye on his soldiers. He feared what his men might do sequestered this way and short-supplied. His fear of Lyons, a big man with discipline issues, was greatest. As the mood declined each day, Alvorez spent a lot of time on the VHF radio demanding a confirmation date for a rations drop from headquarters. He could at least show his men he was trying, even if his constant radioing only resulted in annoyance from whoever was on the other end of the airwaves. But if a shipment didn't materialize soon, Alvorez feared the men—each young, cocky, seasoned with a Middle East tour under his belt, and weaponed— would mutiny.

On November twenty-first, Alvorez had to ration supplies down to one MRE meal a day; they were accustomed to getting three. Yet this only extended their supplies for one week. After that, they would be out of food. Finally, Alvorez got HQ to promise a food drop, but it wouldn't come until December first—three days *after* their rations ran out. There was also no mention of cigarettes coming in the drop. Emotions flared.

"I'm taking a Humvee and Baxter into town. I'll be back in an hour," declared Lyons, clearly beyond the point of respecting any chain of command.

Alvorez stared hard at Lyons, contemplating his answer. He finally said, "I cannot let you do that. Leaving the property is strictly forbidden. And even if—well, if someone saw you leave, it could spark an attack."

"With all respect, Lieutenant, if anybody wanted to attack now, there aren't enough of us to stop 'em."

"I still cannot allow you to leave. Now get back out on patrol, soldier!"

Lyons turned to leave and then stopped. He looked at Alvorez with contempt and said, "Were not finished with this conversation." With that, he launched through the door and slammed it shut.

The next evening, Alvorez prepared for his evening rounds. He put on his Kevlar armor over his winter fatigues, grabbed his personal M-16 and a radio, and set out to walk the perimeter. Lyons, feigning sleep, waited for the door to close before getting up. He waited until Alvorez appeared on a monitor that showed him headed for the northeast corner of the fence line before he opened the weapons locker. He knew that he had less than twenty minutes to get in position. Lyons grabbed the long rifle case. Using its sling, he threw the case over his back and exited the bunker.

He'd ascended the ladders on the tanks before, so he knew he could be on top of one in less than five minutes. And he'd already secretly met with his six subordinates outlining his plan and warning them against raising any alarm. They feared him, so there were no objections. He just hoped he had chosen the tank that would give him the view he needed.

After reaching the top, Lyons quickly opened the case and took out the M-90. It was almost fifty inches in length. He uncapped the infrared scope, locked the magazine into the body, and fed a cartridge into the firing chamber. The M-90 had been his weapon of choice when he did his tour in Iran, and he felt confident that he could hit his target if it was no more than 800 yards away. The M-90 had a bipod attached about halfway down the barrel and Lyons used this to steady it. His gloveless hand exposed to the abnormally cold wind. He peered through the scope, scanning the fence-line. He saw no one. He stood and darted towards the southeast edge of the tank. Dropping onto his belly, he scanned again. He saw what he was looking for, a figure moving along the fence. In two minutes, the man would walk out of his field of view. Daylight was fading, and he couldn't be sure that it was Alvorez, so Lyons pulled out his radio and keyed the transmitter, "Lieutenant Alvorez, request your location."

"I'm midway down the eastern fence line," came the reply.

Lyons watched as the figure re-pocketed his radio. It was him. He took careful aim at Alvorez's face. Suddenly, Alvorez dropped to a knee and pulled the sling of his M-16 over his head. The lieutenant had become suspicious. Lyons watched as Alvorez rolled into a drainage ditch and dropped out of sight. But Lyons only needed to see him for a few seconds, so he waited, breathing steadily, keeping the sight focused on the ditch. At the same time that he saw the top of Alvorez's helmet appear over the edge, radio to his face, Lyons heard the "Mayday, Mayday, Mayday" come from his own radio. He shot, enjoying the sound of his rifle. The .50 caliber sniper bullet pierced Alvorez's Kevlar helmet before the sound of the shot could reach him.

As Lyons climbed down the ladder, he could see the other six men standing outside the bunker. Their watchful stance told him that they didn't openly disapprove of his action but were waiting to see what came next. He jumped from the last three rungs and landed standing, ready to draw his pistol. He directed two of them to dispose of the body and when they jumped to action, Lyons knew he'd have no problem. He'd promised them they would be able to leave the refinery, and he was delivering on that promise.

The next day "the tank" was left unattended as both Humvees and all seven men went in search of supplies. Lyons led in the first Humvee. After discovering that Ferndale was all but a ghost town with not much left to steal or scavenge, they headed south towards the Indian reservation, where most had bought cigarettes back before they were confined to their duty. The trailer-turned-store was still there, but it didn't look open for business. Then again, without power, nothing looked open for business any longer. Light from a candle, though, flickered through a window.

Lyons killed the engine and turned to the three men riding with him. "Let's get us some cigarettes," he said in a gloating fashion. All four men climbed out of the vehicle as the three in the other Humvee kept watch. Using hand signals, Lyons sent two men around behind the trailer. A face appeared in one of the windows, then disappeared briefly before the door opened and an older native peered out through the screen door. He didn't speak.

"We wanna buy some cigarettes," Lyons demanded, his rifle casually down by his side.

"I need ten pounds of food for each carton," the man said, looking nervous.

"Well that's just too bad, old man." Lyons raised the barrel of his M-16 and fired. The elderly man was blown backwards into the depths of the trailer. Lyons and the others listened for a moment, hearing nothing, then advanced to the open door. With several cases of cigarettes in their possession, Lyons and the others high-fived all around. Mission accomplished.

It was still early, so on their way back to the bunker, a farm with fruit trees and chickens in the yard caught the attention of the soldier in Lyons's Humvee. Lyons pulled over, the other vehicle following him. Lyons motioned for everyone to get out of the vehicles, wanting all of them visible to whoever was inside.

"Anybody home?" he shouted towards the house.

A moment later, an elderly woman appeared in the doorway. "Can I help you?"

"Yes, ma'am. We're on duty not far from here, and we ran out of rations. Can you spare any food?" asked Lyons, ingratiating himself to see how far it would get him

"I'm sorry, but I don't have enough for myself," she replied, seeming to be genuinely concerned for the men.

As if on cue, Lyons gave a sneer; his polite demeanor instantly dropped, and pointed his rifle at the woman, pulling back the bolt.

The other soldiers followed suit. The woman dropped to her knees and began sobbing.

Lyons pushed past her and entered the house. In the kitchen he found ten eggs on the counter and a box of apples on the floor. Pulling open the cabinet doors, he discovered several jars of homemade canned pickles, corn and green beans. He walked back to the door and held up three fingers. The closest three soldiers followed Lyons inside and came back out with their arms full, intentionally knocking into the woman as they passed. She stayed on her knees until long after the Humvees backed out of her driveway.

After the first day, the trips to obtain food had almost become a competition. Confident they'd encounter no obstacles and almost giddy from their new freedom, the soldiers now headed out in two separate directions each morning. At the end of the day, the men would compare their bounty, which now included liquor, wine and other things that took their fancy or that had value, and they'd laugh while telling their stories of manipulation and fright. They no longer even feigned asking for handouts. They just demanded, and had no qualms about killing if someone resisted.

On the afternoon of the ninth day, the storm arrived. The rations drop never happened.

Chapter 9

Only after James securely locked the door did he remove his hood, mask and layers of gloves. Stepping over to Lara, he gently took the gun from her trembling hands, while keeping the barrel directed towards the small figure on the couch. The man, dressed in a miss-match of garments that were clearly too big for his small body, lifted his face. James was startled to see that it was only a boy—maybe in his early teens. The face was so thin and dirty and still, reminding James of old photos taken by American soldiers after they liberated a concentration camp. James lowered his backpack to the floor with one arm as he held the rifle with the other. Guessing the boy could not be a physical threat, James leaned the rifle up against the wall and looked at both the boy and Lara, taking a deep breath.

Lara gained control of her sobs and finally spoke, "I heard the wind. And when you didn't return, I got scared and peeked outside to see if I could see you. I guess I forgot to lock the door again. A little later," she pointed to the boy, "he came in pointing a knife and demanding food."

"Where's his knife?"

Lara reached into her coat pocket. She pulled out a small paring knife and handed it to James.

James looked at the boy and demanded, "What's your name? Where did you come from?"

The boy just stared in silence. James could see that he was more scared than Lara was. This time he toned his voice down and asked once again, "Can you tell us your name?"

"I wasn't going to hurt her. I only wanted some food," he whimpered.

James was relieved by the boy's contrition and evident fear. He made a plea, "If you tell us your name, we'll share some of our food with you." He opened the top of the pack and removed one of the two food bags. That captured the boy's attention.

The boy watched as Lara roused herself to throw more wood in the stove and open the dampers to get the fire going stronger. Finally the boy turned to James and said, "Skyler. My name's Skyler." James, whose fingers were still numb from cold, blew on them and nodded to the boy.

"Were you the one that broke in here a few days ago, Skyler?" Lara interrupted.

The boy didn't answer.

James looked at him and said, "Come on, kid, we need to know if it was you or someone else, because if it was someone else, we have even more to be worried about."

The boy looked down at his feet before whispering, "It was me."

"Good. Okay. Now, how old are you?"

"Thirteen," Skyler replied sheepishly.

The pot on the stove was simmering loud enough to signify that it was about to boil. James got up from the crouching position in front of the boy, grabbed the food bag and walked to the kitchen. He busied himself pulling the inner bags out, gathering spoons and bowls, and measuring out two cups of oatmeal. He watched the near-boiling water for a moment, looked to Lara, then eyed the boy again. "Do you live alone?"

The boy nodded his head up and down.

"Do you live in one of the houses on this street, Skyler?" Lara asked with a gentle, encouraging tone, their earlier frightful encounter now a thing of the past. Again he nodded before adding, "I'm sorry I scared you. I thought you were my mother."

At that second James stirred the oatmeal into the boiling water and the smell, though subtle, filled the small room. It grabbed Skyler's full attention who avidly watched James work. When James finished stirring the oats, he sprinkled a pinch of sugar into the pan and dished up three equal bowls. Lara appeared as ravenous as Skyler, finishing hers first. Even though James was as hungry as the other two, maybe more so after his long and arduous morning, James divided up the last of what remained in the pot between Skyler and Lara, and then finished his own. James made sure the boy downed a few cups of water, too.

After their silent meal, Skyler gave a contented sigh and stared at Lara a moment before saying, "I used to live with my mother in a house about a half a mile from here. But then she had to leave."

Lara knitted her brows, "Why did she have to leave?"

"We didn't have any more food, so she went looking for some."

James became interested and asked, "When was this?"

"The day before the wind started," replied Skyler. "She told me to wait and she would return that afternoon with some food, but she didn't."

"But that was five weeks ago! Then how did you end up here?" asked Lara.

"I went looking for her the next day. When I was walking past this street, it got really cold and windy." Skyler paused as he stared at the floor as if he was recollecting the chain of events. "I ran up the street and was looking for a house to hide in. I saw you putting plywood on the windows," he said as he looked towards James, "so I kept running."

James thought back to that day. How could he have missed seeing someone running up the street? But then, his attentions were pretty focused.

Skyler continued, "I found an unlocked house up the street and nobody was home, so I snuck in there. Then the wind got *real* bad and blew the windows out."

"You were in a house with no windows and you're still alive?" James was incredulous.

"I shut all the doors and stayed in a closet."

"How did you keep from freezing to death?"

"I dragged some mattresses in to put against the walls. And I found candles, lots of candles."

James couldn't envision living alone in a closet for that length of time. But he looked to Lara who had a turned-in look to her expression. She had an idea of what it was like. "Did you have anything to eat?"

"I found a bag of Christmas candy. That was all I had except for water."

"How did you have water?"

Skyler looked back up, "From the candles. I melted snow with them, and they helped keep the closet warm. If I burned two candles at once, I could read a book."

James remembered that he was missing two candles after he and Lara returned from the farm, when his door had been kicked in. "Is that why you broke into my house, to get candles?" he asked, trying not to sound upset or aggressive.

"No, I needed food. I couldn't find any so I took the candles and matches."

Lara cut into the conversation, "Do you know where your mother is now?"

"Not for sure, but I think she must be home by now, waiting for me."

James and Lara exchanged glances; the possibility of this was slim to none. He was surprised that Skyler had survived, and in a damaged house exposed to the worst weather they'd seen yet. "Your house is only about a half mile from here? Maybe in a few days we can go there."

"Can't we go now?" asked Skyler eagerly.

James smiled apologetically, "No, right now the wind is too deadly and I think you're too weak. Let's get you stronger and go in a few days on a morning when there's no wind."

To keep Skyler engaged, Lara asked, "What does your mother look like?"

"She's real pretty and nice. Her hair is really long and it's brown like mine."

James harbored doubts that Skyler's mother could have survived the storm unless she was taken in by someone that was better prepared. He was ready to stop the questioning when a thought crossed his mind. "Was she dressed warm when she went out that day?"

"I think so. She had on her favorite coat." He fished around in his coat pocket and pulled out a crinkled photograph that he stared at for a moment, then handed to James. James looked at the photo and his heart sank; he saw a tall lean woman, gentle wind blowing a few wisps of hair across her face, wearing a long, bright red coat smiling back at him.

James tried to conceal his surprise, a pang of heartache for the boy, so hopeful that his mother was home waiting for him. It was less than an hour ago that James had spotted the dead woman in a red coat, half buried in the freezing snow. Changing the subject, he asked, "Why did you come here with a knife? Why didn't you just come and ask for help?"

"I was scared that you were mad. I saw you looking in houses and I thought you were looking for me."

Skyler went on to tell of his final days in the closet. Over the last few mornings, he said, he had noticed the wind die down for a bit and had occasionally left the closet to peak outside. He saw James leave early one morning, so he took advantage of his absence and broke down the door. The next day he looked out and was watching when the man returned with a second person. Skyler looked sheepishly at Lara, "I couldn't tell if you were a lady or a small man." During that week he noticed that they sometimes came outside together, and that James was making trips to the more destroyed homes; that's what made Skyler think he was searching for whoever broke down his door. Worrying about being found out, having no food, and knowing that he would soon be without candles, which meant no water, had made him fearful. And when his last candle sputtered out, there was nothing else he could do: Skyler made the decision to ask for help.

Skyler recalled that the wind was calm again that morning. "I watched the house for almost two hours before I saw you," he pointed to Lara, "come out the door looking towards the other end of the street. You're so much smaller that I wasn't as afraid of you as I was of running into him." He tipped his head toward James but kept looking at Lara. "On my way out the door, I grabbed the knife, just in case. I saw you go back inside right when I was sneaking out, so I didn't know if you saw me or not." Skyler took a deep breath, shaking his head back and forth, then continued. "My legs felt so wobbly, I could hardly walk, and then the wind picked up and I almost fell flat in a snow drift. I didn't know if I was doing the right thing, but I couldn't go back to that closet and I figured if you wouldn't help me," he shrugged his shoulders, "I would just keep on moving and try to make it for home and my mom."

"I don't remember pulling a knife from my pocket," he looked sheepish. "And I was so tired and cold once I got to the door, I don't think I knew what I was doing or even where I was. I remember hearing someone inside moving around and thinking it was my mother, that she had come home." He looked down to the floor. "I know I grabbed the doorknob and it wasn't locked, but then it was all dark, and I heard screaming and someone shouting something at me. When I could focus, I saw you pointing something at me. And all I could think to say was, "I want something to eat.""

The three were thoughtful for a moment, and Lara saw the boy struggle with his memory. "You were probably in such a blur from starvation, Skyler, but I remember vividly what happened next. You shocked me so much stumbling in the door. I didn't realize I hadn't locked it! You were so disheveled, and with your arm raised, holding the knife—I couldn't tell whether you were a child, a man, or a woman. I just panicked and fired. But the sound. I had no idea it would be so loud from within the room. And then you dropped the knife and collapsed."

Lara looked at James. "I hadn't really aimed, but I thought I had killed him. I just froze. But I had to do something, so I pushed him onto his back with my foot and saw that he was just a boy and that he was breathing. I was so relieved when I couldn't see any blood or sign of a wound." Lara paused here, the memory was so sad she didn't want to speak it. "When he had stirred, the boy had muttered 'Mom?' with such a weak voice, it nearly tore my heart out."

"I remember you helping me to the couch, holding the gun and crying. I wondered why you were sad. That's when he came in."

James nodded, glad to have heard the whole story. He looked at Skyler; he had never seen another human so emaciated and guessed his weight at less than sixty pounds. Knowing what he did about the boy's mother, James didn't have the heart to turn him out, even though it created a dilemma: he'd now have three mouths to feed out of the food that he'd intended to last him through the next few years. He looked at Lara. The expression on her face made it clear that she'd gotten over her shakiness and warmed to the boy, another human like herself, caught up in a bad situation and needing James' help.

By the time the light coming through the holes in the window coverings diminished, the boy had fallen asleep. James and Lara stepped into the kitchen so their conversation would not disturb him. James relayed what had happened when he went after the food, about the smoke coming from some houses, and how they now had an ATV to use until they ran it out of gas. "Do you have a problem with the boy staying with us until he's stronger?"

"No, not at all," she said. Then added, "Maybe we'll find his mother."

James said nothing.

They made rice for dinner and, once again, James did not limit either Lara's or Skyler's portions. He reiterated to Skyler that he could stay with them to build his strength, and that they'd take the half-mile journey to the house that he lived in with his mother soon after. James secretly hoped that they'd find Skyler's mother there. The image of that red coat contradicted this hope.

Keeping the stove stoked up and having three people sharing the main rooms kept the house noticeably warmer. They no longer had to wear their coats when inside. The next morning, with a couple of meals, a full night of sleep, and his tattered coat removed, Skyler seemed like a different person. James discouraged the boy from venturing outside just yet, to allow his body time to recuperate. But the boy was too excited to cooperate. The wind had abated like the other mornings, the sun as bright as ever, and the boy was intent on going outside. James relented. They did need more firewood, and they'd used the last of the water for breakfast, so James welcomed the help. James also wanted to figure out why the ATV had died.

Lara lent the boy her down coat and mittens, and the two men went outside. Skyler was excited to see the vehicle and wanted to know if they could ride it up to his house. "I want to see if Mom is waiting there for me!"

James unscrewed the cap and peered inside the gas tank before answering. "This thing isn't going anywhere. It's out of gas," he said, perplexed. He remembered checking the tank and thinking that he had plenty before he left the storage area.

"There's some gas at my house!" Skyler quipped. "We had almost four gallons saved up. We were going to trade it for food."

"Sorry, Skyler, but we don't have enough gas to get there," replied James. He knew it was inevitable, but didn't look forward to telling the boy that his mother might be dead. The vision of the woman in the street flashed through his mind. He fixed his gaze on the boy and said, "Let's wait a couple of days, then we'll walk over there and see what we can find."

The boy nodded eagerly, his optimism breaking James' heart, and the two set off to find wood for the fire. They were also going to look for a table and a few chairs, a request Lara had made after reflecting that with only the one couch, the room seemed incomplete now that there were three of them. They pirated the new furniture, along with several books, and Lara clapped her hands in pleasure.

Over the next couple of days, the three settled into a routine of scavenging that revolved around the wind. Most of the houses offered little to take; they were empty shells with nothing left inside except for the endless garbage from their former inhabitants. Garbage pick-up had ceased completely over a year before, and mounds of waste filled garages, porches, and even closed-up bathrooms and bedrooms. Even though there was no sign of humans, James and Skyler would enter each house cautiously. Skyler turned out to be adept at finding hiding places that usually revealed something of interest. They found an old set of silverware tucked behind a false wall in a bathroom cabinet that James wanted to save; just the fact that it was real silver gave it value and might someday come in handy. They brought back paintings for Lara to hang. They even found enough clothes so Skyler could change out of his rags.

Once they opened a door and found a frozen body. James made no attempt to hide the dead man from Skyler; he wanted the boy to understand that often death was a result of not being prepared, and only a thin line separated those that survived and those that didn't.

Lara had seen one too many frozen bodies and no longer wanted to be part of the house scavenging. So while James and Skyler were out pilfering, she spent her time cleaning and sprucing up their living quarters. The table and chairs added a nice touch, but to her mind the place still resembled a prehistoric cave. She thought of how nice it would be to take the plywood off the windows. If the winds would ever allow it, having daylight shining inside was one of the first improvements toward regaining a normal life, an improvement on a list that grew longer each day.

In the afternoons when they were prisoners of the wind and sequestered inside once again, James included his new housemate in the book-reading periods. The three of them would get absorbed in a story and forget about the wind and cold and destruction. Meals were also enjoyable with the added supplies, and James didn't ration the food, at least not yet. Both Lara and Skyler had been under nourished and he wanted them to have the extra nutrition. Granted, he was also under nourished, but compared to his roommates he was the strongest of the three.

Three days did wonders for the boy's strength, and James decided it was time to visit Skyler's old house. They downed a breakfast of plain oatmeal and weak coffee, dressed in their heaviest garb, said their goodbyes to Lara, then stepped out to a morning of clear skies and no wind. James sensed that the temperature seemed just a bit warmer than the previous few days. He wondered if this winter from hell was actually releasing its grip a little. Yet the clear day only did a little for James' outlook. He truly was reluctant to wander into another housing development. The world around him had changed so much in just the last year that he couldn't know what to expect. While he presumed not everyone was bad, no one could be trusted. He preferred to avoid any contact with others, but James needed Skyler's gasoline and was forced to take the risk. He was confident that, if needed, he could drop his pack and have his bow ready in just seconds. However, he still packed the pistol in his coat pocket just in case his bow wasn't enough of a deterrent.

Once they'd crossed the snowdrift by the entrance to the development, they turned west into an area unfamiliar to James. Skyler was highly excited and kept trying to convince James to pick up the pace. He talked about the gas waiting for James and about how happy his mother would be to see him. "I might even get to stay in my own bed tonight!"

Breaking the truth to the young boy was going to be difficult, so James focused on watching the road ahead and the small, older houses lining the street, alert to any possible threat. Each house looked far too damaged for anyone to survive in. Like in his own neighborhood, the construction of these houses must have been with the intent of keeping the building costs to a minimum, because each house had lost all or most of its roof and several had complete walls missing. James and Skyler had to climb over large pieces of debris, including power poles. There was no way that they could have ridden the ATV down this road.

James thought of how Skyler had described his neighborhood, and from the sounds of it, most all the houses were two-story and much newer than what he was living in. He assumed that since the houses were constructed when the building codes were actually enforced, maybe they were able to withstand the high winds.

But when they reached the entrance to Skyler's development, they stopped short: the damage was worse than either of them had expected. Skyler let out a cry of dismay. All of the homes within sight had severe second story damage. It was as if a physical force had punched the top half of each structure. Nothing appeared intact. From where they stood, they could see that none of the windows had been boarded; their sills were dark gaping holes. Besides debris from the structures, there was human debris—pieces of beds and other furniture, fabric, house wares, even toys were scattered or were stuck under the wreckage. Skyler stood there without any expression and James worried that he was going to start crying. Instead, Skyler looked up and said, "Come on, let's find my house."

The two walked down a gentle slope and stepped around large sections of walls and roofs. Skyler pointed out his house; it was a beige one, about a block and a half straight back on the left side of the street. Like the others, the roof was gone and the windows were without glass. As they drew near, they stopped in unison, both seeing the same thing: a silhouette of a heavily-jacketed man inside the broken-out living room window. The man was facing away from them, seemingly unaware of their presence. James motioned to Skyler to move close to him against the side of the house. James removed his bow and fit an arrow onto the string.

"Did you recognize that man?" James asked Skyler.

Skyler replied quickly, "No."

Suddenly a shot rang out; James could tell it came from within the house. He dropped his bow, quickly pulled the pistol from his pocket, and waited. There was some shouting and it sounded like two men arguing over something. Then a man came out the front door, limping heavily; blood covered his left pant leg. James pushed Skyler back against the wall and watched. When the man limped in the opposite direction, James released his grip on Skyler's shoulder. There was still at least one man inside the house—one with a gun. James waited silently. Almost thirty seconds passed before he heard footsteps in the snow. Skyler heard too and tensed up as he leaned back to stay out of James's way. The man walked right past James and Skyler without noticing them. When James saw that he carried plastic gas can in each hand, James pointed his pistol towards the man's back and yelled, "Stop right there or I will shoot you!"

The man halted but didn't turn or speak. James sensed that the man was contemplating his next move and said, "Any movement other than setting those gallons down and I'll shoot you before they touch the ground."

The man turned his head slightly and said without any tone of fear, "If you're after this gas, I'm willing to split it with you."

"This house belongs to my friend, and so does that gas. We call that looting," replied James. He hoped the man could not sense just how scared he really was and stepped around in front of the man. Holding his pistol tightly while pointing it at the man's chest, he reached out with his free hand and patted his pockets. The man's pistol, an old military .45 caliber semi-auto, was in his coat pocket. James glanced at it briefly before slipping it into his own pocket. He then stepped back a few feet and, still aiming at the man's chest, said, "Now—set the cans down. And if you're smart, you'll run back to where you came from."

The man didn't move. Looking at James, he pleaded, "If you keep my gun, you know you're sentencing me to death."

"Like you just sentenced your friend in there to death?" James asked.

"He found the gas and wasn't willing to share. I only wounded him."

The man had sunken cheeks like he'd had almost nothing to eat for the last several weeks. Any other time, James would have considered handing back the gun minus the bullets, but he knew that if he did, the man would find more bullets and use it against him at another time.

Then out of nowhere, Skyler's voice said very loudly, "I will count to three. One . . ."

Before Skyler could say "two," the man turned and saw an arrow aimed at his temple. He dropped the cans before he turned and ran up the street in the same direction that the wounded man had gone.

James realized that he was shaking badly. The man *must* have sensed this. It was only thanks to Skyler that the man thought twice about his survival. He looked at Skyler. The boy stood there holding the undrawn bow. Why didn't he seem afraid? James finally said, "You know, that bow shoots much better if you pull the string back."

"When we get back, I want you to show me," Skyler said excitedly. Handing the bow to James, he added, "I need to look inside for just a minute." The boy disappeared into the house. Knowing that the boy would not find his mother inside, James let the boy go in alone while he stood watch. Skyler didn't return for almost five minutes and when he did, he had a pillow case filled with small items. He dragged a small plastic snow sled behind him. Skyler dropped the pillow case onto the sled and motioned James to set the gasoline there. Looking back at his old house briefly, he turned to James and said, "We can go home now."

Chapter 10

Lara was emptying the waste bucket when she heard a gunshot in the distance, faint but most definitely a gunshot. She looked off down the street. Did it come from where James and Skyler had gone? This was only the second time that James had left her alone for more than a few minutes and with the sound of the gun, she felt that familiar wave of fear and uncertainty, an unwelcome emotion, overcome her. It would grow into an ugly monster. It always did. Since James had rescued her, she had beaten back the anxiety and tried to keep it hidden.

Since the night the soldiers had attacked her friends, a deep pain was seeded within her. The time she spent alone in the dark, dank cellar fixed that pain, driven by the certainty that she was going to die a slow death. James's appearance at the top of the stairs had been like a miracle; that he didn't leave her but freed her from her prison was a godsend. He gave her something to live for and, as yet, asked for nothing in return. However, whenever he wasn't near her, distracting her from her thoughts, she would start to dwell on her future and everything would once again seem hopeless. It was this hopelessness that overwhelmed her now, with the sound of the shot, spurred on by her fear that something bad had happened to him. Without him, Lara was sure she would become a victim of the next predator that came her way. At that moment, Lara just wanted to die, to have it all over with. She wanted a stiff drink or strong drugs with which to drown these demons, but such "pain killers" were no longer available. She was forced to live with a cancer that targeted her soul.

Lara had shared only some of her past with James, never mentioning that she harbored anxieties that pushed her to extremes. As the economic deterioration increased, so did her depression. The almost five weeks she had spent locked away in that subterranean prison was the first time in three years that she had gone more than a few days without getting shit-faced on vodka or Valium, or whatever else she could lay her hands on. The nursing home had been a great source of medications. Her patients were old and they didn't miss their pills. After he rescued her from the cellar, James had replaced the drugs as her crutch. His afternoon readings made her forget the ugliness of the world and the uncertainty of the future. She was able to sleep through the night only because she knew he was nearby.

Her friends at the farm knew nothing of her hidden habits. She'd volunteered to spend the night in the chicken coop, as she did at least a few nights each week, for only one reason. It had been the only place she could drink a bottle of wine without being labeled an alcoholic; she feared she'd be asked to leave if they found out. The five weeks in the cellar had forced her to sober up, but the pain of uncertainty never swayed and actually became worse as each day passed. She was living in a time that had no guarantees about tomorrow, and there was nothing she could use to dull the pain.

She was hugging her knees to her chest and rocking back and forth when the door opened less than an hour later. It startled her to see James and Skyler standing there; she had convinced herself they would never return. James knelt beside her and placed a hand on her back and just started petting her as he spoke softly in reassuring tones, looking deep into her red swollen eyes. Skyler stayed by the door not knowing what to do, any adult sensibilities years away. James turned to Skyler, quietly asking him to bolt the door before the wind picked up, and helped Lara move to a chair at the table. "You heard the gunshot?"

She sobbed, nodding. "What happened?"

"Nothing. It didn't involve us. Two men were looting a house and one of them shot at the other." He intentionally downplayed the event.

"Did you see them?"

"Only briefly," again he lied.

With James at her side, Lara slowly regained her composure, embarrassed by the state in which they'd found her. She watched as Skyler unloaded a pillow case with his mementos. He arranged them on the top shelf of a bookcase he'd dragged across the snow only yesterday. At the center of his belongings he placed a framed photo; it was of him and his mother riding in a Ferris wheel. The photographer had been standing below the big wheel with the camera pointed vertically. Mother and child were leaning out the front of the cart and smiling towards the camera. Lara wondered if Skyler's father had taken the photo and another swell of depression flooded through her. She didn't ask about his father. She didn't ask about his mother either; it was all too obvious.

By noon, her anxieties dissipated somewhat, Lara boiled water for their meal of rice and set out three bowls. She looked up in surprise when James handed her a few strips of beef jerky to add to the rice.

"I was saving this for a special day, but then I figured that every day is special," he said quietly.

His attentiveness was reminding her of someone taking care of a sick person. He took over and dished up the rice. He put an extra piece of jerky in her bowl. He offered her the final spoonful. She didn't want to be a sick person; she wanted to forget the events of the morning and move on. After James made her stay put while he began clearing the table, Lara was about to scold him but couldn't think of a gentle way. Finally, in an attempt to change the subject, she turned to Skyler and said in a light-hearted conspiratorial way, "What if we ask James to start reading just a little earlier than usual today?"

Skyler's face lit up and he looked to James.

"Sure, I can do that. We have all afternoon." replied James; he stopped what he was doing.

Lara worried that the earlier scene had damaged her connection with the boy. Feeling the need to re-establish their relationship, she went over to where Skyler was sitting on the couch and curled up next to him. He made no attempt to move away. As James read, they both focused on the story almost as if they were watching it. Eventually, Skyler leaned his head on her shoulder.

The next morning, Lara watched as James poured one of the cans of gasoline into the tank of the ATV. They all breathed a sigh of relief when the motor started; the battery had retained enough of a charge. James pulled the generator out of the large box in the back and placed a cushion there for Skyler and Lara to ride on. Whether it was because he didn't want a repeat of yesterday's drama or for some other purpose, Lara was grateful that James wanted her to go along with him and Skyler to "get stuff"—that's all he'd said. But she didn't care. She just didn't want to stay home and wait alone.

Watching him work in silence, Lara realized that James was in somewhat of a dark mood. Was he upset over her breakdown? At the last moment, James tied Skyler's small sled to the rear hitch of the ATV. The boy was too excited about riding in the ATV to bother asking why.

They drove quickly over the drift and turned left onto the road that led down to the center of town. The ATV bounced around on the uneven surface; Lara and Skyler had to hang onto the rails with both hands to keep from falling out. A couple times they had to stop briefly in order to drive over or around an obstacle as they made their way down the hill. Once again, the sky was a vivid blue and cloudless. Lara hadn't seen it snow since coming out of the basement, just that the snow drifts changed each day from the afternoon winds. The cold also didn't seem as biting as when they walked away from the farm, and telltale signs hinted that the snow was even starting to melt: cars that had been completely buried now had parts of their roofs and windows exposed. The wind would blow the snow off a small patch of glass or metal, and once an area was exposed to the sunlight, it would act as a natural solar collector to warm the car from inside.

Lara could see houses here and there above the road that had smoke seeping from their chimneys. She wondered who these people were and just how they were coping without amenities. She pointed so that Skyler would notice the smoke. Maybe he'd realize that they weren't the only ones to survive the winter and give him hope, as it did her.

It took them maybe ten minutes before the ATV neared the bottom of the hill. James turned left on a short road that led to Second Avenue. He drove slowly, clearly scouting the street for something. He steered around the end of a utility pole and stopped. She was partially hidden from view by the pole, but her face and red coat were even more exposed than when he'd seen her before. James killed the engine and stepped off the ATV, pausing only long enough to see that Skyler recognized what he was seeing, his eyes suddenly wide. Lara, too, understood what was buried in the snow, and she realized why James had brought her along. At first Skyler didn't move; Lara and James stood by and watched, helpless. Slowly Skyler stepped towards the body of his mother and knelt down on one knee beside her. He didn't speak or look up to his friends. Lara swallowed hard as she watched Skyler touch his mother's frozen hand, almost as if he looked for some sign that she might still be alive. He finally turned towards Lara and said, "She came down here to find food. She did it for me. She did everything for me."

Lara didn't know how to respond, so she just looked deep into Skyler's eyes, sharing with him her silent understanding about this change in his life.

Skyler turned to James and looked at him woefully as he collected his thoughts. "We need to take her home. Will you help me?"

They drove slowly back up the hill following their morning tracks. Skyler leaned against Lara, her arm around his shoulders, as he watched the sled holding his mother trailing behind in the snow.

As they approached the top of the hill, Skyler reached inside his pocket and pulled out a large khaki-colored button. He showed it to Lara. "This was next to her hand."

Lara leaned over to look at it. "Was it hers?"

"No. None of her clothes had buttons like this."

Though the khaki button conjured thoughts of the night her friends were attacked, she was silent. There was no reason to suggest anything that might give Skyler worse visions than he already had of his mother's death.

Skyler slid the button back into his pocket and continued staring towards the sled.

Once they arrived back at their block, Skyler and James pulled the sled to the front yard of the house where Skyler had holed up for so many weeks while he waited for his mother's return. It was only fitting that the house that had provided him protection during her absence should in some way be his mother's final place. The sled came to rest with a quiet thud against a small bank of snow. Lara stood back and watched; waiting for the time she knew would come when Skyler would need her. A boy his age could not get through this alone.

Since the ground was too frozen for digging, it was Skyler's decision to cremate his mother's body. They used wood from the frame of the garage and house to build a platform for a funeral pyre. After the base was assembled, they set some boards off to the side before laying her body on the deck of the platform. They set the remaining wood on her body. They were gentle. When they finished resting the last few pieces, Lara arrived with the can of kerosene that James had asked her to retrieve. James took the can and carefully doused the stack of timbers with the kerosene.

Skyler said quietly, "James? Do you have a match?"

"I have one," Lara said, and gave it to Skyler.

Just before striking the match, Skyler turned towards James and Lara, and said, "Her name was April and she was the best mother anyone could wish for."

With that, Skyler struck the match and threw it onto the pile. The flames grew quickly as the afternoon wind kicked up. Lara stayed close behind him absorbing the heat as the pyre became totally engulfed. The boy stood as close as he could, almost as if the warmth was the one last gift from his mother.

Finally, he stepped back and turned to face Lara. She saw his lip quiver. She stepped up closer to him sensing what was about to happen. For the first time since he found his mother, Skyler wept. She took hold of Skyler's shuddering body and held him tight as she cried along with him.

Chapter 11

Winter was definitely receding. Seven weeks had gone by since Lyons had liberated his men from what he considered the lieutenant's unreasonable control. Two weeks had passed since their only calendar became outdated. Each morning since then, there had been a brief window that the wind simply disappeared. The soldiers embraced the chance to get outside and stretch, if only for a few hours. As cold as it was, there were still outdoor tasks that needed attention. One of their surveillance cameras had completely succumbed to the high winds. Two just needed to be re-directed. There wasn't any hurry in doing it now; the afternoon winds would just shift them once again. Most everything else, including their bunker, remained unscathed. The food they'd acquired before the storm was now in short supply, and the food drop that HQ promised had never materialized. Since killing Alvorez and assuming command, Sergeant Lyons hadn't taken on any of the duties inherent to the position, including attempts to contact HQ about the missing drop. His excuse was that radio reception was weak, suggesting their antenna may have suffered the same fate as the surveillance cameras. As soon as the winds and temperature allowed it, they'd need to get someone on top to fix the communications gear. So far, no one was volunteering.

The two Humvees had been sitting in the garage for over six weeks. They had killed time by performing the required periodical maintenance on both vehicles. That was their only diversion besides playing cards. First on the list would be restocking their supplies.

Cigarettes were still plentiful, at least for now, but they all wanted meat, Lyons complaining the most about its absence to their diet. The stash they'd acquired before the storm was strictly vegetables.

They had plenty of work to do before the Humvees could navigate the roads again. Except for tree limbs and debris carried by the winds, the scene inside the refinery property had not changed much. Outside the refinery was a different story: every tree and power pole was down, littering the snow covered pavement and leaving the roads impassable. Nothing was left standing except the security fences surrounding the refinery. Enormous snowdrifts filled in the recessed areas, further altering the landscape.

Each day, they were able to venture out further after using the Humvees to tow obstacles from their access to the main road that ran north to south on the east side of the refinery. Once they cleared the way out to this road, they split up into two teams: one cleared the northern route, the shortest route to Ferndale; the other went south. The team that went north was led by Sergeant Lyons, and the three men clearing the southern route, the three Lyons disliked the most, were glad to be away from him. Throughout the six weeks of seclusion, Lyons had referred to them as 'government fuck-ups,' verbal abuse he found humorous, but that weighed upon them. They feared one day the abuse would turn physical. The removal of their rule-rigid lieutenant was supposed to make things better, not worse, but the last several weeks had turned into a living hell for the three men.

Especially for the crew on the northern route, it was tedious and obstacle-ridden work clearing the roads, tangible obstacles as well as logistical. Power poles criss-crossed the road, tangled up with fence posts, tree stumps, and whatever else was abandoned or blown in. The Humvees could only tow so much before they slid on the ice-covered the asphalt, and without the luxury of a chain saw, any cutting had to be done with handsaws. Each day, snow blew up against solid objects and created huge drifts, which they had to shovel, sometimes more than once if the night's wind was bad.

The shoveling seemed endless. Time was also against them. They had to be sure to be back to the bunker by 10 a.m. or risk having a Humvee caught out in the wind. Generally they made it a rule that when the temperature combined with the wind chill dipped below minus thirty degrees Fahrenheit, they would retreat into the bunker for the day; they couldn't be sure just how much cold the antifreeze could withstand. To lose a Humvee, their only means of transportation, would be disastrous.

Lyons observed that each morning, it seemed the time the winds picked up came a little later. He finally had one of the men start recording the times when the wind stretched above the twenty mph mark. He found that with each passing day, they gained almost five minutes of calm weather.

On some days, the guys on the northern route were only able to clear some forty to fifty yards. The crew clearing the southern route encountered fewer obstacles and made better time. They followed the eastern fence line towards a four-way intersection. Once they made it there, they turned onto Slater Road and continued clearing the route to the interstate. Through a once-fertile valley, this route passed a few farms, which meant they might encounter survivors.

Grateful for the morning reprieves from Sergeant Lyons, the three men on the southern route had been at their road clearing for most of a week when they passed a driveway that led to a large home. From their distance it appeared vacant, yet it had suffered no visible damage from the high winds. Like most houses, the windows had been covered with boards and large sheets of plywood. None of the men saw any reason to venture down the long driveway. It was severely cluttered with downed trees that had once lined its long entrance. The following morning, as the same soldiers drove past that same area, one of the men noticed smoke coming from the house's chimney. The driver brought the vehicle to a sudden halt and they all surveyed the scene. With thoughts of their depleted and now rationed food supply, they donned their Kevlar and sunglasses, checked their weapons, and started walking through the snow-covered field towards the house. It didn't look ominous, but their experiences in Iraq and Afghanistan had taught them that traps never looked like traps.

The smallest of the three soldiers was twenty-two year old Jason Carter. He had been in Iraq for two tours before getting sent stateside and assigned to guarding the tank. His main skill in Baghdad was performing drive-by ambushes, but he excelled in close-quarters combat. Lyons hadn't bothered to place any of the three in charge, but Carter seemed to be the only one that took the initiative.

As they neared the front entrance, Carter pointed out several foot prints, large and small, stamped into the wind packed snow. Some of the tracks were fresh. He placed his back against the wall just outside the frame of the front door. He reached out and knocked loudly three times before pulling his hand back. The other two soldiers stood about twenty feet out from the door with their rifles pointed towards the door. Almost a full minute passed with no response. Carter could not hear any sounds coming from within the house. He was about to knock again when he saw his two compatriots swivel their heads and their weapons to the right. Carter followed their aim and saw a man step out from behind the corner of the house. The man was brandishing a shotgun. He was well past fifty years old, larger than any of the soldiers, and his skin was the texture of someone who had worked outside all his life. The man kept his eyes on the two soldiers in the yard, not seeming to notice Carter against the wall. He was obviously angry, yet he did not have a finger on the trigger. "You sons of bitches get off my property!" he shouted.

Carter swung his muzzle around and fired two shots. Both bullets entered the man's temple and pierced his brain before exiting. The man's shotgun hit the ground only a second before he did. Without hesitation, Carter kicked in the front door and motioned the other two inside, covering their flank as he followed them in. The room was silent and dark as a cave; the only source of light coming from the open doorway. They held their weapons ready and switched on their headlamps. A large bed was positioned in front of a fireplace Carter noticed a bra amidst the pile of clothes near it. There was also an odor present that was not unpleasant. The man had been eating grilled meat for breakfast.

Using hand signals, Carter motioned one of the men up the staircase. He instructed the other to check down a hall towards three closed doors. This man had clearly not lived alone, yet the search of the other rooms came up clean. Where was the woman? Carter cautiously stepped into the kitchen, the smell of meat stronger, and observed the back door slightly ajar, indicating the way that the man had exited the house. With the barrel of his gun, Carter coaxed the door open further. Outside were two fresh sets of foot prints in the drifted snow. One pair traveled around towards the front of the house; the other pair, smaller, went straight out, towards a barn. Carter raised his weapon to his shoulder and followed the smaller prints.

The barn had suffered extensive damage, with most of the roof torn away. Tracks showed that whoever had headed this direction—he guessed it was a woman from the boot size—had circled to the left towards the back of the structure. Carter turned right and crept towards the first corner. He pulled out a small mirror and held it past the edge of the structure. She was not in sight. He moved quickly to the next corner and peered around the backside of the barn. Her tracks indicated she had stopped there before continuing out into the field. Carter spotted her as she stumbled through the snow, her back towards him. She fell once, but recovered and slowly continued her plight. Carter set his sights on her lower spine and waited for her to falter once again. She was less than sixty yards away when she fell a second time. The woman stood back up and stayed motionless. Carter took his shot. The bullet pierced her lumbar spine and instantly her legs folded. She went down again. Carter smiled to himself. The wound itself would not be fatal, but she would die when the winds returned. He'd paralyzed her from the waist down.

Carter returned to the house to find that his men had discovered where the couple stashed their food: a chest freezer parked outside the back door contained at least eighty pounds of frozen beef and pork. The individual parcels were wrapped in plain white butcher paper and stamped with the name of a meat cutter and the type of cut. Inside the house, they found steaks and sausage thawing in the refrigerator, now used just for storage. A pantry in the corner of the kitchen revealed canned corn, pickles and cherries. "These people ate well," grumbled Carter.

Instead of leaving, they stoked the fire in the stove and cooked three of the steaks for themselves. Over their loud chewing, they could hear the faint cries from the woman out back. It did not bother them. Afterwards, they set about filling bed sheets to carry the food back to the Humvee. Carter left one package of sausage in the refrigerator for tomorrow when the three would be back to clear more of the road. He closed all the doors, noticing from the back door that the woman's cries had gotten quieter, before joining his men at the Humvee. Instead of heading further to clear any more of the road, they drove back towards the refinery.

They arrived at the bunker ahead of Lyons's crew, Carter expected them to arrive within the half hour; the winds dictated this. Carter grabbed three small packages of partly thawed steaks and left the rest of the meat stowed in a corner of the cold garage. Using their small electric stove, he began frying the steaks. While they sizzled, he filled two bowls with cherries and pickles and set plates and silverware out onto the table. They had something to celebrate, and Carter wanted to surprise Lyons. He wanted the big man to see that they weren't fuck-ups after all.

Chapter 12

"Tomorrow's St. Patrick's day!" Skyler announced one morning. James and Lara laughed at the loud way he'd made the announcement. He'd obviously been keeping track of the date. Yet they were completely aware that over the course of the last two months, the temperature had gradually warmed while the wind speed had diminished in proportion. James and Skyler took advantage of this with longer and longer periods of time to explore and scavenge together. They even had time for chores that didn't involve going into abandoned homes, such as when James removed some of the plywood from the windows to allow more light into their house. Lara often joined them for the opportunity to get fresh air. Instead of huge mounds of white snow along the streets, a variety of colors from the abandoned cars and SUVs began emerging with the thaw. They siphoned gas from the more accessible vehicles if they could get through the snow to the gas cap. If they couldn't, they would dig out the underside and pop out the tank's drain plug to get what remained inside. James had grown accustomed to using the ATV on his and Skyler's expeditions, and the two gallons from Skyler's home had gone quickly.

Mornings after the chores were done, for most of an hour, James taught Skyler how to shoot a compound bow, one they'd found in a garage about four blocks away. Compact and powerful, it was intended for hunting in tight brushy woods. The small bow was just right for Skyler, and James was able to reduce the draw resistance enough for the boy to handle. Even though Skyler had gained weight with a steady supply of food, his arm strength was lacking, so James made him draw the bow and shoot thirty arrows each day to help build up his arm strength. They had not seen any living birds or animals, but James wanted to be sure the boy knew how to hunt; it would likely be a necessary part of his survival for the rest of his life. Someday there wouldn't be any bullets left. The bow-and-arrow, dating back to before written history, would become the dominant hunting tool once again. It would also be the dominant weapon, and James wanted the boy to be able to defend himself.

For Skyler's training, James had constructed a makeshift target and shooting range. He'd found an old thick oriental rug, heavy enough to stop arrows without damaging them, and hung it over a clothes line. While Skyler would need to learn to shoot in any conditions, for training, a solid platform was needed. Recent ice and snow melt had left pools of water atop the frozen ground. The permafrost created a barrier that didn't allow the water to seep downward, leaving the top two inches a sticky mud that clung to everything. A thin sheet of plywood, too thin to be worth saving for boarding up windows if the winter winds came back next year, but strong enough to hold the boy's weight, acted as a shooting platform. It could be moved easily to increase the difficulty or to experiment with the sights for different distances.

Every day, Skyler would have to show his proficiency to Lara and James. The challenge was to shoot his last five arrows into an eight-inch circle painted on the center of the rug. Whenever he'd hit all five, James would gently tighten the bolts that controlled the draw strength. The shooting platform would also be moved back a foot or more. His progress impressed James. Sometimes they would compete, James shooting from ten yards further away than Skyler, for who could place their arrow closest to the center. As each week passed, it became more difficult for James to win every contest.

One morning, Skyler requested their presence for a demonstration. The sky was overcast and the temperature was mild. James picked up his mug of tea and followed the boy outside. Lara pulled on her coat before stepping out. It was above freezing, but not by much. The ground beneath their feet had softened even more. James spotted an alteration in the usual eight-inch target on the rug: Skyler had used tape to secure a cardboard toilet paper tube to the center of his target. There was so much tape that the circle was completely covered. James wanted to say something to Skyler about wasting supplies, but held back. His curiosity outweighed the need to lecture the boy. There was a slight breeze that gave the rug a gentle, swinging rhythm. Before retreating back to his shooting deck, Skyler stuffed the tube with wads of aluminum foil.

"Why the foil?" James asked.

"So my arrow won't bounce out of the tube."

"Do you honestly believe that you can hit that small an area in these conditions?" James pointed towards the rug swaying with the breeze.

"You'll see." Skyler picked up his bow with a single arrow equipped with a target tip. He moved to his shooting deck that sat twenty yards from the target.

What was the boy up to? James knew that from twenty yards, a moving target that was less than two inches in diameter was a near impossible shot. Skyler stood on his usual platform eyeing the target. He hadn't drawn the bowstring yet. Skyler turned towards James and grinned. The smile looked almost diabolical. And then Skyler walked back to James's platform. He was now a full thirty yards from the target. James shook his head in disbelief. Skyler drew his bowstring back. While the target swayed a few inches one way and then the other, Skyler didn't waver his aim. After a few seconds, he released the arrow. The impact shook the rug. The arrow's shaft protruded from within the cardboard tube.

James was stunned, but he decided to have a little fun with the boy. "Better lucky than good," he quipped.

With that remark, Skyler pulled a second arrow from his quiver. He quickly drew back the bowstring a second time. This time he released the string almost instantly. Two arrows were now imbedded within the tube.

Lara went to the boy and put her arm around his shoulder, giving him a squeeze and tussling the hair on his head.

James clapped three times slowly, again shaking his head. "I'm impressed!" And James truly was. The boy had mastered the skill in such a short period of time—from the moment of that fearless act when he'd raised the undrawn bow at the man stealing gas from his home, to now, nailing his target from such distance and in variable conditions. He hadn't expected such skill and accuracy this quickly and was proud of the boy.

"I think it's time I can leave you to defend yourself, Skyler," James said. With more signs of survivors now that their world was thawing, and with food in short supply, it wouldn't be long before someone started searching the storage lockers and James wanted to be sure he had his goods. He looked at Lara and thought of her anxiety crisis the last time he'd left her alone, then back to the boy. "How about you stay here with Lara when it comes time for me to retrieve more supplies and food from storage?" Skyler grinned wide and nodded vigorously at James. Lara's own subtle smile indicated her appreciation.

James made four trips down the hill into Ferndale, which meant four trips back—each time struggling up and over the large snow drift, still unmelted, at the entrance to the development. He was tempted to shovel a path through the drift until Lara pointed out that even though he'd not seen anyone on any of his recent trips, people could be out there, watching, and just take cover when they heard the ATV. Clearing the entrance to their road would make it too easy for someone to enter the development for scavenging, or worse. James nodded in agreement, and the predicament made him realize two important things: they weren't really safe in this development since it only had one way in and out. And if they wanted to grow vegetables, this was not the place to do it.

James had not recovered everything from the three lockers. He'd left a sizeable amount of goods in one that he considered safe. Anyone wanting to get into the locker's contents would need power tools. Included in what he kept back were bags of corn and other vegetable seed. These were best left in a secure place until the prospect of spring and growing weather was a reality and not just a hint. He'd also left a handgun, another compound bow, some of their heaviest winter clothing, and about one third of the food in the last locker. It was his cache if by chance he lost everything else.

James and Lara divided up the food he did bring back to the house into smaller bags. Each held about a week's worth of staples, and James felt that all but one bag should be left in the lower part of the house at a time. The rest would need to be stored in a safe and dry place. The crawl space had thawed and became extremely wet. James had already moved everything out of there. He also didn't feel safe keeping the stores hidden somewhere in the main house, in case someone had witnessed his trips with the ATV. It was Skyler who thought of the small attic, and offered to help move the bags there; he was smaller and more agile. He stuffed the bags beneath the blown-in insulation. Should someone search the place, James hoped they would only glance around the attic, see nothing, and not look under the level of the rafters.

By mid-April, most all the snow had disappeared, yet there were still no signs of any plant life other than grasses. Shrubs and trees that normally would exhibit buds prior to blooming were just brittle, dead sticks. The fact that the grasses seemed unaffected left James with hope that eventually other plants would survive the harsh conditions. He didn't know if the new spouts came from windblown seeds or from last year's roots. The internet could have answered that question in a snap. It was a shame that modern technology had followed the same fate as the dinosaurs. Even without a computer search, James knew that there were plants that could survive in the tundra under similar circumstances. Maybe then it could also happen here.

Around the third week of April, Skyler was out practicing his archery when a crow flew overhead. Two days later, both James and Lara spotted three of the large black birds; they landed in the field behind their house. Either these birds had survived the winter or they had migrated here—maybe from a place that had not been altered in the same way as this area had. James and Lara looked at each other with hopeful eyes. Such signs of life could mean that other living creatures may also have survived. It also meant a potentially new supply of protein.

The next day, James hid himself by lying on a patch of semi-dry turf under an earth-colored rug, slightly tented with a stick so he could see out, a few yards from the smelly remains of a dog. With his bow and two arrows, James waited almost thirty minutes before finally being rewarded. A single crow landed on a fence post just a few feet from the dog. A second crow appeared a few seconds later. It landed on the ground much closer to the carcass. Probably a mated pair, James thought. The second bird appeared to be wary of danger; it began walking a half circle towards the dog's body. The first crow seemed content just to sit on the post and watch.

James's breathing became more rapid and his palms got sweaty. He waited for the crows to become distracted by the possibility of food instead of being cautious of their surroundings. His patience drew thin. The ground beneath him that once seemed almost dry now felt mostly wet; the cold mud had become uncomfortable. He couldn't wait any longer. James quickly stood and drew the bowstring as fast as he could muster. The instant he let go, he knew his arrow would miss its target. Getting to a standing position in order to draw the string back created just too much commotion. And the crows were too wary of danger; they naturally took flight the split second they sensed movement. The arrow disappeared in the thick dead grass, and for all his efforts to find it, it was lost.

James couldn't afford to waste one arrow, let alone any more arrows. Using a gun was out of the question; it was imperative he have the bullets for more critical times. What he needed was a bow that was pre-drawn and could be shot from a concealed blind. He put his mind to the requirements and came up with a possibility. First he found his small crossbow. To the underside of its riser, he added a fishing reel. He modified the head of a frog gig he'd taken from someone's collection of diving gear so that it could mount on the tip of an arrow. Once this was firmly fitted to the arrow, he tied the fishing line through a hole in the shaft. The small crossbow should work better than his larger compound bow, as the string could already be drawn and just needed someone to pull the trigger to release the arrow.

James and Skyler tried a few practice shots on a target. A paper cup filled with water represented a crow on the ground. This crossbow was altogether different than shooting a bow in that it felt more like a pistol, and Skyler was able to hit the small target more often than James. James decided to let Skyler test out the weapon on the crows.

About fifteen yards from the dog's carcass, they set a small rug over the mud to protect Skyler from the damp and cold. Once Skyler positioned himself, James laid the other rug over him before spreading some dead grass over the top of this. The boy was well hidden. James returned to the house and watched from one of the windows. Skyler was there for almost two hours, and James was about to go tell him to give up for the day, when a pair of crows landed in the field. They tentatively waddled their way over towards the rotting carcass. There was no movement under the rug and James worried that the boy had fallen asleep, yet he kept watching with anticipation, his heart racing as if it was himself under the rug. Finally, one of the birds hopped on top of the carcass and began tugging on a piece of the hide. James focused on Skyler's position, but there still wasn't any sign of movement. Suddenly, the crow shot backwards, thrown several feet when the prongs pierced its chest. The other bird froze for only a second before it flew off frantically without its probable mate.

Skyler sprang from under his cover and ran back to the house with the bird in his hand. He was breathing hard and smiling. "I got one, I got one!" he shouted.

"Skyler, you never fail to impress me. I was afraid you'd fallen asleep."

"No. But my legs were beginning to cramp. I don't think I could have lasted much longer."

"Well," Lara added from the front porch, "since it's your first kill, it's your job to clean the bird. I'm expecting crow for dinner tonight."

Skyler didn't argue, knowing James would show him. His mood was elevated knowing that he could put meat on the table, and with only a small amount of assistance from Lara, Skyler even cooked most of the meal himself. It wasn't a lot of meat, but they ate it, along with some rice, and relished the change.

The following day, the winds picked up, but not to the magnitude that they had experienced during the earlier months of the year. Still, there could be no hunting. With a few hours of daylight left, the trio retreated into the house, as they had been accustomed to doing, for their daily ritual of listening to James read aloud and letting their fears and sad memories be carried away by the story. James briefly paused between chapters to look at the two listening. They'd both experienced such loss, and he felt lucky that he didn't have a loved one to mourn, but then living with Lara and Skyler had shown him just how much he had missed in his life when he lived alone.

James had removed the plywood from the living room window, so their quarters were flooded with natural light. Lara had done well refurnishing the three main rooms. With the increased temperatures, they had been able to open up the rest of the house, the small wood stove able to heat it now. However, all three of them still chose to sleep on the two mattresses on the living room floor, even with the option of having their own rooms to sleep in.

James closed the book for the afternoon, and when he did so Skyler jumped up to stoke the fire. Watching him, James realized something about the boy, a change. It wasn't something tangible that he could point out to Lara, so he didn't say anything. But he noticed that now Skyler did chores without being asked to help. They weren't assigned to him, he just did them. He knew when to light a fire, he kept the wood box full, and he started the stove to boil water when it was near meal time. Skyler was no longer dependent on them. They couldn't look at him and see the small boy who had lost his mother. He was truly a full member of their household who carried his weight and who at the same time could manage on his own, if needed. James had to wonder how much longer the boy would be with them.

Chapter 13

Nearing the end of April, James started seeing more signs of people who had survived the winter, but there just weren't that many left. Those who did survive were in a constant search for whatever they needed to continue their existence. The snow drift out by the intersection had melted away and there was finally a clear access in and out of the development. On a few occasions someone, always a man, would wander part way in towards their house. Once this person saw that only one house was habitable and the clear evidence that it was occupied, he'd turn and continue on in another direction. It was as if there was a stigma associated with encroaching on another human's bit of territory. Only one man wandered past their house; he walked all the way up to the end of the cul-de-sac. He was old, very thin, and moved slowly. He'd stopped and looked at a house that had lost its roof and windows. He didn't venture into it, but instead just stood there starring at its empty shell. James thought it looked as if the house contained some memories for the old man and he was trying to recall them. James wanted to ask what his connection to the house was, but the man looked so very hungry, and James didn't want to risk being asked for food, so he kept silent and just watched from his window. After a short bit of time, the man slowly wandered back toward the main road and James did not see him again. But the presence and threat of others made him nervous. Everyone he'd seen was close to starvation. And the thought of that man they'd encountered in Skyler's old house—James was sure that he would not easily forget what happened. He knew that it would only be a matter of time before he would have to defend his home, his supplies, his companions.

Almost two weeks after he saw the old man come into the neighborhood, James was startled awake by a rattling. As his mind became focused, he realized that it was the middle of the night. Lara and Skyler sat up in alarm as well. Someone was working the door knob on the living room door. All three looked at each other in fear when the rattling turned into a loud pounding, someone ramming, shoulder against door. James assured Skyler and Lara with a calming hand; the door was solid and would not give in easily. Then he picked up his small caliber pistol that he always kept handy under his pillow and yelled, "Get away from my door!"

The ramming continued. James motioned for Lara and Skyler to cover their ears, and he fired the .22 into the floor. The commotion on the other side of the door ceased and all became quiet. James breathed a sigh of relief, assuming he'd frightened the would-be intruder away. Suddenly, there came a much louder blast. The explosion tore a hole in the middle of the front door, sending splinters flying into the room. The three inside hugged the floor. With the only light in the room from moonlight filtering through the drapes, James could see little and felt the urge to use the large hole to find the intruder. He realized that the intruder would be using this hole for the same purpose. He looked at the .22 in his hand; this was not the gun you wanted to use in a gun fight, and if he did fire, he couldn't be sure the bullet could penetrate the thick hardwood.

They lay there, not making a sound as they waited for what would happen next. James kept his pistol aimed towards the door. A minute passed. Suddenly, the large glass window of the living room exploded inward, showering the three of them with shards of glass. Something heavy thudded onto the floor, a rock maybe, pinning the drapes under it. James scanned the floor for the object but gave up quickly. The three of them, not wanting to move, were sprawled in front of the large opening and a dim light was now flooding the room. James crawled over to where he'd stashed the older military .45 caliber. He knew it only had three cartridges left in its magazine. He was so angry by the assault, James felt the urge to charge the door and attack whoever was on the other side Then James heard a sob. Lara was crying silently but uncontrollably. In the low light James could also see Skyler; his face had such expectation on it that James would be able to take care of the situation. James went to them and motioned for Skyler and Lara to follow him, staying low in a crawl, to the kitchen. He handed Lara the smaller pistol. "If you have to use it, use it. Don't be afraid." He quietly pulled the back door open and slipped outside.

He cursed himself, knowing that he could have walked into a trap: was there one man trying to enter his house or twenty surrounding the place? Lara and Skyler were his responsibility, yet he didn't know what to do to protect them. James waited a few seconds for his eyes to adjust to the moonlit night before moving towards the corner of the house. There were absolutely no sounds. He held the .45 out in front of him and stooped down low before looking around the corner to the side of the house. No one in sight. James felt hot, even though the night air was cool; his heart raced as he'd never felt before. He didn't like the wave of fear that this intruder had instilled upon him; he needed to put an end to this event.

James silently crept along the side of the house to the corner that bordered the front yard. He listened intently; still no sounds. James glanced out into the twilight looking for anything that might be out of place. Nothing caught his eye. He peered around the corner towards the front steps. Again, no one in sight. Then he heard a noise behind him. For a split second he thought it was Skyler and felt some anger because Skyler shouldn't have left Lara alone. Then he heard the distinctive sound of an automatic pistol-slide being pulled back. He turned around slowly to see the silhouette of a man. James froze when he saw the moonlight glisten off the barrel pointing at him.

"You think you're some kind of big shit with that gun, don't you!" the man growled angrily.

James was so afraid, the gun pointed at his face, that he couldn't say anything. James's own gun was pointed outward and he didn't dare move the arm that held it. Just when he was about to try and reason with the man, James heard a twang; at the same instant the man's head jerk slightly. The man stood staring towards James with a quizzical look on his face like something was wrong and he wasn't quite sure what it was. The stand-off lasted for almost ten seconds before the man looked down at his pistol and let it drop from his hand. He then dropped to both knees just before falling on his face. In the twilight, James saw an arrow protruding from the back of the man's skull. Then he saw Skyler standing only twenty feet behind the man with his bow drawn. The second arrow was aimed at the man on the ground.

"Skyler, I think he's dead," said James.

Skyler slowly released the pressure on the string and let the arrow drop to the ground. He stood staring at the man before him. He finally looked up at James and said, "I saw him follow you. I was afraid that he was going to kill you."

"I'm sure he would have if you hadn't stopped him," James said. He nudged the body with his foot, "I'd be in his place if it wasn't for you."

Skyler picked up his arrow and set it back onto the string of his bow before looking up to James, "I didn't want to shoot, but I didn't know what else to do."

James nodded, then gripped Skyler's arm and spoke quietly. "We need to make sure he was alone. I'll circle the house. You go back inside and make sure Lara is OK." James waited for Skyler to disappear around the corner before picking up the man's gun and placing it in his own pocket. Then he moved back toward the front of the house. With his pistol pointed out in front of him, James slowly circled the house checking for any signs that the man wasn't acting alone. He finally made the loop and returned to the back door.

As James stepped back into the house, he saw that Lara was still huddled on the floor of the kitchen. Skyler was stooped down next to her, his hand on her back. For a moment James thought maybe she'd been hurt, but then he saw her body shudder with a sob. James pushed the dining room table aside and lifted one, then the other, mattress to shake off the glass shards. He situated the mattresses where the table had been and with Skyler's help, got Lara to her feet and onto a mattress. It took some time to get her to calm down, fear overriding her ability to control her emotions. James was also shaky; who wouldn't be, he thought? He looked at Skyler. The boy appeared calm. James was in a state of disbelief over Skyler's actions. This kid was thirteen and he had just terminated someone. He also seemed ready to do it again if necessary. Yet Skyler seemed emotionally unaffected by the fact that he had ended someone's life. James wondered if Skyler had always been like this or if his mother's death had changed him somehow.

Lara raised her head and asked James, "What happened to that man?"

"He ran off. He saw my gun and got scared," he lied. For some reason he was hesitant about telling Lara all that had happened. James looked over at Skyler. The boy remained silent.

When Lara finally settled down, James told her that he and Skyler were going to check outside once more. They walked in silence to the corner of the house. Then James whispered, "You OK?"

"Yeah, I'm fine."

"You sure?" James asked sounding concerned.

"Yeah, I'm OK. It's over with."

"We need to move the body. We can drag it out behind the wood pile for now," James said. "I don't want Lara to see it."

"Why'd you lie to her?"

James paused, "I needed her to calm down. If she knew that there was a dead man out here, she might not handle the thought of a body lying outside our house."

Skyler stood there for a second as he contemplated this. He followed James around the corner. In the moonlight, they could see the dark lump of the man, and the silhouette of the arrow standing almost straight up. They each grabbed a leg and started pulling the body towards the corner of the yard.

Skyler stopped. "Can we roll him onto his back for a minute?"

"Why?"

"I want to see his buttons," Skyler said.

James wondered why Skyler would want such a thing, but didn't ask. Skyler put a foot on the man's back and jerked the arrow from his head. James grabbed one of the outstretched arms and rolled the man onto his back. Skyler looked at the man's torso and nodded that he'd seen enough. With the moonlight coming out from behind a cloud, James could see the man's face clearly now. It wasn't the same one they had encountered at Skyler's home. They each grabbed a leg and finished pulling the body back behind the woodpile.

James spent the rest of the night pondering all that had happened and what he should do next. He also kept an eye on Lara, who remained restless but seemed to sleep a little. He worried that she would have a relapse. Skyler sat with his back against the wall, his thoughts clearly to himself, and only a few times let his head drop. When the sky lightened with the new day, James announced that they needed to move as soon as possible; he no longer felt safe in their current location. Lara didn't question this announcement. She looked so tired as she nodded in agreement.

While they ate a breakfast of plain oatmeal, James didn't' waste any time. "I need the two of you to round up all of our supplies and move them into the living room, ready to move. I hope to have us in a new house by tonight."

"So soon? Are you going to leave us alone?" Lara asked, almost shrill. She had a look as if she was about to cry again.

"Don't worry, Skyler will be here with you, and I'll leave most of the guns with you two."

His plan was to take the ATV and head back down towards Main Street. Instead of traveling east across the river, he would go west towards a more rural section of town. There he would scout the houses for one that was unoccupied, specifically one with some arable land for growing vegetables, food that would see them through the next winter. The ideal house would need to be away from other structures. He didn't dismiss the idea that he could burn down any adjacent house to enable their privacy.

After gassing up the ATV, James filled an old bread sack with rice and set it in the box behind the seat. He figured it might come in handy as a bartering tool. He also threw in a small bag with enough coffee to brew one pot. With the .45 hidden inside his coat, he sped away towards Vista Drive, the road that would lead him back into town.

James had not ventured down this road for at least three weeks and wondered if these people had dealt with the same problems he had. It was mid-May and anyone left alive would have been out of their dwellings. At one point he thought about finding a house in this neighborhood, specifically to be close to other survivors with whom he could unite for protection. But the thought never settled with him, and he couldn't put his finger on the reason—whether it was because he was used to being independent and didn't want to rely on someone else for his safety, or because he didn't want someone else to rely upon him. While Lara and Skyler had proved their value and he had no regrets about taking them in, he wasn't sure he wanted to take on more responsibility.

Most of the obstacles in the road had been moved and James speculated that others had found fuel to drive the vehicles away, or found means to cut the power poles up for firewood. When he reached the bottom of the hill and turned right on Third Avenue he saw that here the carnage from the storms was still cluttering the streets. Once he'd maneuvered the ATV around the debris, he paused to look at the downtown area. Without the snow cover, the extent of damage from the winter's constant storm was glaring; this small city was beyond repair. Turning the handle bars to the right, he drove the ATV into the outskirts of town, the road he'd driven daily on his way to work at the refinery.

Chapter 14

The same morning that James set out in search of a new place to live, a tan colored Humvee rolled to a stop at the crest of the hill overlooking Ferndale. The soldiers had taken over three months to clear the almost five miles of road between the refinery and town. Less than a half-mile stretch remained, yet they felt no hurry to complete it. The last stretch could wait until the following day. Their need to reach the town had diminished, their food, alcohol and cigarette supplies growing each day as they cleared more road and had access to homes and farms with families that had survived the winter and stored food when the future looked bleak. One family had actually walked out to greet the soldiers. They ended up losing most of the remainder of their food supply by doing so. As he looked out from the top of the hill, Carter, who'd been rewarded with a seat in Lyons's Humvee after acquiring the supply of frozen meat, spotted someone on an ATV turning off the main road and pointed it out to Lyons. At the same time the other Humvee radioed that they had made a big find. Lyons glanced at the ATV but shrugged his shoulders. "Let's worry about the locals tomorrow and get back to the refinery. I want to check out what the others scored."

James was so focused on the houses on either side of the road that he didn't notice the Humvee parked about two hundred yards up the hill, or when it turned to disappear over the far side. And the loud four-cycle engine drowned out the throaty rumble of the military transport. Slowly ascending the long hill, James passed several blocks of apartments that he instantly ruled out. Next was a trailer park that was severely damaged, some of its trailers blown clean down to the frame. James continued further up the hill and saw a two-story house that was missing its upper level. He stopped the ATV and scanned the area. Further back off the road was a large two-story house that appeared intact. It stood by itself at the edge of the hill, so it had little protection from the wind. However, the upper level was still unscathed. It lacked a chimney, which James knew meant that it also lacked a wood stove. But he could add a stove for cooking and heating at anytime, and installing a metal chimney could easily be done using hand tools. This house interested him. He drove in closer, few obstacles in his path, and turned off the engine in front of the house.

James dismounted and stood in front admiring the size of the place, marveling again at the lack of damage. All the visible doors and windows were still boarded up. This house isn't being used, James thought to himself, otherwise the boards would have been taken down with the warmer weather. The lower half of the house appeared to be mostly one big garage with three large doors on the north side. The doors were without exterior handles. James bet that without electricity, there wasn't any way the doors could be opened from the exterior. They could store a lot of firewood in there. He nodded to himself, then scanned the surrounding area. There were open fields on three sides of the house. A person couldn't very easily sneak up on the place without being seen. On the west side of the house, through a row of dead cedar trees, there was a similar house; it also looked intact. James started towards the backyard when he heard the distinct click of a pistol being cocked to shoot.

"Where the hell do you think you're going?" The voice came from near the end of the house. James had to look hard before he noticed the barrel of the pistol and half of a face protruding from around the corner.

"I'm not here to hurt anyone," said James. "I'm just looking around, looking for a new place to stay." The fact that a stranger was pointing a gun at him made him wary, but he wasn't terrified. Something about the man made James think he was not much different than himself. The guy was being defensive, especially because he probably saw the compound bow strapped to James's back, and not aggressive. He'd obviously survived the winter and wanted to avoid trouble as much as James did.

The man didn't hesitate. "This place ain't for sale, so get on your scooter and leave."

James almost turned to leave when a thought struck him. "What would you say if I could offer you some food and protection?" James asked.

"If you don't leave, you're the one's going to need protection."

James walked over to the ATV and was about to climb back onto the seat. Instead, he stopped, looked back at the man, and reached into his coat pocket. The man with the gun still had the barrel pointed in James's direction. James lifted a small brown bag into the air and asked, "Can we talk about this over a cup of coffee?"

When James returned home, he found Lara and Skyler impatiently waiting, all their essentials and belongings stacked in the living room, as he had requested. James looked at the pile, gave a slight nod, but didn't say anything. He was enjoying his little secret. Lara and Skyler watched him intently, waiting for him to tell whether he'd found a better place to live, or not.

"Did—" Lara started, but James raised his hand to shush her.

James glanced about their small quarters looking for anything that might have been missed. Finally, he picked up a box of books and went towards the front door. He stopped, looked over his shoulder at his two housemates, and said with a grin "Why are you just standing around? We're moving today!"

Both Skyler and Lara began bombarding him with questions about the new house. James simply responded, "You'll see when you get there." With a partial load in the ATV, James headed out with Lara to the house, leaving Skyler behind to guard the remaining supplies until James returned. Lara had to ride on top of the boxes and was able to place her hands on James' shoulders to steady herself.

James had no worries about leaving Skyler alone for an hour or two; the boy had shown his courage and abilities more than once. And as they drove, he assured Lara that she would be okay to unpack and begin getting settled when he left for the second load. "We'll be living next to another couple. They'll be anxious to meet you."

Lara sat silent for a moment as she digested what he'd just said. With some concern in her voice she asked, "Are you sure this is safe?"

"I had coffee with the guy. His name is Mike. I pointed out how vulnerable his situation was with the house next door being vacant. I was able to convince him that we could look out for each other. A half hour later, we were taking the plywood off the front door of the house."

"Is the woman his wife?"

"My guess is that they aren't husband and wife. Appears to be a big age difference and they didn't act like a couple would. Her name is Cindy. She was pleasant enough but she really only said hello before she disappeared. I thought that was a little odd."

"What did you tell them about us? I mean, did you tell them that you lived with a woman and a boy?"

"No, I only told him that I had a family. He didn't ask for specifics."

He finished his tale, explaining how the clincher to the deal had been when James pointed out to Mike that if he was attacked from more than one side, he probably wouldn't win the battle. Before James left for home, he tossed the bag of rice to Mike and said, "Thanks."

As he and Lara drove with the loaded ATV, the sky had continued to darken and the air felt cooler than it had earlier, even though it was not yet three in the afternoon. Although it was mid-May, everyone knew that snow was still a possibility. Lara was quiet as she scanned the sides of the road. While James had explained all about how he'd gotten Mike to agree to their moving, he hadn't told her about the house.

"Oh my God, it's huge," Lara exclaimed as they pulled up to the house and stopped. "How are we ever going to heat this place?"

"Don't worry, we will."

James was like a proud new owner as he pointed out the size of the place in comparison to his old house, the intact siding and roof, that because the house was newer it would be better insulated, and how it was so well situated, far from other houses besides Mike and Cindy's. A large staircase ascended the left side of the garage to a large deck about ten feet off the ground. The only door leading inside was at the top of the stairs.

"Can we look inside?"

"Not yet. I should introduce you to Mike and Cindy first."

James led Lara through a line of brown cedars to the neighboring house. Mike was warm to meeting Lara, while Cindy appeared reserved and only nodded when Lara asked, "Can you show me around the other house? I'm anxious to see it."

The four of them left for the house, with James and Mike stopping at the ATV to grab some of the boxes.

James noticed that neither Mike nor Cindy appeared malnourished, but he didn't ask about their food supplies. Instead he commented on the plywood over all the windows. Mike told him that he had taken down the pieces from his southern facing windows to allow the sunlight in but had left the plywood on the north side. He suggested that James do the same so that the house didn't appear to anyone out on the road that it was occupied.

As James reached the top of the stairs, he nudged open the door with the corner of a box, letting the low afternoon light into the room. He saw Lara and Cindy in the living room, Lara looking dumbfounded. He surveyed the place himself. Even though during his first visit he'd removed the sheets that had covered the furniture, he was seeing the place with fresh eyes. Except for a thick layer of dust on the uncovered areas, the living room was clean and well furnished with leather couch and chairs. The tables were of polished wood. He was pleased with Lara's evident approval.

"And look," she said, "We can even see Mt. Baker and the Cascades." Her arm stretched out towards the east pointing through the window.

Mike came in behind James and said, "This house belonged to a college professor that lived back east. He and his wife used the place as a summer retreat. I haven't seen them in four years." Mike went on to say that three years earlier, a handyman showed up and started boarding up the doors and windows, telling Mike that he worked for a bank and that the house had been foreclosed upon. He also said that there would be an auction for the furnishings followed by another for the house itself. "That was the last time anyone came to the house."

Even though the house didn't have a chimney, a corner of the living room was occupied by a large faux stone fireplace; it was fueled by natural gas and was only vented out the back wall. As a fireplace, it was basically useless now. The kitchen, living room and dining room were actually one large room with a single vaulted ceiling with a large fan. Also useless, and without the fan to push the heat down, James noted, it would mean having to burn more wood. There were two bedrooms, each with a queen size bed, dresser and end tables. One, the master, was on the south side of the house and had a bathroom with a toilet that appeared intact, since it was dry of any water. The other bathroom, near the north bedroom, had a toilet that had cracked from the extreme cold.

Between the two bedrooms were a laundry room and a staircase leading to the lower portion of the house. James lit a candle and led Lara downstairs, Mike and Cindy following, to a large family room furnished like a gym. No light leaked in through the plywood window coverings, but in the candlelight they could see weights along one wall, with a treadmill and exercise bike in the center of the room. Without electricity, the treadmill was junk. Everything here was covered with a layer of dust; no one had thought to put sheets over the equipment. Off of this room was a small bathroom with another cracked toilet. There was also a very large bedroom. Like the ones upstairs, it was furnished with a queen size bed that was covered with a bedspread. The room was clean except for a thick layer of dust on all surfaces. As they turned to leave the room, James noticed another gas fireplace and was about to comment on its waste when he realized that it could be good for hiding food since it was vented. He didn't say anything about this aloud.

They took a quick look into the large garage, accessible by a door from the exercise room, and found no cars or work benches, but in one corner was an almost-new gas-powered lawnmower and weed whacker. Two kayaks were suspended from the ceiling above the middle bay; James speculated they were hung in such a way so they could easily be dropped onto a car or truck. The ropes that suspended them led over to an eyebolt drilled into the wall. James made a mental note that this was another good place to stash food. Lara wandered over to a wall rack and took a quick inventory of the shovels, a hoe, two types of rakes and two garden hoses. Her smile of approval was now quite broad and James felt proud to have been able to make her happy.

James looked at his watch with a jolt of alarm; it was getting late and Skyler was waiting with the rest of their supplies and belongings. He asked Mike to help him unload the last of the boxes, and then checked the ATV's gas. There was about a quarter tank, just enough to get him back up the hill, but not much further. He had some gas at the old house saved for the second trip. James estimated that it took just twelve to fifteen minutes to cover the distance between the two houses, so with time to load up, he'd be back to the new house with Skyler well before nightfall. He was gratified that Lara was content staying behind to get settled. Everything was working out.

James was almost all the way back up the hill of Vista Drive when he heard something over the ATV's engine, a loud popping sound. He quickly killed the engine and stopped to listen. There were no new sounds. He started up the engine and eased the throttle forward as he slowly inched his way up the hill.

Suddenly, he noticed a body lying in the yard of one of the houses he knew, from chimney smoke earlier that spring, to be occupied. He stopped again, but this time kept the engine running. A second later, two very thin men in tattered clothes came out of the house dragging a woman. A third man followed them. All three were armed. They tossed her body out onto the yard alongside the other body. She appeared to be dead, though not stiff like someone who had been dead a long time. One of the men looked up and saw James. He said something and the two others also looked towards James. One of the men raised his shotgun. James was about seventy yards away, and before the man could fire, James released the clutch and made an accelerated turn back down the hill.

James could feel his pulse racing as he sped away. He knew the shotgun's range was limited to maybe one hundred yards at the most, but one of the other men was carrying a rifle. Its range was only limited by the scope he'd seen above the barrel. James hugged the handlebars and kept his head as low as possible as he aimed for the bottom of the hill. Worry escalated his already high heart rate. He had to get to Skyler, less than a mile away—too close to the murderous men for comfort, yet impossible to reach without going past the same threatening men. How was he going to get safely back up the hill to retrieve Skyler and then bring him back to the new house? Going by way of Vista was no longer a viable option.

James maneuvered through the intersection of Third Avenue without slowing, then turned onto Main Street in the direction of the new house. Though James didn't relish the thought of maneuvering on roads that he hadn't traveled before, he had to be open to it, and hoped Mike knew of a different route up and over the hill. He also had to warn Mike about what he'd just witnessed, but how could he do it without alarming Lara? Events like this were going to be more commonplace now that the weather had improved, and even in a new home, stress levels would remain high. Still, there would be nothing to gain by upsetting her just yet.

James drove up Main St. and passed the road that led to the new house. He kept going towards the driveway that led to Mike's house. He was counting on the boarded up windows diminishing the sound of his engine, and that Lara wouldn't hear him drive past. Mike's driveway was significantly longer than James had expected, with two sharp turns giving it an 'S' shape. At the second turn, Mike had piled a lot of tree debris on the driveway, obviously to discourage visitors. But James maneuvered around this by driving into the tall grass. As he neared the house, he cut the engine, and the ATV coasted up onto a concrete pad. Cindy stuck her head out the door but didn't say anything.

"Where's Mike?" he asked.

She pointed a finger towards the other house, and merely nodded when Mike said, "Still helping Lara, then, I take it?" He quickly formulated a reason to be back so quickly.

Lara was putting food containers into the cupboards as Mike stood by watching her. Mike looked surprised when James appeared at the doorway.

"Mike, I can't take the ATV up Vista to get to the old house," he announced. "Do you know another way?

Mike pondered the question for a few seconds. "Yeah," he paused, thinking it through. "There's a shorter route. Across from the end of my driveway is Church Road. It leads up and over the hill and it looks to be unobstructed. I don't know what kind of shape it's in beyond the crest. Once the road levels out, you go maybe another quarter mile to a four-way intersection and turn right. That'll lead back over to the upper part of Vista."

Lara looked alarmed. "What's wrong?"

"Nothing," James said lightly. "Just some old cars blocking Vista now. Not sure why," he lied, "but I couldn't find a way around them."

It was pretty obvious that Lara was unconvinced, but she didn't question him. James assumed she wanted to believe that all was okay and left it at that. He was about to leave and then casually snapped his fingers. "Hey, Mike, do you have any gas I could borrow? I have enough at the other house to reimburse you."

"Sorry," Mike replied, "but I no longer use the stuff."

Desperate to get back to Skyler, James was about to risk the run on what gas he had left when he remembered the lawnmower in the garage. It wouldn't have been run in over four years. Maybe there was some gas left in its tank. James lit a candle and headed downstairs. Once he was in the garage, he paused and looked about. Dangling from the top of each garage door was a cord for unlocking the door from the motor driven carriage. Choosing the middle bay, James pulled the cord and lifted the door to fill the dank room with low afternoon light. The small draft blew out his candle.

He easily removed the gas cap on the mower; the tank was about half full, maybe a quart at the most. Not enough to get the ATV over the hill. He glanced at the weed whacker which, when he'd looked at its opaque plastic gas tank earlier, he'd thought it was bone dry. Then he confirmed that the reason he hadn't seen a fuel level was because it was filled to the top. He glanced around further. An old stained and dusty oil pan could serve as a container. He blew out what dust he could and then poured the gas from the weed whacker's tank into it. The gasoline looked and smelled good and there was almost a quart. He then pulled the pan over to the lawnmower, which he had to lift completely off the ground to get all of the gas out of the tank. Stepping back into the dark hollow near the bottom of the stairs, James yelled up that he was leaving again. James closed the garage door most of the way, carried the pan carefully over to the ATV without sloshing out any of its precious contents, and emptied it into the tank. It was now almost four in the afternoon, only a few hours of daylight left. James knew Skyler was probably concerned, but he also knew the boy well enough to count on him keeping a cool head.

As he drove back out the driveway, James couldn't help but wonder why Mike was watching Lara unpack. Why hadn't he followed James down into the garage to help? Surely he must have heard the garage door open and close. Maybe Lara liked having someone around besides him and Skyler. He didn't give it more thought once he reached the end of the driveway and crossed Main Street. Church Road was a long hill with a steep grade, but manageable. James saw only one church; he glanced at it briefly on his way past. Its roof was caved in like a cardboard box that had been stepped on. He was lucky that the road ran a north-south direction, the same as the heavy winds had blown, so the power poles and trees were lying mostly parallel with the road. Only a few partially protruded onto the asphalt. As James crested the top of the hill, he came to a hard stop. Here, telephone poles stacked like Lincoln Logs formed a barricade that stretched across the road.

Chapter 15

James scanned the structure; clearly not something caused by the wind, and wondered why somebody would go through the trouble of creating it. It would have taken some heavy equipment to lift the logs, and the joints were obviously carved with a chain saw. There was a path around the eastern end of the barricade so, not seeing anyone, he inched up closer. It was wide enough for the ATV and more. James steered onto the path then back onto Church Road. He was cautious, especially after what he had witnessed earlier, and took a quick survey of the surroundings. Houses were situated all about this part of the hill; many were badly damaged but he could detect the smell of wood smoke and saw that some were still habitable and occupied.

As James continued slowly on the road, he couldn't help but feel that he was being watched; though, other than the smell of wood smoke, he did not detect any signs of life. The top of the hill was like a plateau, flat with almost no grade. James passed a few side streets that led into groups of houses and noticed that much of the debris had been cleared from the streets and stacked off to the side. He guessed there must be at the least a handful of survivors living up here and obviously working together. And whoever had placed the barricade across the road had intended for it to stop vehicles, not someone on foot. The trail around the barricade was too obvious. Then a thought occurred to him: was the reason that he wasn't seeing anyone because they were off raiding other survivors? Could the men he'd seen earlier on Vista have come from here? It was only a mile and a half or so away. He shook himself, realizing his conjectures could lead to nothing and that he was just scaring himself by thinking up all the possibilities. Best to just keep alert and keep moving.

James kept his speed down but was ready to hit the throttle if necessary. He went a little further without incident when he saw another barricade ahead on his route, blocking the road just like the other one. When he reached it, he saw that it also had a trail around the end. He maneuvered the ATV around the logs without stopping and saw an intersection in the road. The white painted stumps from what used to be stop signs indicated it was the four-way stop that Mike had told him to look for. He turned right onto what he recalled was once named Thornton Road and recognized the opening of the development that Skyler used to live in. Did the man they found in Skyler's house live in the community behind the barricades? It was only a fifteen minute walk between the two places and was very possible.

The road leading towards his old house was still blocked with downed power poles, but with the snow completely gone, James found it easy to navigate around them by following the sidewalk or driving through some of the yards. His progress was slow, but he was near his destination.

James arrived at the development and could see that everything looked as it should. He drove up to his yard and turned the engine off. James was surprised that Skyler did not open the door to greet him, being able now to both hear and see through the windows of the house. James looked all around, dismounted, and strode towards the door. A shot rang out behind him. A bullet splintered the door frame next to his head. James dove for the door handle, grateful it wasn't locked from within. He slammed the door shut as another shot rang out, shattering the wood of the door behind him. He lay prone on the floor next to the pile of goods that were to be moved to the new house. James looked around.

"Skyler!" he half shouted. There was no response.

James still had his bow strapped to his back, but it was no match for someone with a gun. He looked at the heap of belongings. He needed to move fast. Whoever had fired those shots could be coming through the front door at any second. He kept as quiet as possible while he gently lifted bags and boxes from the pile. The rifle lay hidden near the bottom in its waterproof bag and James pulled it out. "Skyler!" he called out again, half shout, half whisper. Where could he have gone. Was he OK? "Boy, I hope you were smart enough to run away at the first sign of danger," James muttered to himself.

With the rifle in hand, James crawled over to the living room window to peer out towards the street. The day was still bright enough to see, but darkness would start its descent within the hour. At first, everything looked like it should—quiet, no movement. Then James noticed a body standing in an alcove of the house directly across; it was unmoving and unidentifiable. The sun was behind that house so the shadows made it almost impossible to see. James considered firing to make the person move into the open. Then he saw the person's hand come out of the shadows horizontally and push down, a gesture he had taught Skyler. Before he could react, another shot rang out and splintered the window frame near his head.

It must be Skyler, in the alcove, James thought, and he could apparently see whoever the shooter was. Or shooters; there was no way to know if there was more than one. He peaked out. Skyler quickly held up one finger, then pointed it towards the garage end of the house. Once again he gave the motion to duck down. James immediately rolled to his right as another shot was fired. The bullet pierced the wall right where he had been positioned. No way could he escape through the front door, and he couldn't know if someone waited for him out back. Then he realized that as long as the shooter was firing, Skyler would know the shooter's whereabouts. James pulled a fishing rod from the pile of supplies and quickly tied some rags onto its tip. He was able to make the rags barely appear over the windowsill about six feet away from himself. Another shot was fired. The bullet penetrated the wall just below the level where the rags had appeared. James had an idea. He shouted like he had been shot and was in pain, then let his moans die away and listened.

Chapter 16

Skyler had been patiently awaiting James's return, and wondering what was taking so long when a gun shot came through the opening of last night's broken window. Skyler had just walked past it; the bullet missing him by inches. He dove for the floor. The shot, loud, sounded like it had come from across the street. Skyler crouched low and peered out the corner of the window. He had been afraid, but also angry: Why did everyone they encountered feel that they had to kill other survivors? He saw movement in the carport of a collapsed house and heard another shot. The frame of the window exploded just inches from his head. Skyler had rolled back towards the dining room.

Skyler following his first instinct had grabbed his bow and headed out the back door. Once outside, he had moved behind all the structures of the development unseen. He knew he needed to hurry—James would be showing up soon and this man would probably try to shoot him–but it had taken him about ten minutes to walk the wide arc to come in behind the shooter.

Skyler had moved silently as he tried to get into position. He needed to be close enough to shoot an arrow, but without being seen. From behind the empty house, he couldn't see the shooter; the collapsed carport made it impossible to get a fix on his position. There was no way to get a shot at him unless he stood directly in front of the carport, but that wasn't acceptable. He had to get himself into a position where he could release an arrow from the side as soon as the man stepped out of his hiding spot. Skyler remembered that the front door of a house off to the man's left sat in an alcove that was recessed inward. This would give him a good place to wait. Very quietly he worked his way to his goal. Every few steps he stopped to listen. He glanced around the front: no sign of the shooter. Skyler inched his way along the wall and reached the alcove, where he waited until sounds from the carport confirmed that whoever was doing the shooting was still in there.

Skyler heard the ATV before he saw it. His bow was ready if the man stepped out. He watched James drive up the street and leaned out, waving his bow to get James's attention. James wouldn't look in his direction, and Skyler couldn't risk shouting. Skyler drew the arrow back and partially stepped out of the alcove. He was ready should the shooter go after James, his arrow aimed at the carport's opening. James shut off the ATV and walked towards the door.

Skyler heard the shot; the bullet missed James by inches. Another shot rang out and passed through the door as James slammed it shut. Skyler ducked back within the alcove. He waited for James to peer out, hoping he'd see him in the alcove. Skyler had to release the tension on the bowstring so that he could signal James when he did look his way. It worked; James saw Skyler's motion and got down before the bullet could hit him. The second time he saw James peek out, he held up one finger and pointed towards the carport. As he did this, he heard the metallic noise made by the bolt action of a rifle. Skyler motioned to James to duck again, and the bullet entered the wall below the window. Had it hit James? Again he held off the urge to charge the carport and waited. A few minutes passed by. Then there was movement in the corner of the window, but it didn't seem like James's head. Another shot rang out and pierced the wall below the window. Skyler heard a deathly moan from their house. He gasped. Was James hit? Skyler drew back on the bow, remaining hidden from view. He calmed his anxious nerves and held the string taut as he worked out what he needed to do. If he shot an arrow and missed, his location would be made evident. He would be in trouble. And if he didn't miss—what if there was more than one shooter? Either way he was trapped.

He peaked out around the corner and saw a man aiming a rifle at their house as he slowly walked towards it. He had his back towards Skyler. Skyler stepped out, aimed for the middle of the man's back and released the arrow. The arrow was aimed accurately, but it disappeared from view and he feared he had missed entirely. The man didn't change his course at all, but kept moving towards the house, one step, two steps, then stopped. He dropped the rifle and stood still for a few more seconds before glancing around slowly as if in a daze, looking for something. His last sight was of Skyler with another arrow drawn and ready to shoot. The man collapsed to the ground and didn't move.

Skyler kept the arrow pointed at the downed man and waited. The street was entirely quiet. He edged his way out of the alcove and slowly walked towards the body. Skyler glanced about but kept returning his sites to the man on the ground. He could see no one else around. "James!" Skyler shouted. "Are you OK?"

James's head appeared briefly in the window. With rifle in hand, he cautiously stepped out the front door. He scanned the street before walking down the driveway. Skyler stood with his bow drawn as he also scanned the block. Neither one of them spoke. They only listened and looked. Skyler took a moment to stare at the body in the street: it was a younger man, his face smeared with dirt. A large bloodstain covering his jacket was the only sign that the arrow had penetrated his heart. A hunting rifle lay just beyond the man's hands. Skyler noticed that it lacked a scope and was thankful for the absence. He headed over to the carport where the man had been shooting from.

Skyler was bending down to open a small backpack when James approached him. It was a kid's school pack. Skyler reached into it and James watched with quiet curiosity as the boy pulled out a box of rifle shells, a large hunting knife, and an old pop bottle filled with water, laying each on the pavement next to him. Then he pulled out a bundle of newspaper that was partially saturated with what looked like blood. Skyler unrolled the wrapping and instantly tossed the parcel away as if he was repulsed by what he saw. James stepped over to it and nudged the paper aside with the toe of his boot. He saw a human forearm.

Skyler looked terrified as he asked, "What was he doing with that?"

"I wish that I could say that I didn't know, but I can take a good guess," replied James. "He was going to eat it." Skyler walked over to the body in the street and picked up the rifle. Skyler looked around the body and then quizzically at James. "Where's my arrow?"

"It went right through him—probably stuck somewhere near one of those houses over there" James pointed at the structures just south of his own house.

"He wasn't a good man, was he?" asked Skyler.

"No, he wasn't."

Skyler glanced at the man's clothing. He checked his buttons. "Skyler, are you OK?"

"Yeah, I'm OK. Why?"

"You killed a man last night. And now you've had to do it again." James gave a big sigh. "In both cases, you saved me from getting killed. And for that I'm forever grateful. But I'm worried how this will affect you."

"I didn't have a choice."

"I know. And I know you're not a child any longer and can face facts. Just—let me know if you need to offload on me or something, okay?" James changed the subject. "Listen—while I load the ATV, will you take the rifle and bullets and hide them someplace real good?"

"Why can't we take them with us?" Skyler asked while admiring the rifle.

"Because Lara would ask where we got them."

Skyler nodded his head, understanding.

"Now let's get moving so we can be on the road before it gets any darker," said James.

It took them only five minutes to stack most of the remaining supplies into the cargo box. James filled his backpack with the rest, which meant his bow and rifle had to be strapped down with everything else. He still carried the pistol in his pocket. There was just enough room for Skyler to stand at the rear of the box; he would have to hang onto the straps that secured the load. As they pulled away from the house, not bothering to look back at it or the body in the street, James filled Skyler in about the detour through the neighborhood with the barricades. "Be on the lookout, but don't react if we see anyone unless I tell you."

They made their way back to the intersection near the barricade without incident. James paused the ATV long enough to see that no one was guarding the narrow entrance. He edged the vehicle around the large pile of poles and continued slowly up the road. At first, the scene looked as quiet as it had before, with no signs of life except for the smell of smoke. Then they saw the sign. In the middle of the road, someone had constructed a crude easel supporting a large sheet of plywood. James stopped the ATV long enough for both of them to read its warning.

"YOU ARE TRESSPASSING ON PRIVATE LAND. ANY ACTS CONSIDERED TO BE UNFRIENDLY WILL MEAN CERTAIN DEATH FOR YOU."

James released the clutch and continued forward without speaking. Skyler swiveled about, looking for any clue as to who wrote that warning, but there was none. The sign didn't seem aggressive to Skyler, just a warning as to what would happen if you weren't friendly. He thought that maybe these people would be OK and made a mental note to someday return to see if he could make a connection with the people that lived here.

When they arrived at the new house, Skyler let out a whistle and patted James on the back as if saying "well done" to him. The garage door was still slightly open, as James had left it, and with Skyler's help, they raised it the rest of the way. They pulled the ATV into the garage, securing the door behind them. James switched on his headlamp and as they started to untie the load, Lara stepped into the garage. She was holding a candle and didn't look happy.

"What's the matter?" James asked her.

"It's our neighbor. Mike. We need to talk." She had a severe scowl on her face as she helped James and Skyler unload the supplies in silence. In a matter of minutes they all headed upstairs.

"The entire time you were gone, Mike followed me around like a lost child," Lara exclaimed.

James took the minute to explain to Skyler who Mike and Cindy were.

"Maybe he is just lonely for someone to talk to?" suggested James, turning back to Lara.

"I was thinking that too, until I told him I needed him to excuse me so I could pee."

"So?"

"So—" she paused, embarrassed and then angry, "—he asked if he could watch."

"Jesus, I'm sorry. I thought he was OK. What do you want me to do?" asked James.

"I don't want you to do anything."

"Nothing?"

"I finally lied to him and said that we were married, and that I would pretend that he never asked me, and that I would not tell you as long as he never spoke to me in such a way again."

"What did he say?"

"He said 'fine' and left." She paused for a few seconds. "I hope that'll be the end of it. But what's with Cindy? She hasn't said two words to me."

James shrugged his shoulders; he didn't have an answer for her.

Skyler listened in but made no comments. He wondered if their new neighbors were going to be trouble. So far, everyone they had come across was trouble.

Rain began to fall just as dusk was turning to dark. Their water supply was low and they hadn't had time to scout for a new source, so Skyler took it upon himself to pull a tarp out of their gear and spread it on the deck. He tied the corners to the rail so that all the water it caught would run to a bucket at the lowest corner. Even though it was dark, he could see a long way in almost every direction and was eager to come out in the morning and have a better look around. He was hungry, but when he went inside, James asked if Skyler would help hide their food first. Even with a sense of security in the new house, James said it was necessary; no use taking chances. He showed Skyler the pulley system to lower the kayaks in the garage and they stuffed the boats with almost all the food before hoisting them back up and tying off the ropes.

That night they ate a dinner of rice with a small amount of crow meat stirred in. Since they wouldn't have a wood burning stove until James found and installed one, they were forced to use the mountaineering stove and tap into their limited supply of kerosene. And they would have to endure sleeping in an unheated house.

After dinner, James found the book they had been reading. With a single candle glowing, he read for the next two hours. The soft sound of rain hitting the roof was calming for all three.

Skyler took the bedroom at the north end of the house while James and Lara shared the other. The three had been sleeping side by side for almost five months so it felt odd to Skyler to not be sleeping in the same room with them. He soon got over the strangeness, especially after he slipped under the sheets. It had been over six months since Skyler had slept in a real bed with clean sheets. While the sheets were cold, there were enough blankets to keep him warm. "I could get used to this," he said to himself as he adjusted the covers around him.

Skyler laid awake for some time thinking about the day's events and heard James get back up and wander through the house. It sounded like he was checking the dead bolt on the upstairs door. Skyler wondered if James was having trouble sleeping like he was. His mind wouldn't shut down. So much had happened in just the last twenty four hours: the man who tried to break into their house and the man with the human arm in his pack. Neither one had buttons that matched the one Skyler carried in his pocket. He thought of James and Lara and how lucky he was that he had met them. They were good people. It sounded like Mike and Cindy might be sort of strange, and nobody mentioned if they had children. His mind then flitted to the fact that they would need more meat. Could he find crows near this new place? Maybe up by the neighborhood they'd passed through. He thought about the barricades built there, and the sign in the road. He would go back up and try to connect with whoever lived there. But what if they were bad? He finally fell asleep wondering if he would ever meet a stranger that wasn't filled with hate.

Chapter 17

All three of them slept longer than they had in months. Sometime during the night, the rain had ceased. When they awoke, the sky was cloudless and the morning sun was warming their new house very quickly. Skyler retrieved the water captured by the tarp. There was more than enough for their breakfast and tea.

A part of James was frustrated for sleeping in, he had so much that needed to get done that day, but the rested looks on both Skyler's and Lara's faces reminded him the extra sleep was helpful. Even though they didn't have a wood stove yet, James commissioned Skyler to start rounding up firewood, to carry or drag what he could manage to the yard for them to cut down to smaller pieces later. James wanted a minimum of three cords stacked in the garage by fall. He laughed when Skyler rolled his eyes when James reminded the boy to keep his bow with him in case birds appeared. James should know better by now about Skyler's resourceful nature. Lara busied herself by building a small fireplace for cooking behind the house. They needed to conserve their kerosene. She stacked stones into a U shape and pulled a rack from the oven to act as the grill.

James left the ATV in the garage and took off on foot to find a wood burning stove. Most homes had built-in fireplaces, mostly natural gas or propane, while some added free-standing wood-burning models when fuel prices skyrocketed. He needed at least one free-standing stove but could use two to keep things warm in their larger house.

James left his bow at home so that he wouldn't intimidate any locals, but kept his nine millimeter pistol in his coat pocket.

The first house he came to was right off of Main Street, not far from their new home. The entire second floor was gone so he couldn't see if there was a chimney, but he wanted to check anyway. He approached the house from the rear and entered through a sliding glass door that had been broken out. The inside of the house was very wet, with sheetrock hanging from the ceiling or covering the floor and furniture with sodden paper and gypsum. James didn't see a stove and was about to leave when he noticed a wood box on the floor next to the back door. James had grown up in the country, and his parents' home had been heated by wood. They also kept a wood box by the back door to hold enough wood to last a day or night; they could bring in one big load at a time and avoid multiple trips to keep the fire burning. The kitchen was partially hidden by a sagging sheet of ceiling material. He tore the sheet down and saw a large wood stove with an oven on the side in one corner of the small kitchen. Seeing the stove brought back memories of when he was small and stayed with his grandparents. They had one much like this one. This one had rust on some of the surfaces, but it appeared intact and undamaged, though it definitely would be heavy; he estimated almost three hundred pounds. He knew that getting the stove out of the house and into his own was going to take a Herculean effort, but it would be worth it.

James quickly cleared the area around the stove to make sure everything was intact and then went around to the front of the house to a side door into the garage. He tried to turn the knob and discovered that it was still locked. James raised his right foot and slammed his sole against the door. He heard a crack from the frame, so he kicked the door once again. The frame shattered around the deadbolt. The door swung open revealing a damp, dark, putrid abyss. The two-car garage had been used to store waste when the garbage trucks had quit running. He held his breath as he stepped in and worked his way over to the main door for the vehicles. He unlocked this and hoisted it up over his head. The light from the opening revealed some tools still hanging on the walls. What he needed most was a crowbar, and he could see one hanging at the back of the garage

As he started wading through the garbage, he heard a throaty rumble and turned to see a Humvee park right in front of the open door.

James froze with fear. He recognized the vehicle as one that was used to guard the refinery while he'd worked there. All four doors opened as four men stepped out, three with rifles and a forth wearing only a sidearm. They were wearing camouflaged uniforms, body armor and sunglasses. These could very well have been the same men that Lara had told him about. They made no gestures of friendliness. The driver, the name above his breast pocket showed 'CARTER,' stepped forward and stared directly at James, then beyond James at the sea of garbage. "Do you live here?"

James swallowed and mustered a quiet "No."

"Then where do you live?"

James wanted to lie. He wanted to tell the soldier he lived over the hill. But James was afraid what they would do if they later found he had lied to them. He realized that he had stalled too long to tell them anything but the truth. "I live just up over there off that road." He pointed to the southwest. He then added, "We just got there late last night and we need a wood stove. That's why I'm here."

Carter looked at James skeptically and asked, "How much food do you have?"

"Hardly any," James answered. "That's why we had to move. We were robbed the night before last." This time he had no problem lying. After a few seconds, he added, "Three men took our food. They had guns and they live over on Vista."

"Where on Vista?" The other men were silent as Carter continued the interrogation.

"I think it's the brown house, 'bout three quarters up the hill," James replied. He hoped that this might interest the men so they'd leave him alone. Acting innocent, quipped, "Hey! Can you guys help me pull a stove out of the kitchen?"

The men just continued to stare. Finally Carter turned towards the Humvee and uttered, "I don't think so." He looked back over his shoulder and added, "I suggest that the next time we meet, you have some food for us."

James stood wide-eyed and, continuing with his innocent approach, gave a nod. Carter climbed back into the driver's seat and the three others followed his actions. They were about to back out onto Main Street when a second Humvee pulled up. James watched as the men in the second Humvee stared at him while they spoke through the windows to the men in the other vehicle. It was impossible to hear what they were saying over the rumble of the two engines, but James had no doubt that he was the topic. Eventually, both Humvees backed out and slowly headed down the hill towards the center of town.

James realized that he was shaking badly after they'd left. Maybe he'd been lucky and spurring their interest in the house on Vista; maybe they were headed that way now. He took a big sigh to calm his nerves then proceeded to retrieve the rusty crowbar before walking back to the kitchen.

Getting the stove out of the house on his own proved to be impossible. He finally had to go back to enlist help from Skyler and Mike. Mike was nervous about leaving his house and wandering out towards the road, but James assured him that everything would be done from the rear of the house and no one would see them. Besides, they only needed Mike to help move the stove outside; once outside, he and Skyler could find a way to get it back, and Mike would only have to be away from home for a short while.

The three of them pushed and pulled the bulky stove through one doorway. Their progress came to a halt at the back door, where there was the lip of the sliding glass door and three concrete steps to overcome. Mike muttered something about 'being right back' and took off for his house. Five minutes later he returned, pushing a hand truck. Mike controlled the hand truck as James and Skyler helped to lift the wheels over the rail and down to the first step. When they landed it on the concrete walkway, Mike bid them goodbye. James was thankful that Mike left the hand truck with them. Wheeling the stove back to their house would now be much easier, but they still had to get the stove up that tall flight of stairs. Didn't Mike realize this? James was starting to lose all respect for his new neighbor.

By the time Skyler and James had pushed the stove the two hundred yards to their house, they were exhausted and had to take a break. Besides, they had to figure a way to ascend the stairs. Lara was in the back yard hard at work digging up a garden and James didn't bother her for help; he needed more than extra hands. He remembered that he once pulled a large man from a crevasse following a climbing accident. He had used a rope and pulley system and was able to use the system to reduce the weight being hoisted. He tapped Skyler on the shoulder and had him follow him to the basement. They lowered the two kayaks down and took the nylon ropes off the pulleys. Between the two systems, there might be enough ropes and pulleys to rig a Z-system that could assist them in getting the stove up the stairs.

An hour later, they had the stove on the deck. James was sweating so badly that he needed a break, but he knew that he still needed to find some cinderblocks for the stove to sit upon, plus some sections of insulated chimney and stovepipe and all the pieces needed to install a chimney before the stove could be used. Retrieving the stovepipe would have to wait until tomorrow. The hunt for cinderblocks could also wait. For now, they could use the stove outdoors for easier cooking than what Lara's makeshift fireplace offered. The only urgent task was to re-hang the kayaks and the food hidden within their hulls. After that, he wanted to help Lara with the garden. She had pressed upon him the importance of getting it started now that the ground was warming enough for seeds to germinate.

Picking up a shovel, James asked Skyler if he would go hunting. They were out of meat. It might take Skyler a few days to figure out the best places to hunt around here, so even a scouting expedition would be valuable, as they also needed to find a source of water. The two plastic jugs they had would last a day at the most, and his plans for diverting the drain pipes from the gutters into buckets would only provide water when it rained, water that would need to be shared with the garden when it became dry. Though it was unnecessary, James reminded Skyler to stay low and avoid any contact with strangers. Skyler returned empty handed and apologetic about it. "I saw a pair of crows off in the distance. But there wasn't any chance for me to move close enough to get a shot."

Lara had built a fire in the stove for cooking their rice. When she saw the sky darkening with clouds, she returned to the garden to get some seeds planted to benefit from the rain, while James worked on the downspout rain collecting system. The three of them stayed up for an hour after dark as James read another couple of chapters from their book. He looked at them over the pages of the book, both with eyes closed to better listen and imagine the story. They were as content as he had ever seen them. This made him content.

The next morning, James was jarred awake by the sound of an engine. He quickly rose and headed towards the windows on the north end of the house. Lara was also alarmed but she didn't leave the bedroom. Per Mike's instructions, James had left the doors and windows on the street side of the house boarded up, and James searched each window until he found a crack that he could peer through. Out in the driveway sat one of the Humvees. It just sat there with its engine running. None of the doors were open. James watched. Then the two rear doors opened and two soldiers clad in body armor stepped out and started for the stairs. James ran to the bedroom and told Lara to stay there and not come out. From the other side of the house, he could hear Skyler moving about. The boy had to know the Humvee was here, it was parked just below his boarded up window. He walked back to the kitchen and waited. Scanning the room, he didn't see their bows or guns in their normal spots. Where did they go? He was certain he'd left his bow by the front door last night. He heard the loud footsteps of the men walking along the deck, evidently scouting the layout of the exterior. Finally, there were three thumps on the front door. James tried to act calm but his fear was overriding all other emotions. He glanced quickly around and couldn't see anything incriminating. He opened the door, and was faced by a soldier holding an M-16; another soldier stood back a couple feet and watched. Just then Skyler walked into the room rubbing his eyes as if he'd just woken up, looking confused. James noticed that the boy was fully dressed like he'd been up for awhile.

"Can I help you?" asked James.

"Mind if I come in?"

"Ah? Sure," replied James nervously.

James recognized the soldier as the same one that had confronted him yesterday, Carter. The soldier took two steps and stopped in the entry. "How many persons live in this household?"

James looked at the man, quickly deciding the best way to answer. "Just three of us. This is my son. My wife's still in bed. She's pretty sick."

"You look like you haven't starved through the winter" the soldier intoned to James. "What is your source of food?"

The question confused him. Did Carter mean what type of food? Or where did they get it?

Carter added "I mean, where can we purchase food?"

"There's no food for sale anywhere that I know of," replied James. "I had some saved up, but like I told you yesterday, we were robbed. We had to move out. We moved in here only two days ago." James worried where this was going and wanted to distract him by asking if they had gone over to Vista but he didn't. His hands were beginning to shake. The soldier stepped into the house to scan the room. James noticed that Skyler's eyes looked to the man's torso and not his face, and kept following the soldier, only occasionally glancing the other standing outside the door.

Carter brushed past James and headed towards the kitchen. He opened several cabinets, revealing dishware. He switched to the drawers and in the first one found a plastic bag with about four cups of rice. He then lifted a second bag with about the same amount of oatmeal. As he lifted it, James said, "That's all we have left."

The soldier gave him a look of disinterest. He dropped the bag back in the drawer and slammed it shut, but left the cabinets wide open. James saw that Skyler was watching the soldier intently, eyes unafraid. The soldier turned to walk towards the bedroom where Lara was. Skyler and James followed.

Carter was about to enter the bedroom when he noticed the stairway leading downstairs. He stopped and pointed, "What's down there?"

"Just a big room with a bunch of unusable exercise equipment, a bedroom, and the garage," answered James.

Carter changed course and started down the stairs instead of opening the door to where Lara was hiding. He pulled a small flashlight from a cargo pocket and illuminated the stairway. Skyler headed back to the main room and James followed Carter downstairs. As they entered the garage, James found it hard to conceal his nervousness. The soldier swept the floor and walls with the small light. The ATV and the lawnmower were the only things he paused at, seemingly disinterested in the garage's contents. He backed out the door and headed up the stairs. James hid his relief.

Ascended the stairs much faster than his descent, Carter proceeded to the front door without hesitation. He pushed past Skyler who was at that same moment coming back inside. Ignoring James and Skyler, Carter requested his partner inspect the perimeter for any additional storage places. The other soldier descended the stairs and disappeared around the corner, while Carter walked the length of the deck to open the oven on the stove and inspect its empty space.

James knew what he was looking for, but pretended to be ignorant. "Is there something you're looking for?"

Carter didn't answer. A moment later, the other soldier came back up the stairs. He gave Carter a negative nod of the head. Both men then began to descend the stairs when Carter stopped and turned to face James. "We'll be back periodically to check on you. If you find a source of food, and I hope you do," he said somewhat threateningly, "we'll want to be informed of it on our next visit." Without waiting for a response, he turned and continued down to the Humvee.

James breathed a sigh of relief and drew his hands along his cheeks to his mouth, holding them there, prayer-like. As the Humvee disappeared down the road, he turned to Skyler, "Do you know where my bow is?"

"It's under the pillows on my bed, along with mine," he replied. "As soon as I heard them turn down into the driveway, I gathered everything we needed and hid it as best I could."

"Good move," said James. Just then, Lara stepped out of the bedroom, eyes wide in terror. James rushed to her, putting his arm around her shoulders, and helped her over to a couch. Fear was clearly overriding her ability to think straight, to even move. Skyler watched the two, a quizzical look on his face.

Once on the couch, Lara lost all control and began sobbing. James didn't say or do anything other than just sit with her. Finally she quieted down and looked at Skyler, saying, "I'm so sorry."

"That's okay, Lara. But you really shouldn't be so afraid."

"I'm sure I must seem like a freak," Lara half laughed through her sobs. "But there's something you don't know, Skyler. I should have told you sooner why I'm so on edge all the time, so fearful. It's just that—" she gave a big sigh, then went on to tell Skyler about her time on a farm with friends, how they happily sustained themselves growing their own vegetables and raising chickens, and sharing camaraderie. Then she told him about the late night visit from the soldiers, and how she was the only one to escape.

Skyler nodded in understanding, looked kindly at Lara, then turned to James, his face brows knitted. "Where do these soldiers live?"

James looked up, surprised at the directness and intensity of Skyler's question, "Out at the old oil refinery near the storage tanks."

"How many are there?"

"I counted seven yesterday when they drove past the house where I found the stove." replied James. He was careful not to mention that they had actually stopped and questioned him. Lara didn't need to know this.

"What are they looking for?" asked Skyler.

"Food." Both Lara and James said it at the same time.

"Like everyone else," James continued, "they're probably out of food. Hard thing is—they have such gun power and, obviously, they have fuel to get around, and I'm sure they have no qualms about taking what they want if someone resists them." James looked to Lara, knowing this could set her off. But he needed Skyler to understand.

Skyler stuck a hand into the pocket of his jeans, evidently considering James's answer and nodding to himself. "That's kind of what I thought." He pulled out the button and held it in his open palm, staring at it. "I found this next to my mother's hand."

Chapter 18

Skyler's mind was filled with so many questions but he knew the answers would be hard to find. The button he carried matched those on the two soldiers' uniforms. If there were only seven soldiers, then one of them must know what happened to his mother. His mind jumped to the conclusion that one of them had killed his mother. But then, he reminded himself, maybe not. Maybe they'd just come upon her, or maybe even they tried to help her but they were too late. He just couldn't know, but he was sure they were somehow connected to his mother's death and needed to find out more about them. He needed a plan, a plan that he'd have to keep from Lara and James; they would not approve if they knew.

Clouds had reappeared, signaling another rain storm could happen soon. Skyler shivered; the house was still cold. He was about to ask how he could help with installing the chimney, but saw James and Lara begin collecting seeds for planting in the garden. Skyler noticed that James was staying close to Lara, who was still pretty upset. She even snapped at James a few times. Finally, he asked James, "When are we going to move the stove inside?"

"Tomorrow, we need to finish planting the garden first."

That night they ate rice with soy sauce. There was no meat to share with this meal. After their small meal, Skyler declared that he planned to hunt for birds the following day. "But—I want to look west of the house," he said nonchalantly, not wanting to call too much attention to his plan. "The fields around here are too open and any birds are going to stay away." James didn't offer an opinion. It was like he didn't hear a thing Skyler said, his mind elsewhere.

Finally James spoke. "We need to find a better place to hide the guns and bows. Today's search was a close call."

Lara instantly snapped at him. "What makes you think that we'll survive another encounter with those men? Or any other person who wants what's ours? Another 'close call' could be our last call, James! I mean, we're planting a garden. Why? So that they can come back and take what we grow!"

"We'll just have to find a better way to hide our food," said James, calmly.

"And what happens when they notice that we aren't starving? Do you honestly believe that they'll leave us alone?"

James didn't answer. He excused himself from the table and headed downstairs. Skyler felt awkward watching this exchange, but didn't say anything. He had not seen Lara remain this upset for this long. Normally the tensions dissipated with James offering some comforting words. Skyler was tempted to follow James when Lara placed a hand on his shoulder.

"I'm sorry for being so upset. I'm not mad at James or you. I'm just so very afraid of the situation we're in."

"I know, the whole thing—it's all so . . . ," Skyler struggled for words. "It's just hard. And I don't want to move if we don't have to. I like this place."

"I like it too," Lara said, smiling at the boy.

The next morning, Lara seemed almost back to her normal self. She didn't harp at James about anything and even hummed a bit as she waited for the water to boil. James promised that he would have the chimney installed and house heated by that night. Before heading out to find chimney parts, James went next door to alert Mike about the visit from the military. He returned ten minutes later with a look of resignation on his face.

"What's the matter?" Lara asked.

"Mike said he heard them drive up. He claims that the soldiers would never do anything harmful to anyone. That their job is 'to serve and protect.'" James said scornfully. "He says that he has all the confidence that they will do only good things for us."

"He's wrong," Lara flatly said. "Did you tell him about what happened to my friends?"

"Yeah." James shook his head. "And he says you're mistaken." James put a hand on Lara's shoulder as he saw her look of contention. "I know, I know. I tried to warn him, that he's got to be wrong about the soldiers, but it's clear he's not going to listen to reason."

While Lara and James talked, Skyler dressed himself in a camouflage jacket he'd found at a house near their old place. He had his bow, a quiver of arrows, and a bottle of water. All three left together: Lara for the garden as if expecting indication of growth since last night's rain; James headed for the house where he'd found the stove, tools in hand and Skyler for his hunting expedition. Skyler, though, had a second agenda: he still harbored a desire to see who lived up on the hill and felt that the telephone pole barricade had something to do with the soldiers. He would head there first; maybe someone in that community had answers. Staying off the main road, Skyler scouted the housing development on the east side of the barricaded road. The houses on the west side, he remembered, were all severely damaged. He knew that he was looking in the right place when the wind shifted and the strong smell of wood smoke drifted his way. He sat hidden behind a downed tree for an hour, watching a road within the development from a gap between two houses, and saw two different men, a woman, and three children move past.

Skyler didn't make contact. If he went walking in wearing his camouflage and carrying a bow, they'd for sure react defensively. But if he had something to give them, or exchange with them, they might be more welcoming, or at least open to talking with him. He thought about asking James for a small sack of rice or flour, but nixed that idea because James would want to know why. Besides, he agreed with James: it would be better if no one knew that they had surplus food. A bird or a fish, just caught, would do the job.

Skyler retreated back down the hill and headed west up the main road that led towards the refinery. His goal was not the refinery, not just yet, but a pond that he remembered sat in a low area between two farms. Skyler's best friend in elementary school, Marcus, had lived at one of the farms. He'd lost touch with Marcus, so didn't know if he'd lived there when the storm came, but before the storm, Skyler often visited Marcus, and they spent many summer days swimming and fishing in the pond. If there were still some fish there, there might also be birds.

As he neared the property, he could see the devastation at Marcus's place. Both house and barn had been almost flattened by the strong winds; debris was scattered across the landscape. Like everywhere else, plant life was nearly nonexistent except for areas where grass was beginning to sprout, small patches of pale green. He considered trying to get through the debris to see if any food was left in their kitchen, but he could find no viable access. Skyler turned his direction to the adjacent farm. Somehow, likely because someone had had the foresight to board up all the doors and windows, it was not destroyed and appeared habitable. Whether someone was there or not, Skyler couldn't tell yet. The boards were still up on the side he could see and he was about to check the other side for access when a movement caught his eye: there was a ripple on the pond. He froze in his tracks and watched.

Finally Skyler saw a large Canadian goose step out from between clumps of dead reeds. Intent on gathering reeds for a nest, it had not noticed Skyler yet. Not caring how it got here, Skyler quietly lifted his bow and fit an arrow on the string. He noted that if he shot from this position, the arrow would pass through the bird and be lost in the water, so he waited until the bird had turned its head away, then silently moved around the pond, positioning himself where he could shoot the bird and the exiting arrow would impact against a dirt bank. It was only a twenty yard shot and it was a big target. He drew back on his arrow and was about to release when he caught another movement along the far bank. A lone duck sat at the water's edge not far from where his arrow would land. Skyler released, and before either bird could react, he pulled another arrow from his quiver, drew and released. The first arrow passed right through the goose's body so quickly that it didn't even flinch; the second arrow hit the duck before it could take flight. The arrow's fletching protruded from the duck's body, its tip stuck into the dirt, holding the duck in place. The duck started flapping wildly, which caused the goose to panic and take flight. It was in the air for only a couple of seconds before it dropped and landed on the pond maybe twelve feet from shore.

After retrieving both birds and his arrows, Skyler hid the birds in the reeds and continued on the task of investigating the other farm house. He circled it wide, coming in on its north side, and saw a porch, its door not boarded. He walked closer to the house, listening intently for any sounds. If someone still lived there, they might have heard the ruckus. There was nothing. He could not detect any scent of smoke, either, nor was the yard a mess of debris like most other places. Skyler couldn't be sure if that was because someone had cleared it, or if it was just because the place had not been so violently damaged. Something about the situation did not settle with Skyler, and his heart started racing with fear. He moved to the side of the house and worked his way around to the door. He placed his ear against the exterior wall. Still no sounds. As he got close to the door, he found that it had been forced open and was barely hanging on its hinges. He crept through the doorway and into the living room. It smelled bad, but not like human waste—something he couldn't put his finger on. Someone had obviously lived here, and it wasn't that long ago. Two beds situated around the cold wood stove meant that more than one person had been here during the cold winter. He looked around the living room once more then stepped into the kitchen. Skyler gasped loudly. There were four bodies lying on the floor; two young boys and two adults. Before Skyler turned away in horror, he could see that each had been shot—either in the head or the chest.

Skyler's fear festered. He desperately wanted to flee. Yet something held him back as he looked at the scene. This was not a suicide-murder where the parents kill their children before killing themselves, a not uncommon method of escape during the collapse. There was no weapon near any of the bodies. Then Skyler noticed the bullet casings lying on the floor. There were no less than eight within sight. He picked one up and pocketed it before putting the scene behind him. Before leaving the farm, he placed both the goose and duck in his pack, then headed east to try and find some answers.

An hour later, Skyler stepped around the barricade at the top of Church road and walked towards the opening of the development. As he turned onto the main street intersecting the rows of homes, he caught a glimpse of someone ducking between two houses. He stood still for a full moment. Nothing moved. He finally, and very slowly, set his bow on the ground and took the goose from his pack, holding the heavy with both arms outstretched. He wanted to be sure someone saw his offering. He considered leaving the bird and coming back the next day, but he had too many questions and didn't want to lose the opportunity, or take the risk that they'd want more. Finally, two men with rifles came out from between houses about a half-a-block ahead of where Skyler stood. They weren't pointing their rifles at him, but they could within a second. Despite how skinny they looked, Skyler noticed that their clothes were clean, not the dirty rags he'd seen on most other survivors.

"What do you want?" called out the taller man.

"I brought you a bird," said Skyler. "I came through here two days ago on our ATV. I saw your sign."

"You didn't answer my question. What do you want?"

"Just some answers and you can have this bird," Skyler said, holding it up higher. "I shot it less than an hour ago."

"How do we know you aren't setting us up for an ambush?"

"I don't know. I mean, I guess you don't know. But I don't want to ambush anyone. I just want to meet good people."

The men moved forward. He was clearly out gunned and outnumbered. However, he didn't sense that the men were dangerous. They introduced themselves as Brent and Petar, and he told them his own name. It felt odd to Skyler, since the only people he'd exchanged introductions with, the only ones he'd given his name to since the big change, were Lara and James.

"I'm glad to meet you two. Was it you who put up those barricades?" Skyler motioned toward the one behind him.

"We put those up to stop the Humvees," said Petar, the taller man. "The soldiers from the refinery came up here last fall and took a lot of our food. We almost didn't make it through the winter."

"How many live here?"

"That's none of your business," Petar answered curtly. He must have realized the rudeness of his answer because he added, "Sorry. We're a bit nervous about any strangers knowing too much about us. You got to understand."

"What about you?" interrupted the one named Brent. "Where do you live?"

Like the two men, Skyler was cautious about divulging too much information, so he just pointed to the south. He fished the bullet casing from his pocket and held it out in his palm. Brent reached out and picked it up. He inspected it briefly before dropping it back into Skyler's palm.

"Where'd you find that?" asked Brent.

"At a farm, about an hour's walk from here. Do you know what kind of gun this came from?"

"I should, I spent two years in the Middle East firing one of those guns. It's from an M-16, the standard weapon used by our troops."

Skyler nodded slowly, his thoughts internal for a moment. He didn't mention the four bodies he'd found on that farm. He knew too little about these men. Then he took a deep breath and said, "Well, here. Sure was nice meeting you." He handed Petar the goose.

"Nice bird," Petar said. "Here's a bit of advice: If you see a Humvee, get out of sight as fast as possible. They don't like it when civilians are carrying weapons. They'll take your bow away."

Skyler thanked him and had turned to leave when Petar spoke again, "Son, how old are you?"

Skyler paused for a few seconds. "What's today's date?"

Brent and Petar looked at each other and Brent said, "May . . . twenty-fifth I think? Give or take."

"Okay. Well, then I guess I turned fourteen last week." Like most children, Skyler usually counted down to his birthday. And his mother always made sure the celebration was a good one. A flood of memories opened up.

Skyler swallowed, holding back emotions, and thanked the men again. He picked up his pack and bow, said he would return again soon, and bid them good-bye.

Lara gave him a big smile at sight of the duck when Skyler returned. There was still plenty of daylight, so Skyler left the duck on the kitchen counter and went back outside to help James with the stove and chimney.

Chapter 19

"A duck?" asked James while they worked. "Where did you find a duck?"

Skyler stood at the kitchen counter with the bird stretched out before him. "Up the main road and over the hill, there's a pond that I used to swim at."

"Yeah?" James's face lit up. "Were there more birds? Did you see anything else while you were out we should know about?"

"No, nothing," Skyler lied. There was enough tension because of the appearance of the soldiers, so he changed the subject. "Do you know what today's date is?"

James looked up with a furrowed brow; the question caught him off guard."Why do you ask?"

"My birthday's May twentieth. I think today must be around the twenty-fifth."

"I guess we've lost track of the dates. Maybe we should've marked the days better." James glanced towards a calendar hanging on the wall. It was five years old. The last calendar he'd seen was the one in his checkbook, right before he used it to start a fire back when he was living alone.

Lara finished wiping the soil from her hands, "What do you want for your birthday?"

Skyler thought for a few seconds and gave a sad laugh. "The things I want can't be found anymore, not even in someone else's old house."

"What about a cake?"

"A cake? Can you make me a cake?" A glimmer of a smile escaped from the boy.

"Maybe not a real cake, but we can have pancakes for dinner tomorrow. I found a can of baking powder in the cupboard."

"They also need eggs," said James. The smile on Skyler's face disappeared and James regretted the words as soon as he'd said them. "But maybe we can find something to use instead," he added, trying to rectify his first statement.

James offered to get the duck ready for dinner. He took the bird outside and began plucking the feathers, which the wind took and spread across the landscape. James watched them and wondered if there was a good use for them—if he should save them as he'd gotten in the habit of doing with most everything of potential value. He couldn't think of a use right then, so didn't bother to retrieve the flown feathers. Instead he let his thoughts get carried away by the idea of meat with their rice the next few meals. He remembered how good the goose tasted earlier that year. As he finished pulling out the last of the feathers, he decided that this bird should be cooked over an open fire.

With the stove's installation finished, Lara was quick to get a fire going inside. The warmth it gave off made the house feel very different—homey, and eliciting good memories. Things just felt better. The warmed air also lent a cozier quality to the already comfortable leather couches—another luxury that was close to extinction. And with last night's heavy rain, they had enough fresh water to last a few days. It was almost as if she could relax a little. James came in the door then, stomping his feet out of habit, shaking the imaginary snow off his boots. Lara smiled at this. She never pointed James's quirk out to him. "Remind me not to cook outside again." In his arms was a metal pan with the spit—roasted duck.

"Why?"

"I bet you could smell this duck a mile away," he replied. And with that comment, Lara's brief sense of security faded.

By the time they finished dinner, the only light remaining came from a single candle on the table. James reached for their current book, but before he opened it, Skyler asked him, "Can I go back out hunting tomorrow?"

"Sure, by all means, Bwana!" James laughed.

"What's Bwana?

"It's what the natives called the great white hunters in the old Tarzan movies."

"Who's Tarzan?" asked Skyler

"Never mind, it was from a story a long time ago." James made a mental note to keep an eye out for an old Tarzan book. "But, sure—if you can hunt for more meat, that would be great."

"I remember there were some ponds near the old aluminum plant; I want to hike out that far and see if there might be more ducks out there. Maybe even some fish."

James looked up abruptly. He knew those ponds; there was once an archery range there, where he learned to shoot a bow. They sat between the old aluminum smelter and the refinery. "Just don't go near the refinery, OK?"

Lara looked up at that, her already worried crease between her eyes now deepening. That single word—"refinery"—subdued everyone. He quickly opened the book and began to read.

The following morning right after breakfast, Skyler readied for a long day of hunting. Besides his bow, he packed water, a collapsible fishing pole, and an old jar of salmon eggs. James urged him to take the small crossbow that he'd found useful for hunting crows. Skyler insisted on taking his larger compound because it was more accurate at longer distances.

Lara added, "Make sure that you are back before dark," she said, handing him a small bag of cooked rice to add to his pack. "I'll have a surprise for you." It almost sounded like a normal mother-to-son exchange, considering none of them ever stayed out even close to dark. Skyler gave her an appreciative nod.

James watched Skyler leave before pulling on his own boots. Today's goal was to find a water source closer than the pond Skyler mentioned yesterday. They had enough water to last a couple more days. But it wasn't going to rain today, and if it didn't rain within the next few days, they would need a back-up source. Where did Mike get his water? James hadn't noticed him walking anywhere with a container. He thought about stopping at Mike's to ask, but decided not to. There was just something about him that made James uncomfortable and James wanted to keep his involvement with his neighbor to a minimum. Once he dropped down below the house, James looked back up the hill. He noticed the proximity of his house to Mike's. It didn't seem that close when he was at home, because they rarely saw Mike since the first day. Plus, the dead cedar trees, kept standing by the shelter of the two houses, created a false sense of isolation. But in truth the houses were pretty close together. He was glad that Mike kept to himself.

.

The fields south of their house stretched for a half mile before being dissected by another county road. James headed in this direction. He'd encouraged Lara to come along with him, but she declined, saying she'd be OK if he wasn't gone too long. He'd promised her that he'd be back within the hour. There was a housing complex about a mile off to the south. He wished he had his binoculars so he could see it better, but he hadn't been able to find them before he left, guessing that maybe Skyler had them. Reaching the complex was part of his goal for the day. Even from this distance, James could see that the damage there was extensive, but he wasn't interested in the houses; he wanted to find their run-off pond. All newer developments had them, where rain water could be diverted. The ponds used to create small ecosystems, providing habitat for fish or aquatic plants.

The older tall grass of the fields had been flattened by the winter storms. But James was pleased to see a new crop of grass sprouting up through the old, casting a green hue over the tan carpet. James scouted the ground for any new growth other than grass; he even listened for the quiet rustling of field mice. There was nothing else. There were no trails for him to follow, so his path was a bit encumbered as he headed in a general direction of the road. Just before reaching the edge of the asphalt, he thought he heard a faint quack. He stopped and looked around. The sound could have come from anywhere. He listened intently, nothing but silence. Nothing in sight on land or in the sky.

He crossed the road and continued south. Travel was easy on the level ground and James soon reached the development. It showed the worst damage he'd seen so far. None of the houses were habitable, most totally collapsed. James felt his nervousness increase. He pulled the bow from his pack and nocked an arrow but didn't draw the string back. He cautiously stepped down the center street, zigzagging through thick debris and keeping alert for any indication of life. He kept turning around, half expecting to see someone following him. There was no one.

The street began to turn, which signified that he'd reached a corner of the development. He was close to his goal. Any diversion pond would be at the outside edge and, if it was still intact, possibly within a chain link fence. James located a clear path between two houses and left the street. Once he was behind the development, he relaxed a little. From this vantage point, he was able to watch for anyone coming from the development, and he could see what was left of the chain link fence about a hundred yards to the southwest of him.

Pieces of garden sheds, walls, and other debris carried by the wind had adhered to the fencing, creating a near-solid wall for the wind to push against and ultimately flatten. The entire half of the fence that faced the northeast was downed; the rest was down in small areas. James worked his way to the berm that bordered the pond and stopped. It wasn't what he'd wanted to find. People had been using the ponds' crater as a garbage dump. Any patches of visible water revealed a sheen that signified the contamination by petroleum products. This would not work as a source for water.

His watch indicated that he had been gone from the house a full twenty-five minutes. It was time to turn back. Besides, he really needed to find a water source closer to home, somewhere more towards the east or west. It would have to wait for another time. James found another traversable gap between two houses and stepped between them to reach the street. Out of habit, he was cautious and paused near the front corner of the house before stepping out in the open. He saw movement—a few houses to the north. At first he thought it was a very sick dog, but then he noticed the bushy tail and realized it was a coyote. James slowly raised his bow and began to draw back the string. She turned to the side and James saw her sagging torso. She was a female, and by the state of her teats, James surmised that she had a litter hidden somewhere nearby. She was skinny from malnourishment, thinner than any canine he'd ever seen. He slowly relaxed his pull on the string and remained unmoving, watching her.

Drawing the bow on the coyote brought back a memory that had been a major turn in his life. When he was twelve, he'd lived with his mother on a farm out in the county. Across the highway from them lived an old farmer named Frank. Old Frank had a terrible speech impediment. It had taken James a couple of years to learn "Frank's language" and understand just what the old man was trying to say. Once they could communicate, James worked for the old man, milking cows, haying, and any other job Frank threw his way.

One day, Frank came running over. He looked frantic. His arms were waving about and he was stuttering so badly that the only word James understood was 'gun.' James grabbed his Montgomery Ward shotgun and followed the old man. He'd never seen old Frank move so fast. He followed him past the house and behind the barn towards the orchard. They arrived at an orchard of some twenty or more apple trees. Frank was pointing a shaky finger at a bifurcation in the tree at the center. Where the trunk split into two separate limbs sat a huge porcupine. Frank was spitting as he shouted, "Shoot it, shoot it."

James did just that. His first shot wounded the animal, knocking it from the tree. As the porcupine hit the ground, it made a feeble attempt to crawl away. James reloaded and fired a second shot. The porcupine laid still. Frank calmed down and was sporting a wide grin as his head bobbed up and down with approval. James, on the other hand, felt ill over what he'd done. The porcupine hadn't been a threat to anyone. There wasn't any reason to kill it. James recalled turning his back on the old man and walking away, confused by his emotions. When he was home again, he'd put the shotgun back in its usual place in the hall closet. He never used it again.

As weak as she looked, the coyote's movements were still graceful. She had appeared from an opening in a collapsed door frame on the opposite side of the street. The house's walls were collapsed but the roof retained a section that was still intact and peaked at its center, her lair. Smart dog, James thought; she had figured out how to survive. He watched as she darted in between two houses, then shot out towards the open field. It looked like she knew where she wanted to go. Maybe she'd found a source of food.

When she was out of sight, James walked towards the structure where she seemed to have come. He put the arrow back into the quiver and his bow to his back. He was no longer worried that any human was in the area; the animal had confirmed this by leaving her lair. As James reached the opening, he crept silently and crouched down low, listening intently. At first he heard nothing. Then he heard a weak, whining growl followed by another at a slightly lower pitch. There were at least two pups—probably no more than two pups, as the mother would have eaten the others so that these two and she could survive, James thought—and it sounded like they were wrestling. James stood and backed away. He didn't want the pups or the mother to know he'd been here. Walking out of the development, he couldn't help but wonder what she was hunting. For many reasons, seeing her made him feel better.

Once he crossed the road into the large field below his house, James veered to the left. He had covered the eastern half of the field on his way down, now he wanted to cover the western half on the return trip. Already he could see mounds of dirt had been pushed around by heavy equipment. He perceived a large flat area and could visualize the beginnings of a street, another housing project stopped short before even any concrete or asphalt had been brought in. James guessed that the project had probably collapsed long before the banks had. The dirt street was covered with dead grass and weeds, but James could still see the developer's intentions. He followed the path for a short distance before turning towards his house. Lara would be waiting. He'd been gone forty-five minutes.

Entering the field that abutted his new place, he skirted along a berm covered with tall grass. A commotion of quacking and slapped water erupted just twenty feet to his right. The berm limited his field of view, but the sounds told him that he wasn't in danger as two ducks flapped past him, his bow instinctively at the ready but too late to hit a target. James stood and climbed atop the berm. Below it was a rectangular-shaped, man-made pond. But since the project was never completed, it lacked the fence. The water was slightly murky, but James noted that the surface was clean. At the most, it was a ten-minute walk from his house. He'd come back tomorrow.

When James stepped back onto the deck, Lara stood in the doorway with an angry look on her face.

"What? It was less than an hour."

"Mike came back. He must have seen you leave."

"What did he want?"

"What do you think he wanted? He came over to tell me that he had no ties to Cindy. He—oh, forget it!" She flung her arms, not wanting to put into words what Mike wanted, then folded them across her chest. Her angry expression hadn't changed.

James didn't know what to say. He hadn't kindled any friendship with Mike, but Mike had been good enough to allow them to move in. What would happen if he went over there and told Mike to back off? To essentially threaten him? Doing that might create a situation that could snowball into something regrettable—if nothing else being forced to move. Finally, James asked, "How did you get him to leave this time?"

"I told him that if I ever saw him on our deck again, I would shoot him in the balls!"

"What did he say?" James was alarmed.

"He didn't say anything. He just ran down the stairs and went home."

Before James could express his worries or ask another question, Lara added, "I was holding the pistol when I said that." Her folded arms seemed to relax a bit and she began laughing. "I don't think he'll be back."

James couldn't hide his amusement. He wasn't laughing at her for daring to threaten their neighbor. It was because she was laughing. He had never witnessed this side of her before.

It was only mid-morning, so James and Lara decided to explore the few remaining places in the house they had yet to open. They had already been through all of the upstairs closets and had found a few useful items. Now it was time to see what they might find in the lower half of the house. Grabbing a candle each, they headed downstairs. Their first stop was the bedroom and its wide closet that covered an entire wall. They'd opened these doors just once before to look for extra bedding, but there were four boxes that they hadn't taken the time to investigate. With Lara holding both candles, James brought one box out at a time, placing each on the floor at the side of the bed.

They started with the heaviest box. First glance showed several identical books. When they moved a candle closer, they could see that the box contained an entire set of encyclopedias. James hefted this box and moved it over near the door. "These are for sure going upstairs. They can be useful and interesting. Besides, Skyler needs some kind of education."

Of the three remaining boxes, one was packed with old photo albums and personal mementos, another contained law books, and the third was filled with gloves, mittens and stocking hats. James put this last box on top of the box with the encyclopedias.

Next they went for the large closet across from the stairs in the main room. It contained the house's furnace and water heater. The water heater had likely burst during a freeze, as it was empty of all of its contents. A drain positioned below it had kept the basement from flooding. The furnace, though, piqued James's interest. A handle on the front was attached to an electronic air scrubber. As an air filter, it was now useless without electricity. However, when he removed the large drawer with its tin plates, he found a cavernous space below the filter. James estimated they could store at least two months' worth of food in here—jars of preserved vegetables, he envisioned—and nobody would know better. He closed the doors to the utility closet and turned towards the closet under the stairs.

Like every other room in the house, this closet was behind a three-panel craftsman door with a cherry-colored stain. Since it was under the staircase, they didn't expect it to have much space for storage. And when James cracked open the door, a foul smell hit them full on. Once the odor dissipated enough to allow breathing, they poked their heads inside and saw a narrow passage. They went further in, candles aloft, about six feet and found a jumble of items piled up, but behind this, the passage made a U-turn under the lower staircase. James held a candle in one hand and worked with the other to move skis, empty clothes baskets, and boxes of old dishes, passing them back to Lara for further inspection. He wanted to get beyond the U-turn, and there was only room for one person.

Inspecting the assortment of dishes, Lara suddenly heard a 'whoop' of surprise. James scootched himself backwards while holding two large boxes. As he emerged from the doorway, Lara held a candle up to the boxes, the outside of each showing a photo of a sleeping bag by the side of a campfire. The boxes had never been opened.

James was grinning. "There's more." James worked his way back in and almost disappeared around the corner. His second trip out revealed a small tent, two new air mattresses in their wrappers, and two fishing poles. On his third and final trip, he dragged out a large plastic storage container with a tackle box riding on its lid. He opened the tackle box first: inside were lures, hooks, weights, and several large spools of fine fishing line. He was like a boy on Christmas morning. For her part, Lara couldn't wait to see what was inside the large plastic bin; it was two feet wide, four feet long and deep, maybe eighteen inches deep. James popped the lid up and let it slide off to the side. The smell hit them like a strong wind. It was filled with jars and cans containing vegetables, fruits, and condiments. But it appeared that every can and jar had burst after being frozen, the subsequent thaw contributing to the foul odor. However, there were also plastic containers holding smaller items. Lara pulled out one of the containers and opened it. It held boxes of pudding powder, packages of cookies, and a box of graham crackers. The other smaller container had a box of cornmeal, a five-pound bag of sugar, and boxes of both brown and powdered sugar. Some of the packages showed mold, while other packages looked like they had just come off the grocery store shelf. After setting the two containers of dry goods aside to take upstairs, they searched the larger container for any intact cans or bottles. They were rewarded with two bottles of oil, one olive and one vegetable.

As Lara moved the dry goods upstairs, James dragged the larger container through the garage to the outside. James got it away from the house and tipped it on its side, dumping the putrid mixture out onto the ground. Once it was clean, they could use the container for storing food. It could even be buried if necessary. Unless it suddenly rained, James planned on taking it to the pond within the next day or so to wash it out. After closing the garage door behind him, he saw Lara standing there, a big smile on her face. He could tell she was bursting to say something.

"I got an idea! We have enough stuff to make a pudding pie. Let's throw a party for Skyler."

"Best idea I've heard in a long time," James agreed. As Lara threw more wood on the fire to warm the oven, James moved the rest of the found gear to the living room. The cardboard boxes that held the sleeping bags reeked of the rotten food, but the bags themselves were still sealed in plastic and they smelled new. The tent was also sealed in plastic and had not seen any use. James came up with an idea.

Hours later, with the sun now moving towards the horizon, they heard Skyler's footsteps as he ran up to the deck. The door opened and there stood the boy holding a string of crappies high in the air. He looked exhausted, like he'd run for miles to get home. "There's fish in those ponds and they're hungry!" he blurted out, panting.

James stood from where he'd been sitting on the couch. "I can't believe it—you've done it again. Yesterday a duck and today its fish! What is that, almost two pounds of meat?" James patted Skyler on the shoulder, delighted by the unexpected surprise.

"As soon as my hook hit the water, I'd get a bite." Skyler's voice still carried his excitement. "And I only fished one of the ponds. I know they're not huge or very meaty, but I want to go back tomorrow!" He looked to James for approval, then turned to Lara.

Lara had been standing in front of the kitchen counter taking in all of his excitement. When Skyler finally looked in her direction, she moved aside to reveal a pie with fourteen candles sprouting from its surface. The room was quiet as Skyler looked at her, then back at the pie. The boy had gone speechless.

"They're not real candles," she apologized. "I made them by rolling paper into little tubes."

"Is the pie real?"

"Yes, it's real. It's made with chocolate pudding and it has a graham cracker crust."

"Really? How . . . ?"

"We found some food stored away downstairs. Like an emergency supply. Luckily the pudding mix only needed water. There was a box of graham crackers, too, that I mixed with a little oil and baked. I hope you like it."

"Like it? I'll love it!"

"James also has something to show you."

James jerked his head towards Skyler's room and said, "Follow me."

When they reached the room, James stood aside. Skyler turned the knob and gently pushed the door wide. There, next to his bed, stood a small assembled tent complete with rain fly. The front flap was zipped closed. Skyler stood in awe.

"Go ahead and open it."

Skyler looked up at James, his face beaming with joy. The excitement he carried in with his catch had been renewed with each gift from his friends. He reached for the opening, pulled the zipper up and lifted the flap. Inside was a new sleeping bag laid out on an air mattress. Once again he was stunned. His grin was wide when he stood up to thank James.

They breaded the fish using the cornmeal and some water, and fried it in oil. While they ate, Skyler retold his story about the fish and that he'd also seen a couple more ducks but couldn't get close enough for a shot, plus he would've needed a boat to retrieve them. While Skyler talked, James did a little math in his head. The boy had been gone for about eight hours. It took maybe an hour each way to get to the ponds. That meant that he was at the pond, or somewhere, for almost six hours. But the boy said that he fished for maybe only a half hour. What was he doing for the other five and a half hours? James decided he'd wait before questioning him and see if Skyler would tell more himself.

By the time they got around to cutting the pie, Skyler had finished the account of his adventure. All three savored the chocolate dessert as if they'd never eaten anything so delectable. James took advantage of their silence to share his own day's adventure about his trek to the development and his encounter with the coyote. "I don't want you shooting any coyote if you come across one, okay? In fact, don't shoot any animal except birds when we need the meat. We need to give the animal population a chance to grow and survive."

"Aren't coyotes dangerous?" Lara asked, more curious than concerned.

"Not really, they're usually afraid of humans."

After they finished off the pie, James tossed the book to Skyler. "It's your turn to read."

"You want me to read?"

James pulled the three large spools from the tackle box. "I'm hoping you will. I need to see if I have enough fish line here to make a net, and then make some calculations and a drawing. So if you'd read, I can get some work done." James listened to Skyler's voice but only half heard the story as he read the label on each spool and did the math. There was over three miles of monofilament line before him. It was more than enough.

That night, Skyler moved his new camping gear onto the deck and slept there. James watched as the boy got situated, then went to his and Lara's room. As he crawled into bed, he tried not to disturb Lara. He'd thought that she would have already been asleep. She rolled over to face him.

"Thanks for rescuing me. Today made it worth it."

"Even after Mike tried to get into your pants?" he teased.

"Yes, even after that."

Chapter 20

Skyler woke at first light. Not because he wanted to, but because he heard a loud screech from a crow. The orange glow of the tent's fabric told him that the sun had peaked over the mountains. The bird cawed persistently, and Skyler briefly wondered if it was searching for its mate or welcoming a new day. He didn't really care; he just wanted to get a shot at it. Even if he failed, it would be a good challenge, and worth the effort if he succeeded. Crawling out of the tent without alerting the bird was his first hurdle; then he'd need to get inside, grab the crossbow, and make it back outside without the bird taking flight. Slim chance, yet Skyler was game. The zipper made only a slight noise as he gently slid it upward. The crow was making so much racket, Skyler joked to himself confidently, that he could have started a chainsaw and the bird wouldn't have noticed. Yet as Skyler poked his head out, he saw the crow just above him on the nearby peak of the roof. The crow gave out a sound that resembled a gasp and was gone in a second.

Both Lara and James had been woken by the crow too. Lara immediately focused on getting a fire going while James stepped out on the deck looking for the bird. He had the .22 pistol in his hand when he saw Skyler. "Did you see where my breakfast flew off to?"

"He flew west as soon as he saw my head. Next time I sleep outside, I'm sleeping with the crossbow!"

"Not a bad idea," said James. He turned and entered the house, leaving the door open for Skyler.

Back inside, Skyler sniffed the air with a proud smile. The lingering smell of fried fish made him hungry and eager for the day. While waiting for the water to boil for their breakfast of plain oatmeal with black tea, the three shared their plans.

"I'm going to investigate the pond I found in the nearby field. I'm sure it could be a good back-up water source, but I'm thinking we might also be able to trap some ducks there."

"Would you be able to bring a container and lug some water back for the garden?" Lara piped in, not indicating any fear at being left alone. "The sky doesn't look like rain at all, and I need to keep those seeds moist." James nodded; it would be no problem.

Skyler said that he wanted to try fishing in the other ponds by the old archery range.

Thirty minutes later, Skyler was on Douglas Road traveling west towards the refinery. He recalled how his mom always referred to it as "the old Douglas road" or "the Douglas," and he had chosen it because he didn't expect to see anyone on it. The Douglas had always seen less use, and even now, no one had done any clearing; Skyler had to step over power poles and fallen trees. The dead trees could provide him cover if he needed it. The soldiers, he'd noticed yesterday, had been using the road known as Mountain View, which ran parallel to the Douglas Road. Main Street turned into Mountain View right at the crest of the hill as it led out of town. Since Douglas hadn't been cleared, he didn't expect to see the soldiers using it.

Yesterday when he'd gone out to the ponds for the first time, Skyler had used Douglas to reach the ponds, but sidetracked along the way. His curiosity had got the best of him. His route had cut across a large field and stopped just fifty feet from a chain link fence that surrounded the refinery. Skyler had watched the storage tanks from a hiding spot in the ditch but couldn't see much. He had, though, seen the cameras on top of the storage tanks with the binoculars. He had wanted to see more and needed to move closer without being detected.

Skyler's position was not far from the main entrance; he could see the locking gate about a hundred yards up the road. To the right was the large, once-wooded area, covering over a square mile of the landscape, which included the ponds and the old archery range. Dead trees covered the hillside before him. Skyler crawled in the ditch north, away from the refinery, and then dropped down a small hill. The uneven terrain hid him from the cameras. Looking both ways for any sign of the Humvees, he scuttled across the road and quickly disappeared among the maze of dead limbs and twisted trunks.

Moving quietly or easily through the tangled limbs was near impossible, but Skyler managed to work his way towards the area near the gate. From there, he thought that he might be able to see more—where the soldiers stayed, what equipment they had, what their activities were. He had to be careful, of course, but even more so because neither James nor Lara knew he was out this way, and if he didn't return, they would have no idea where to look for him. He suddenly came upon some chain link fencing and dropped to his knees at the sound of an engine, one of the Humvees leaving through the gate. "They must still have a source of electricity," Skyler whispered to himself when he didn't see anyone get out to open or close the gate. Skyler inched further along the fence-line until he could see the bunker. It was a one-story structure with an asphalt skin, making it blend in with the terrain. The only side that wasn't covered with asphalt was the side that faced away from the tanks. Skyler counted three garage doors and one regular door. Two of the garage bays were open: one empty and one occupied by a Humvee. A few moments later, four armed and armored soldiers came out of the bunker and climbed into the waiting Humvee. They left through the same gate as the other vehicle.

Skyler didn't need to see inside the bunker but he wanted to. His curiosity still peaking. He looked around the surroundings: the chain link fence, topped with coils of barbed wire, would be hard to cross. Even if he did get inside, how would he get out quickly if the soldiers returned? Going over the fence would not be an option then. Skyler crawled along the bottom of the fence inspecting where fence met ground. He came to a shallow dip; it revealed a six-inch gap. Skyler pulled off his bow and his pack to retrieve his 'poo shovel,' a small gardening spade that he used to bury his waste. He scraped and dug until there was more like ten inches, barely enough to crawl under. Seconds later, he was crouched on the inside of the fence, his bow and pack still on the other side.

Skyler peered towards the road to make sure no one was returning. There was nothing stopping him now. He bolted for the bunker, entering the garage first to check for another Humvee or other vehicle behind the closed door. There were none. He looked about the garage, taking in its contents. A workbench with an array of automotive tools stood against the back wall. There was a large drum of motor oil with a hand-pump sticking out from the upper end. Near an interior door were boxes of home-canned foods, cases of cigarettes and boxes with liquor. Skyler was tempted to grab a few jars of vegetables but stopped himself, knowing he needed to keep his hands free and would have no way to explain them to James and Lara. Not today.

He hadn't been inside the garage for a full two minutes when his fear starting overriding his curiosity. He wanted to take a quick look inside and leave as soon as possible. He placed his ear against the door to what he guessed was the main quarters. Nothing. He slowly twisted the knob, cringing at the slightest mechanical sound, until it would twist no further. He pressed gently, opening a crack wide enough to see that the lights had been left on. Suddenly, a generator behind him kicked on and flooded the garage with its loud noise. It startled him. If a Humvee drove into the compound now, he wouldn't hear it. Skyler pushed the door the rest of the way and entered the interior.

His olfactory receptors were assaulted with a sour odor masked by stale tobacco smoke, and Skyler blinked at the brightness: electric lights lit up the far reaches of the expansive room. Unmade bunk beds, eight total beds, sat in rows at the back-end of the room while a large table and small kitchen occupied the other end. Between these two sections were two couches, one against each wall. A desk sat alongside one of the couches, and above it were three monitors showing views of the surrounding countryside. One of the monitors showed the east end of Douglas Road, but not all of it, Skyler noted. Just before the intersection, the road disappeared behind a low rise in the terrain.

Skyler spotted two doors along one wall and went to them. The first opened up to a toilet and shower. The small room had been stuffed with garbage. "Guess their plumbing doesn't work either," Skyler smiled to himself. The second door was locked. He looked about, but he couldn't find a key. Finally his fear won out and Skyler hurried back through the garage and was about leave when he stopped and looked down at the stack of boxes next to him. He pulled one of the bottles from a box, looked briefly at its label, and stuffed it inside his coat. He ran across the road towards the fence not stopping to see if anyone was coming.

No one followed, and once he was back through the fence, Skyler shoved the bottle in his pack, then hastily secured the pack onto his back while he kicked dirt and sticks into the shallow hole to hide his trail. Carrying his bow in his hand, he worked his way back the way he came and seconds later, heard the distinct rumble of an engine and tires crunching gravel. One of the Humvees was returning. Skyler looked at the horizon and could no longer see any section of the entrance, which meant they couldn't see him. He stopped briefly to catch his breath. Had he been there for another three minutes, he would have been caught. "Stupid," he swore to himself. "Not ever going back there again."

The entrance to the ponds was about three hundred yards north of the refinery's entrance. Skyler stayed clear of the road as he slowly worked his way through the dead timber to a field that gave him an easier trail. However, it also put him in full view from the road. He veered to his left to reach the cover of the trees. Around 2 pm, he finally broke out into the parking lot for the archery range. From here, he knew a single dirt road led to the ponds. Once again, fallen trees slowed his travel, but soon he made it to the first large pond and started fishing, his efforts were rewarded: Skyler caught several small fish. With just enough for dinner, he hurried to get back. Lara had mentioned that she might have a surprise waiting. He hid the liquor bottle behind a sign so he could find it later.

Skyler thought of yesterday's close encounter at the refinery and stuck to his vow to not return. This time, he stayed on the Douglas road until he came to its end. From here he could see the opening to the ponds just fifty yards to his left. Before crossing the road, he made his way along the ditch until he was directly across from the entrance. Skyler was about to cross the street when he detected the noise of an engine. He stepped back, dropped to a prone position in the ditch and waited. A Humvee appeared over a small rise. It was moving very slowly. Too slowly. They were looking for something. Skyler kept his head down and waited for the vehicle to roll past him. He was partially hidden by a large tree limb that had been shoved off the road and hoped that his pack and clothing didn't stand out. The Humvee slowed as it neared the Douglas road, stopped, turned and then slowly drove part of the way down the road. Skyler realized that they must be looking for him. Just before he'd reached the intersection, he'd caught a glimpse of the very top of one of the refinery's tanks, but had thought he was too far away for the camera to pick him out. He must have been wrong.

From where the Humvee had stopped, its occupants could view the fields on both sides of the road. A power pole crossed the asphalt in front of their bumper. Skyler watched, hardly breathing. At one point he raised his head briefly to see if he could see the top of one of the tanks, but the hilly terrain blocked all view from this perspective. They probably saw him from further down the road, Skyler thought, and sent the Humvee out when he disappeared off their monitors.

One of the soldiers climbed out of the Humvee and walked out into the field, definitely searching the ground. Skyler prayed that the soldier didn't walk any further back up the hill. He was well hidden as long as they didn't inspect the ditch. Finally, the soldier returned to the vehicle and the Humvee backed out of the Douglas road and slowly drove on. As they neared his hiding spot, Skyler heard the vehicle come to a stop. Had they seen him? He stayed motionless, afraid to look up. Then he heard the vehicle move forward again. Still afraid to raise his head, he listened intently. The Humvee came to another halt on what Skyler guessed was the driveway that led to the ponds. He heard one of the doors open and close; the vehicle idled. A few moments later, another door opened and closed. Then he heard the transmission shift into gear; Skyler could tell by the whir that they were reversing. When the Humvee was back on the road, Skyler could hear the engine shift to forward and then the sound slowly get quieter as the vehicle slowly went back the way it had come. Skyler waited for a full fifteen minutes before peaking back over the edge of the ditch. His hands were shaking.

Skyler ran across the road and into the trees along the entrance, stopping every so often to listen. He had an arrow riding on his bow string. He couldn't be sure that someone wasn't dropped off when the Humvee had stopped the second time. But he heard nothing that alerted him to danger. He continued further up the trail and over the hill towards the ponds. This time he walked past the first pond towards two others that were even larger. He was unnerved by his close encounter but didn't want to return home empty-handed. So he kept on the alert, looking around as he got his fishing gear together. When the lone salmon egg hit the water, several fish attacked it at once. Skyler had a fish hooked within seconds and his tensions relaxed. He fed this fish onto a string and was about to re-bait the hook but instead, he cast with a bare hook. The fish attacked as before and he reeled in another small crappie. Next Skyler tossed a small stick out on the water. The surface exploded and Skyler let out an amazed laugh. "You guys are starving without insects, aren't you?" he said toward the pond. Skyler guessed that the only reason the fish were alive was that they had probably been cannibalizing off their dead. He continued casting and stringing up his catch for almost an hour before estimating that he had more than twenty pounds of the small fish. That was enough for what he'd planned next.

Skyler found the liquor bottle he'd hidden yesterday and stuffed it into the bottom of his pack. Crossing back over the road was easy enough, but getting home while staying out of the cameras' range was another story. Skyler went down into a ditch and waited ten minutes to make sure the Humvee wasn't coming to look for him a second time. Instead of heading back down Douglas, though, he crossed its entrance and stepped over the downed fence on its north side. From here, his route angled forty-five degrees towards Mountain View Road. Skyler kept looking back to see if the refinery's tanks would come into view. They didn't. On his left, there were several downed trees that afforded him cover from the main road. Still, every minute or so, he would glance back. No refinery cameras and no Humvees in sight or earshot. Once he was about half the distance between the Douglas and Mountain View roads, he quit angling and stayed equal distance between both roads. His speed wasn't much slower than if he'd been walking the road. Skyler finally relaxed a little and congratulated himself on finding a way in and out that the cameras couldn't see. But he wasn't going home yet.

During the four-mile trek, he saw two houses far in the distance that had smoke coming from their chimneys. They were both on the north side of Mountain View, at least a couple of miles away. He pulled the binoculars from his pack and scanned the area. The houses were mostly hidden by the uneven terrain. Skyler told himself that he'd visit another day; right now he needed to deliver the fish. He hoped to reach his destination soon, as the fish had become so heavy, he resorted to putting them inside his pack. He'd wash it out later. At one point he spotted a wedge-shaped flock of ducks pass overhead. They were traveling north. Even if he'd had a shotgun, they were too high to hit.

Reaching the barricade, Skyler confidently walked around it. No one was out in the open, not yet anyway. He continued until he reached the street where he'd met Petar and Brent. He pulled off his pack and waited. Moments later, Petar appeared with a different man. Petar wasn't carrying a rifle this time, but the stranger held one, barrel pointing at the ground. As the men approached, Skyler reached into the pack and pulled out the string of fish. "I caught these for you. Well, most of them. I just need some of them to take back home with me." Skyler looked up from the fish and let out a gasp.

"Hello, Skyler," the one with Petar said, smiling. "I'm glad to see that you have not only survived, but seem to be thriving."

"Mr. Hawthorne! Wow! Am I glad to see you." The man with Petar was Skyler's sixth grade teacher.

"Likewise, Skyler, and you can call me Scott from now on. When Petar told me about meeting you, I had a hunch who he was talking about."

"Where'd you find the fish?" Petar asked.

"Out by the refinery, the ponds that sit back behind the old archery range. They're so hungry, they'll bite anything that hits the water."

Skyler reached again inside the pack and pulled out the bottle of whiskey. He handed it to Petar; it would have felt strange giving it to his former teacher.

Petar looked at the bottle and back to Skyler, "Where did you find this?"

Skyler paused and took a breath before answering. "In the soldier's quarters out at the refinery."

"Are you serious?"

"They weren't there, I made sure. So I snuck in and looked around." answered Skyler, sheepishly.

Scott said, "You could have gotten yourself killed. Those soldiers are like pit bulls."

"What else did you see while you were there?" asked Petar.

"Canned food. Home-made, not store stuff."

"Yes. We've known that they steal food. You were probably looking at some of what they'd taken from us."

"They also have cameras. You can't get close to the place if they're watching the monitors."

Petar pulled a radio from his pocket and pressed the talk button twice. A moment later, a group of people came out from one of the houses. Skyler recognized Brent in the group, and there was another man, two women, and a boy about Skyler's age. When they reached the trio, Brent introduced the three other adults before introducing Skyler to the youth. "Did you say Randy?" asked Skyler, thinking for sure he was addressing a boy about his own age.

"No, it's Brandy with a 'B,'" the girl answered. Her voice could not be mistaken for anything but an adolescent girl, but her hair, clothes and stature were very boy-like.

"She's safer if she hides the fact that she's a girl," added Brent.

Petar showed the group the string of fish and the bottle of whiskey. One of the women thanked Skyler for the fish and took her share back to the house.

Still wondering how many survivors actually lived here, Skyler asked, "Will that be enough fish to feed everyone a meal?"

"It will be plenty for tonight's meal. It will be a welcomed change from our vegetable soup," answered Brent. "You've met about half of our family."

Brandy had picked up Skyler's bow and was holding it like she was shooting an imaginary arrow.

"Have you ever shot a bow?" Skyler asked her.

"No, but I'm sure I could. We just don't have one here."

"James says they're the weapons of the future," said Skyler.

"Whose James?" asked Brandy.

"He's my friend that I live with."

"What about your parents?"

Skyler went silent. It still pained him to be reminded about his mother's death.

He was about to speak when Brandy stopped him, putting her hand on his forearm. "I understand. My parents were gone from home the day the storm arrived. I haven't seen them since."

Skyler desperately wanted to change the subject. "I don't have time today, but maybe I can teach you how to shoot my bow some other day."

"I'd like that."

Skyler noticed that the sun had dropped low on the horizon. He needed to get back soon or Lara and James would worry about him. He said his good-byes and turned to leave when Brandy called his name. He looked over his shoulder.

"Where do you live?" she asked, smiling.

Without hesitation he answered, "If you walk to the bottom of this road, turn left at the intersection. Then walk about another hundred yards and turn right. It's the big house with three garage doors."

Scott stepped away from where he was talking with the rest of the adults to walk with Skyler as far as the barricade. Before Skyler disappeared around the corner, he asked the boy, "I remember your mother well, son. What happened to her?"

"I don't know. She's dead. I know that. But I want to find out what happened." Skyler fished in his pocket. "I found this next to her hand." He showed Scott the button.

Scott lifted the button from Skyler's hand and looked at it. If he knew anything about its origin, he didn't say. He dropped the button back into his palm. "You've made some friends here today. You're welcome to visit us anytime you want."

"Thanks," said Skyler, with a warm feeling in his heart, knowing there were other good people besides Lara and James.

Ten minutes later he reached the bottom of the hill. His eyes stung from his held-back tears. He wanted to tell his mother about all that had happened, the good stuff anyway. She would have been proud.

Chapter 21

It was back. And Skyler was awake by the second caw. It sounded like it was cawing at the tent much like a dog barks at an intruder. Seconds later, Skyler was slowly working the zipper on his tent. This time he had the crossbow with him. The crow continued its loud, rapid cry, a complaint. Skyler whipped his body through the tent opening with the crossbow pointed upward. Just like yesterday, the crow took flight instantly.

When Skyler stepped inside, James was feeding dry sticks into the woodstove to kindle the dying embers and get the stove hot enough to heat the last of their water, enough for the morning's tea and breakfast but no more. It didn't look like it would rain anytime soon, and James told Skyler he planned to haul more water up from the pond.

"I'll help you," Skyler said brightly. "I want to see the pond. Maybe I can figure out a way to transplant some crappies into it."

"I'd like that, Skyler," James said, looking up from the small flame that had caught. "You've been gone most of the last two days; it'll be good to have you around. And I can show you my plans for a duck trap.

Lara served the oatmeal and black tea, and as all the three finished their small breakfasts, Skyler set his spoon down and took a purposeful breath. "Do you remember that barricade we found on top of the Church Road hill?"

"Of course I do," answered James.

"I went back up there a few days ago."

James paused. A flare of anger rose, but he kept it in check. He knew the boy had been doing more than he'd let on and had hoped Skyler would share things soon, maybe even express why he didn't trust his housemates enough to tell his plans before embarking on them. So he was eager to listen to the boy. "What did you find out?"

Skyler smiled, relieved that he didn't get an immediate scolding as expected. "There are about a dozen people up there. They're pretty friendly. My sixth grade teacher, Mr. Hawthorne, he's up there too."

Lara listened but let James do the talking: "If they're friendly, then why the barricades?"

"To keep the Humvees off the hill," Skyler said flatly.

James nodded in understanding. "I see. But it's not fool proof, is it? I mean, what's to keep the soldiers from parking at the barricade and walking in?" James paused. "No, a dozen people would be no match for those weaponed and armored soldiers, especially if the soldiers took it as a challenge. I hope the barricades don't mean they let their defenses down." He shook his head, thinking. "Of those dozen people, how many are men?"

"Maybe half?" Skyler's high spirits were deflated by James's pessimism.

Lara finally joined in, asking nonchalantly, "How many women are there in the group?"

"I met two. There's also a girl about my age. And I know that there are at least two kids younger than her."

Lara reached across the table and touched James's arm. "If we moved up there, we'd be safe from the soldiers."

"No, we wouldn't," James barked. "Didn't you just hear me? Those barricades are an invitation for an attack. A dozen civilians are not enough to fight off two, let alone seven, armed soldiers."

James turned towards Skyler. "What kind of weapons do they have?"

"I only saw hunting rifles, but I don't know what else."

"We won't know how well they're armed unless we go talk to them." Lara sounded almost as if she was pleading.

James knew that Lara wasn't happy with their current situation, especially because of Mike's unwanted advances. But he didn't realize she'd be willing to give it all up. The place was so comfortable. They were eating better. Their garden was planted and growing quite well. Most important, their new house was solid and could obviously withstand the harshest winter. Moving would be asinine. He could see in her eyes that Lara wasn't going to let go of a hope to be part of a bigger community. Didn't she realize that there would be issues no matter where they lived? "Let's talk more about this tonight," was his only answer, but he smiled at Lara. He didn't want her to be upset all day.

James excused himself from the table and had Skyler follow him downstairs. Strung between two posts below the deck was the beginning of a net made from fishing line. It was maybe twenty feet long and about four feet wide. James pointed out that each completed square had four-inch sides.

"What's that thing?" Skyler asked, pointing at a wooden device with fishing line wrapped around its middle that hung at the end of the last row of loops.

"It's called a shuttle. It's a type of a sewing needle for nets. I carved it."

"How big does the net need to be?"

"I want it fifteen feet by twenty feet."

Skyler stared at it a moment. "How's it going to work?"

"I'll be in just the right position and scare the ducks. When I scare them, I'm hoping that they'll run for it. Against the sky it's almost invisible." James could see that Skyler wasn't convinced. "I'll finish it this afternoon and you can help me put it up. Then you'll see how it'll work."

James and Skyler went back upstairs to get some supplies to find Lara sitting on a couch. She wasn't doing anything, just sitting there with her hands between her knees and staring at the floor. James could tell she was dwelling about the people on the hill. He needed to convince her that they were probably better off staying here, keeping separate from a group. But he didn't know how. Finally he asked her, "Do you want to walk down to the pond with me and Skyler?"

"No."

"Why not?"

"I just don't want to go!" snapped Lara. Her anger was sudden and unexpected.

Skyler backed out the door first, grabbing the crossbow from its hook; James followed with some plastic buckets, handing one to Skyler.

"She's mad," said Skyler.

"Yeah, she is."

"What can we do?"

"I don't know." James led the way down the slope and into the field where a path had already begun to appear. As they neared the berm, James put a finger to his lips. This wasn't necessary. Neither of them had spoken since they'd left the house. Skyler could see that James had built a sort of duck blind on the closest berm. It was a simple wall, much like a wooden pallet standing on end. James crouched down low and Skyler followed his actions. They quietly set down the buckets and crept up to the makeshift blind. James peered through a hole in the boards. He nodded at Skyler, who had the crossbow.

Skyler moved into James's position and peered through the hole. Two mallards were sitting on the water about twenty feet away. As ducks often seemed, they looked nervous, ready to take flight. Skyler turned to James for the go-ahead, and James nodded once more. Skyler stood, aimed, and pulled the trigger in one smooth motion. The frog-gig nailed a duck in the head, killing it instantly. The other duck took off skittering across the surface to the far end of the pond. Just before it reached land, it became airborne. Seconds later, it disappeared from view.

"Did you see that? It flew to the far end of the pond!" exclaimed James.

"So?"

"So if we put a net down there and figure a way to raise it up when they take off, we can trap any that try to fly away."

Skyler pulled the line connected to the gig and the bird. It was a drake and slightly larger than the hen he'd shot a few days ago. "It might work," was all he said.

They returned to the house with the duck and almost eight gallons of pond water. James left the two buckets he had carried by the garden, and went to work on the net below the deck. Skyler took his two buckets upstairs. Lara was still sitting on the couch, looking as if she hadn't moved a muscle. He showed her the bird.

"From the pond?" she asked him.

"Yeah."

She stared at the bird without really seeing it. "What are those people like?"

"The ones on the hill?"

"Yeah, them."

"They seem nice. But—I've only been around them for a few minutes," said Skyler with a shrug. He felt nervous about getting grilled by Lara. The last thing he wanted was to become a pawn in this argument. Lara went silent again. He could tell that this was really eating at her. Sure, he thought, they seemed like nice enough people, but he wasn't sure if they were any better off. And they were so grateful for the goose and the fish—what if that was the only meat they'd had in months? Having just him, James and Lara to worry about could be a lot better.

By early afternoon, James had finished the net, and he pulled Skyler away from tending to his quiver. Skyler grabbed the tools James asked for and they headed back to the pond. They dug holes at the far end of the pond and planted two tall alder poles there, situating them so they leaned out over the pond. The two upper ends of the poles were held apart by another alder pole tied in place. The net sat bunched at the bottom of the poles. When James gave the signal, Skyler kicked a board loose, freeing a rock used as a counter-weight. The rock dropped several feet, which pulled the net part-way up the long poles. The net didn't reach nearly high enough.

They took the apparatus apart. This time, James secured the net to one of the long poles. His thinking was that the net could be pulled from one pole to the other rather than try to raise it the full fifteen feet. Their second attempt also ended in failure. James realized that the distance that the rock travelled was equal to the distance that the net moved. He needed to figure out how to double the distance without doubling the height of the rock.

They reset the apparatus the same way as they had the first time, only this time James removed the rock and tied the rope to a tall pole parallel with the ground. He then fixed the opposite end to act as a pivot. He placed the rock on another five-foot tall pole and secured it to the middle of the pole connected to the rope. When James waved to Skyler, the boy pushed the rock. It fell, dragging the free end of the long pole. The distance that the net moved had almost doubled. They reset the trap one more time before leaving for home. They would return in the morning, and if the ducks were at the pond, they could test their trap for real.

That evening, Lara remained quiet and cold. Almost as cold as the dinner, James thought. For some reason she'd cooked the duck and rice while they'd been out building the trap, eaten her share, and left the rest sitting out on the counter. James dished out moderate portions of meat for himself and Skyler and they ate their meal in silence. After they finished, James pulled the rest of the duck meat off the bones and mixed it with a cup of rice. He wrapped this up in some old foil and stuffed it in his coat pocket.

"Go for a walk with me?" he asked Lara.

She looked up in surprise. "Where to?"

"We're going to visit a coyote."

Lara got up from the couch and looked around for her shoes. Other than plucking the duck, she hadn't been outside since yesterday and had not put on her shoes. Her garden had gone ignored for the first time since it was planted. Once she'd donned her shoes and coat, she silently followed James out the door. Skyler wanted to see the coyote too, but decided it was better to let them have some time alone.

Once they were away from the house and headed down the path, James asked her "Can you explain to me why you are still so angry?"

Lara was silent for a full minute, thinking. Then she said in one breath: "It's because we are waiting to die!" She looked beseechingly at James. "What is there to stop the soldiers from killing us? Do you think Mike will help us if we're in trouble?"

"I don't know, Lara. I haven't gotten that far with Mike yet. Either way, I'm just not so sure that those others are better off. And who's to say they'd want us part of their group anyway?"

"Well, we won't know unless we ask." Her tone had reverted back to one of anger.

Once they crossed the field, they headed down towards the destroyed development. Like before, James pulled his bow from his back and rested an arrow on its string. They didn't speak. James led Lara to the structure where he'd heard the pups. He pointed towards the opening. Lara nodded that she understood. As she watched, James removed the foil parcel from his pocket and quietly spread it open and moved towards the entrance. He knelt down and placed the open package on the ground in front of the opening. When he stood, he saw that Lara was staring at something across the street. He followed her gaze. It was the pup's mother. She was sitting on her haunches across the street, watching them, seemingly unalarmed that two humans were near her den. Lara moved closer towards James. He turned to look at her, then started walking back the way they had come. Lara quickly caught up to him.

"That was rather generous of you."

He looked directly at her again, "Before I met you and Skyler, I probably wouldn't have cared if she'd survived."

"What changed?" she asked.

"You and Skyler taught me that when I helped you, I was rewarded in some way. I'm hoping that the same applies here."

They walked on a little further before James spoke again. "If you still want to meet those people up on the hill, maybe we can get Skyler to take us up there tomorrow."

"Thank you."

During the walk back to the house, James told Lara everything he knew about coyotes. He told her that he felt they were actually smarter than humans. "They're true survivors. They only use what they need. You won't see a coyote waste food."

Early the following morning, James was awakened when a strong southerly wind blew in through the gap of his open window. He jumped out of bed, slammed the window shut, and then returned to the warm covers. A faint glow was just appearing over the Cascades signaling the new day. Within an hour, the entire eastern sky was glowing orange. James stared at the horizon and uttered softly, "Red sky in morning, sailors take warning."

"What did you say?" mumbled Lara. She was just in that transition between sleep and reality.

James rolled over to face her. "You know the old saying, don't you? 'Red sky in morning . . . ' means it should rain soon." He rolled back over all the way until his feet were planted on the floor, and walked out the bedroom to the door to the deck. He opened it and yelled towards Skyler's tent, "Get up, boy—no waiting for your wake-up call from the crow! I want to see if there are any ducks on the pond!"

James could hear Skyler stirring, so he turned towards the kitchen to get the fire started. Lara followed closely behind him. This morning's breakfast was to be the first one using boiled pond water. James had done what he could to filter out any sediment and floaters, but the water still retained its brownish hue.

Lara insisted that they taste-test the pond water in their tea first. James stirred the leaves into the boiling water. Two minutes later he filled three mugs. Nobody wanted to go first. Finally, Skyler took a sip. He ran his tongue over his lips and took a second sip, then a third. He put his cup down and said, "Where's my oatmeal?"

After a breakfast they all found palatable, Skyler led the way out to the pond. Every time James tried to close the gap, Skyler would pick up his pace. The boy was anxious to get there. And was disappointed at what they found.

No duck this time. Skyler and James stood at the pond's edge in resignation. Maybe they needed to arrive earlier. It had been daylight for over an hour. James also suggested they could bait the water with something the ducks would eat. "Dry rice might work," he said to Skyler. "Mature corn, if we had it."

When they arrived back, Lara looked utterly different. She was wearing a man's dress shirt instead of her usual grungy sweatshirt. She'd put on clean jeans and her hair had been tied back. James noticed that it no longer had an oily shine to it. Since the deprivation they'd been going through, clean clothes had never been a priority around their house. But Lara had washed up like she must have done in the old days, as if they were going for an interview.

"Shall we go?" she smiled brightly. James looked at the front of his own shirt and pants. He was still wearing the mud he'd picked up while building the trap yesterday. "Give me a minute," he replied.

By 9:30, they were on foot headed out towards the main road. Both James and Skyler had cleaned themselves up a bit. Once they were on Main, they needed only to walk a hundred yards to Church Road and about fifteen minutes to the barricaded area. Despite Skyler's reassurance, they were still cautious as they walked, and James insisted Skyler have his bow strung over his back, quickly accessible if needed. James kept a pistol in his coat pocket. Just as they crossed the road onto Church, Skyler stopped. He heard something. The noise grew louder until the front end of a Humvee appeared at the top of Main

Street's hill. James almost pushed Lara into the deep ditch alongside the road. Skyler followed. They flattened themselves along the steep bank. James crawled up and peeked over the edge of the road. He held up two fingers. Skyler had heard the second engine before James had seen it. James crawled back down and the three waited. If the Humvees continued down Main, they would need to find new cover. They were in clear view of anything coming from the east.

The rumble of the engines grew louder as the vehicles decelerated. Then they stopped completely at the opening of Church Road. Everything went silent. Skyler had already removed his bow and had an arrow in his other hand. James shook his head at the boy. They weren't in a position to fight back.

Lara kept her face buried in the grass, unmoving. The shirt's blue color stood out against the green and brown bank, and James could see that the shirt had picked up some dirt when she landed on her back. James knew she had to be scared. He was scared. He kept his gaze on her as he listened for signs that the soldiers were leaving or staying. He redirected his attention to the road. As long as the soldiers stayed on the asphalt, they shouldn't be able to see the trio hiding just yards away. A moment later, they re-started their engines and drove up Church Road.

James waited until their engines sounded well up the hill. He raised his head above the ditch only long enough to confirm what he feared. The Humvees were headed towards the barricade. Lara finally broke down and began sobbing.

"Let's go back home," said James resolutely.

"No, we need to see what happens," said Skyler. The Humvees had already disappeared over the crest of the hill. They should be arriving at the barricade by now.

"You mean stay here?"

"Not here. I know a way through the tall grass that connects with their group of houses. I went that way my first time up there. I was able to watch them without being seen."

James looked at Skyler then over at Lara. It all came down to what she wanted to do, since she lived with the most fear from the soldiers. This trip was for her. Finally James asked her "What do you want to do, Lara?"

"I don't want to go home and wait for the soldiers to show up there." She took a deep breath to recover some of her composure. "Let's stay away from the road. We can follow Skyler's idea."

It didn't take James long to agree. They did need to see what happened up on the hill. Maybe it was just a friendly visit, or maybe they were there to burn the place down. "OK, Skyler, show us the way."

Skyler led the way further down the hill before turning back towards the north. From here, they couldn't see the road but they would hear if the vehicles returned. Just the act of doing something seemed to relax Lara. She focused on following Skyler. James stayed in the rear. They didn't speak as they worked their way up the hill; they needed to be able to hear everything, engines, gunfire, calls for help. So far, there was nothing.

The slope they passed through sat below a handful of what used to be large expensive homes situated there for the impressive view of the mountains and foothills. Because of their exposure on the edge of the hill, though, they'd all been reduced to splinters. James turned and looked down below. He could see their own house far in the distance. They skirted the damaged houses by heading further northeast and even further from the road. Soon, they'd be too far to hear the Humvees once they did descend the hill. The long dead grass grabbed at their ankles as they made their own trail. It had been over fifteen minutes since the Humvees had disappeared over the crest, and everything still remained quiet.

Ten minutes later, they reached the viewpoint. James could see where the grass was flattened from Skyler's previous visit. All that was visible was the gap between two houses. They wouldn't see anybody unless someone walked past this gap. All three watched for movement. It was like having a stare-down with a ghost-town. James looked behind them. The clouds had thickened. It should be raining by nightfall.

Lara looked towards Skyler. "What do you think?" she whispered.

"Last week, I saw kids playing in that street. Now it looks deserted."

They waited over an hour. James hadn't planned on being gone this long and had not bothered to pack any water. Yet none of them wanted to leave without knowing the outcome; they could handle a little thirst. Finally, Skyler had Lara and James wait while he went to scout by Church Road, where he'd have visibility to see if the Humvees were still there.

Several minutes passed before Skyler reappeared. He was walking upright, not attempting to conceal himself.

"They're gone!" he said.

James and Lara both stood and stretched.

"Follow me and we'll walk in the entrance."

They retraced Skyler's path to where the barricade was. Once there, they walked quietly and cautiously up the road. James felt his fear return. Lara, on the other hand, appeared to be more curious than anything. He was thankful that she was handling this so well and was unaware, or unconcerned, that her clothes were now stained with dirt and grass. They reached the entrance to the street. They stopped and waited.

"This is where I first met two of the men," Skyler said.

It was almost twenty minutes before a lone figure holding a rifle appeared. It was Scott. Instead of moving closer to the trio, he waved them forward to his position.

The last time Skyler had seen him, Scott seemed to have a perpetual smile. Now, his smile was gone. As they drew closer, Scott nodded grimly at Skyler, and then stretched out his hand towards James.

"You must be James. I'm Scott."

"Yes. Hello. But what happened? We saw the soldiers drive up this way."

"Luckily, they didn't catch us sleeping. When we heard their engines, we hid."

"You hid? Where?" asked James.

Scott raised his arm and slowly swung it in a long arc. "This is a large development. We have numerous places to hide."

At that moment, Petar and Brandy appeared. Petar also carried a rifle and moved to Scott's side. Brandy was hesitant to move closer to the trio until she saw Skyler was one of them. When they were all together, Scott made introductions.

James asked, "Is everyone OK?"

"Fortunately, yes," said Petar. "However, they did wreck one of our gardens and they found our house. A couple of windows were shattered, and they tipped our stove over and tossed about some belongings. I'm sure they were angry that we weren't here to greet them," added Petar sarcastically.

Soon a few others from the community appeared. All of the men carried rifles.

"Are you going to be alright? I mean—the garden?" asked James. He knew that losing a garden could be disastrous.

"We can fix the house. The garden was just one of many. We'll be fine."

Lara asked, "You said that they found your house. Do you all live in the same house?"

Petar hesitated before answering. "Only one house survived the winter. We're working on repairing another."

"What now?" James asked Scott.

"First, we need to start posting a sentry. It was by pure luck that we heard their engines. Had we been sleeping, they would have found all of us together."

The trio stayed and talked with the group for another twenty minutes. By then, most—James counted at least ten—had come out of hiding to meet the newcomers. Skyler and Brandy separated themselves from the group. She held his bow in her right hand as he showed her the motion of drawing the string. She tried several times, but didn't have the strength to pull the string back completely.

James was anxious to get back even before they felt the first few drops of rain, and shook hands with Scott, Petar and Brent. "I know we all have to be careful," he said, "so I don't know when we'll meet again, but I can't tell you how good it is to know there are other survivors, good people, around." He looked to Lara and smiled. They all said their goodbyes.

Lara didn't question his decision to return home. It was past two in the afternoon when they left, and they walked back by way of Church Road because it was shorter. Skyler stayed several feet behind James and Lara, seeming preoccupied. Lara was nervous and stayed near the edge of the road. When they reached the bottom of the hill, she stopped. James stopped too and waited; it was obvious she was formulating something to say."

"I'm sorry that I was such a bitch," she said.

"What? It's OK. You don't have to apologize."

"You were right. They aren't any better off than we are."

"I'm surprised that they weren't better prepared."

Lara shook her head. "I can't imagine sharing a house with that many."

They crossed the road together and walked the last stretch without speaking. As they rounded the last corner and their house came into view, James could tell something wasn't right and started walking faster. He motioned for Lara and Skyler to stay where they were and took off running. He'd pulled the pistol from his pocket and held it out in front of him as he ran. When he reached house, it took him only four long strides to ascend the stairs. He disappeared through the front door. It was already open.

Chapter 22

Their surprise visit had turned out to be no surprise at all; there was no one there when they'd arrived. They had split up into two groups to search through the destroyed homes and couldn't find a single person. One of his men had discovered which house they were living in and Lyons had trotted over to check it out. He'd left them his calling card by busting up the place. He was angry. The only reason he hadn't torched the whole damn place was because of food. They would need to harvest food from these people before winter set in. He'd seen their gardens. They could wait, though he couldn't refrain from kicking at all the seedlings in one garden. "Let 'em replant," he'd muttered.

As they drove back down the hill, Lyons directed Carter to make a left turn onto Main Street and take him to the house Carter had visited just the other day. He wasn't ready to return to the refinery just yet. Both Humvees came to a halt in front of the large garage. Before opening their doors, Lyons turned towards the men in the back.

"Would you fine gentlemen go up those stairs and request that the occupants come down here and visit me?" His sarcasm was not lost on them; they knew his anger took time to subside. "And while they're down here, have a good look around the place."

Both men nodded and stepped out of the vehicle. From his open window, Lyons could hear his men pound their fists on the front door several times. After ten seconds, he heard the crack of timber splitting as the door was kicked in. A moment later, one of the soldiers returned and reported that no one was home.

"Does it look like they still live here?"

"Yes sir."

Lyons turned towards Carter. "Let's have a look around outside while they search the house." He turned back to the soldier, "Collect any weapons that you find and take an inventory of their food. If you find a stash of food, leave it there and report back to me. Remember, what they don't want us to find will be well hidden. Get my drift?"

"Yes sir."

Carter and Lyons stepped from the vehicle and motioned the occupants of the other Humvee to stay put. They walked around the west side of the house towards the back yard. In the back, they found a garden that was well maintained. Lyons looked over the rows of beets, carrots, and cucumbers, taking a mental count of the quantity. There were also three long rows of corn and tomatoes that still needed another month or two of sunshine. He intentionally left his boot prints in the soil. On the way back to the vehicles, they had to pass between a thick row of dead cedar trees and the house. Lyons stopped and peered between the trees.

"Carter, there's another house here."

Both men moved closer to the trees to get a better look. From their position, the front of the house appeared deserted with all the windows boarded up. When they looked towards the back, there was laundry hanging over the deck's rail. Then a woman appeared from the door, and after looking up at the increasing clouds, she gathered up the clothes. Lyons looked at Carter and smiled. Lyons whispered, "She's rather plump, wouldn't you say?"

Carter smiled. Lyons seemed to have shed the anger from their thwarted attempt on the hill. "Yeah, I would say she isn't starving."

"Let's come back in a few weeks and do a little shopping," Lyons rubbed his hands together.

"Why wait?"

Lyons looked at him with a hint of contempt, "Because I want to catch everyone at home in bed. Besides, we need their gardens. If we alert them now, they'll just disappear on us, and who'll grow the veggies?" The big man turned and took long strides back towards the Humvee with Carter trying to keep pace. They were met by the other soldiers.

"What'd you find?" asked Lyons.

"We didn't see any weapons, but we did find a stash of food."

Lyons raised an eyebrow as if signaling him to finish.

"There are two kayaks in the garage that are stuffed with bags of rice, flour and other stuff."

Carter looked surprised. "There wasn't anything except an ATV in that garage when I came here."

"The kayaks are suspended from the ceiling. We almost missed them too."

"Will they notice that we've discovered their hiding place?"

"No sir, we tied the boats up just like we found them."

"Good. Let's go back to base for now."

Chapter 23

Lara and Skyler stayed far back from the house until James waved them in. Whoever had opened the door was no longer inside. When they reached the top of the stairs, James came back out again. The door had been kicked in. A boot print just under the door handle told the story.

"Go through everything. Let me know if anything is missing." It was a command more than a request. James looked more upset than he had in a long time.

Lara checked the kitchen first while Skyler went right to his room. James had hidden his bow and the .22 pistol behind a curtain. They were still there. Skyler came back from his room and reported nothing missing. Besides some meager staples they kept handy in the kitchen, they kept most hidden inside the kayaks and the hollow insides of the furnace. Lara found nothing askew in the kitchen, but when she went to the garden, there were two different boot prints among the plants.

"Those are soldiers' boot prints," said James.

"So they now know about our garden!" exclaimed Lara. Skyler saw where this was going, so he returned to his room.

"Nearly impossible to keep that from anyone, Lara. At least it doesn't appear they could find anything else," James retorted, not wanting to get into another debate about where they lived.

The soldiers had to be pretty pissed off, James thought, after their failure to locate the people living up on the hill, or find any food caches here at their own place. He looked at the stand of dead trees. "I better check on Mike and Cindy."

Because of Mike's advances on Lara, James had only been over to Mike's house a couple of times since they'd moved in. It was just too awkward. But James climbed the stairs, reluctant, but loud enough so they wouldn't think someone was trying to sneak up on them. He knocked on the front door and waited, suspecting that one or the other was watching him from another window. Finally, the door opened and Mike stood before him.

"What do you want?" Mike glared.

James was taken aback by the cold greeting. "I was worried about you and Cindy, actually" he paused before continuing. "We were all three out today and someone kicked our door in. Everything OK here?"

"You think I did it?"

Once again James was alarmed at Mike's response. "No, I know who did it. It was the soldiers."

"Well, I'm sure they had their reasons. Anything missing?"

"No, not that we've found." James realized that continuing this conversation would get him nowhere, so he quickly said, "Thanks for your time. I'm glad you're okay" and headed back down the steps.

James was met by Lara at their front door. "How did he react?"

"Like I was there to cause trouble. He was pretty defensive."

"Do you think that's my fault?"

"No. I think it's his fault. He's just that kind who likes to be a tough guy and, well, a jerk."

Over their meatless meal that night, they didn't talk about the intrusion, but about the next day. Skyler said that he would check the pond in the morning, but earlier. If he didn't get another duck there, he intended to hunt elsewhere. James said his first priority would be a better fix to their front door than what he'd slapped together to protect them through the night. Once that was out of the way, they needed to do some more scavenging, especially for canning jars.

"With how uncommon canning was in the recent decade, it might take weeks to find enough jars. Lara," James looked casually at his partner even though his motive for not leaving her alone was serious, "you'll come with me won't you? Maybe we'll even get a glimpse of the coyote again."

Lara nodded, resigned and solemn.

The rain came down heavily that night, enough to fill their buckets and last them for a couple of days.

One day a little over a week later, Skyler returned home looking upset.

"What's the matter?" asked James. He was cutting up firewood and using a wheelbarrow to move it to the garage.

"I was down by Slater Road. I wanted to check the fields there since before this last winter, there were usually a lot of ducks and geese in those fields." He paused as if searching for a way to say what he'd observed. "I saw a group of men with guns."

"Were they hunting?"

"I'm not positive," Skyler answered slowly. "They had two women with them. There were ropes around their necks."

James wanted to ask more questions of the boy, what he thought was going on, what they looked like. Then he realized it didn't matter. So far, only Mike and the hill people knew that their companion was a woman, and his greatest concern was that it stayed that way. "How many men?"

"I counted seven. I think they're living in the old casino."

James remembered the place. It was only four miles to the south. No one could have survived the winter in that large building, though; it was much too expansive to heat. He hoped the group was just passing through. The thought of the women captives worried him, knowing that there was nothing he could do about it.

Two days later, James spotted a group of men on one of the roads to the south. He'd been scanning the countryside when he saw a dark spot that appeared to be moving. He retreated back into the house to get his binoculars. Lara saw him following the group closely.

"Who are they?"

"Don't know and I don't want to find out." He continued to watch their progress. They appeared to be checking every farm along Imhoff Road. They went out of his sight briefly before reappearing on the road just below their house. They were less than a half mile away. James ducked out the door and ran the short distance to Mike's house. He rapped three times on the back door. When Mike appeared, James handed him the glasses and pointed towards the road. No words were exchanged. Mike stared through the glasses for several seconds before handing them back. He looked worried. The group of men was moving west. Mike and James watched until they disappeared up Douglas Road.

That night, James and Skyler took turns standing watch from the deck. James found it impossible to sleep when it wasn't his turn. By morning he was exhausted. Lara wanted to work in the garden, but after James decided to tell her about the women captives, she was afraid of being out in the open.

James finally succumbed to his exhaustion and slept. When he woke, he found that Lara had cut her hair very short. In her standard garb of men's clothing, unless someone was closer than thirty feet away, it would be hard to tell that she wasn't a man.

She was matter of fact when she saw James's look: "I'd rather be shot than raped and eaten."

A few days later, shortly after sunrise, James barely discerned the sounds of distant gunfire coming from the area where the casino was. He was outside on an all-night watch and marked the time that it started. Forty minutes passed before it was over. The last few volleys, he was certain, came from automatic weapons. When it was over, he watched as Mike walked over and stood at the bottom of the stairs.

"What is it?" asked James, heading down the steps, knowing that Lara's threat kept Mike from coming closer. Mike held something black out to James. "It's a G.I Joe Walkie-Talkie. It belonged to my son. It actually works."

"What do you want me to do with it?"

"If you hear gunshots, turn it on. I have its brother. I may need your help or you may need mine."

James nodded in appreciation "Sounds like a good idea, Mike. Thanks" James would have preferred to keep the radios on most of the time, but he knew what it would do to the batteries.

Over the next month, James stood nightly watch on his deck while Mike stood watch on his own. It seemed that the warmer the weather, the more people would be out in search of food, and on a few occasions, someone would move in close enough to earn a warning shot. The warmer weather also brought the frogs, their croaking faint at first because they were few in number, but louder each week, as they moved closer and grew more numerous. Something else lives, James thought.

Skyler made regular trips to visit the community on the hill. While he was friendly with everyone, his true intention was to see Brandy. As much as she looked like a boy, he was aware of her hidden feminine beauty. It came to the point where he was away from James's house more often than not. He would pack his tent and sleeping bag and sometimes be gone for up to a week. Lara and James learned to be okay with his absences, and trust that he could take care of himself.

Brandy liked his visitations, not only because he was about her age, but because he was well liked by the other members of her family. She often heard the men in her family invite him to stay with them permanently. They wanted someone with his hunting skills. But he always answered, "Not until I find the owner of this button." As a result, they referred to him, when he wasn't around, as the Button Boy. They had all seen the button at one time or another; Skyler always had it with him.

When Skyler did return to James and Lara, he always brought some form of food back with him. One day he arrived with a bucket filled with small, fresh blackberries. Both Lara and James were stunned. He'd found a patch of bushes that must have grown from dormant but viable seeds. The bushes were small since they were in their first year, but there were many more patches all around the area. They just needed to look.

Two weeks after that casino shoot-out, James resumed feeding the mother coyote and her pups. Her weight and girth were almost back to normal and she no longer hid from him, though the pups kept their distance from the humans. James thought it was better this way. Lara would often walk down with James to see how the small family was surviving. She was delighted to see that pups had grown to three quarters of their mother's size. After dropping off food, they would spend a short period of time scavenging. Besides books and Mason jars, they also looked for salt and vinegar, items James had not stored away before the storm but that were necessary for canning. They hoped other scavengers might have overlooked such items in their search for true food. The soldiers had kept their distance too. James infrequently saw their vehicles drive up or down the main road. And only on one occasion did they drop in over the summer. James was prepared; he'd kept a bag of beans in the cupboard just for such an occasion. He'd found the ten pound bag in one of the houses in the lower development. Water had gotten inside the package and damaged about a third of them, though they were still edible when cooked. When the soldiers searched his cupboards, James offered them the beans. He said that he'd find more. They took them. The one named Carter even went as far as thanking James. Before they left, Carter walked to the back of the deck to look down upon their garden. He smiled to show his approval.

Lara had stayed hidden while the soldiers were there, but James had been nervous because he'd made reference to a wife and son the first time they'd come by almost three months ago. This time the soldiers had not asked about his wife or son, and James was relieved. He wasn't sure what he would have said if they had asked.

When Skyler returned from his times away, he often brought news about other survivors. Most of them he found by following the smoke. Everyone needed fires to cook. When Skyler would spot a new fire, he'd investigate first. If the family was composed of just men, he'd avoid making contact. However, if there were women and children, he would arrive bearing a gift. Sometimes it was a duck or crow, other times a string of fish. Towards the end of summer, he brought berries. People were always apprehensive at first; the gift was the key to breaking the ice. No one turned food away. Skyler would make a point to remember names and cautiously share what he knew about other survivors—all except for Brandy and her family. He wanted to protect them from any danger.

When Skyler did return home, he would record all the new survivors he'd encountered in a blank book; it helped to remember their names and give a sense of geography to the surviving population. He drew a crude map of the Ferndale area and pinned it behind his bedroom door. Hand drawn stars marked the location of each family. There were also black circles drawn into the map; these marked the places to avoid. The refinery had a black circle.

Near the end of summer, Skyler found another point on his map that earned a black circle. The days were growing noticeably shorter, but were still pretty warm. Skyler had been out hunting ducks at a swamp near the old aluminum refinery. He had been returning home by way of Douglas Road and was passing a gated driveway he'd walked by several times before without noticing signs of habitation. The smell was what had caught Skyler's attention. The long narrow driveway lined with dead trees was uninviting, with only one way in and one way out. This day, though, Skyler clearly smelled the aroma of charcoal briquettes, lighter fluid, and cooked meat blowing in on a southwest wind. His memory was thrown back to summer days when all of his neighbors cooked outside. It reminded him of his mother. Skyler had two ducks hanging from his belt. He could spare one, so he decided to take the chance.

Skyler left one duck in the tall grass by the road and hopped over the gate. Because of the thick dead foliage, he had no choice but to walk in on the driveway, fully exposed. The house was large, with all of the windows still boarded up, and as he approached, he saw three adults, two men and a woman, in the yard. Yet the trio didn't see Skyler until he was standing before them; they each had that look of surprise on their faces. The woman lounged in a chair; she was topless and reached for a shirt, but threw it over her plate of food instead of covering herself. Her eyes were adorned with heavy make-up, something Skyler hadn't seen in these times. One of the men was standing over a portable grill. He was shirtless, with huge arms covered in slate-blue tattoos, and a shaved head. He quickly closed the barbecue's lid when he saw Skyler. The second man was also lounging in a chair near the woman. The thing that made Skyler suspicious was their size: all three were overweight—another strange sight in these times. Skyler moved no closer and said, "I'm sorry if I'm intruding, but I just wanted to say hello. I brought you a duck."

"Well thank you, Sugar!" the woman said with a smile. "Come on in and join us." Her eagerness was also suspicious. The men hadn't uttered a single word.

Skyler stayed frozen to his spot and tried not to stare at the woman. Both men looked towards the porch then back to Skyler. Skyler followed their gaze: a shotgun leaned against the porch rail. The man cooking took a few steps towards the porch without taking his eyes off Skyler. The woman stood from her chair—Skyler saw that all she wore was a pair of dirty panties—and tried to draw Skyler's attention. She pranced toward him, laughing loudly, acting much too happy. Her breasts were bouncing up and down. The third man was slowly pushing himself up from the lounge chair, and Skyler quickly evaluated the situation. If he ran, the cook had time to close the gap to the shotgun and Skyler would not be outside range. A shotgun blast from behind would not be fatal, but it would stop him.

"Besides the duck, I have something else for you." Skyler started taking his pack off as if it held another treasure. Both men halted their movements; their curiosity got the better of them. The woman clapped her hands together like an excited little girl and bounced her breasts even more. With his visible hand, Skyler opened the top of the pack, while his other hand pulled the string that secured the bow. The cook must have sensed what the boy was doing because he turned his eyes away from the pack and lunged for the shotgun. Skyler raised the bow with his left hand while his right hand fed the arrow onto the string. He drew back and quickly aimed. The cook had reached the shotgun, one hand clutching its long black barrel. The arrow that pierced his temple stopped him altogether.

The second man charged Skyler. There wasn't enough time to load another arrow, so Skyler pulled an arrow from the quiver and dropped the bow. The man dove at Skyler, his monstrous sweaty body filling Skyler's vision. Skyler swung his arm around and brought the arrow up to meet his assailant. He felt the man's giant fist collide with the side of his head. The light briefly dimmed as an overwhelming odor of stale sweat permeated his nose. Skyler shoved the arrow upward as hard as he could, not knowing where it would enter. The man landed on top of Skyler then rolled off him. His focus was no longer on attacking the boy but the arrow. Its tip, Skyler could now see, had entered the man's throat just below his Adam's apple. The man gripped the arrow with both his hands and tried to pull it out of his airway. Blood poured from the gap as Skyler fought to crawl out from beneath him. Skyler turned his eyes in time to see the woman running towards the shotgun. Grabbing his bow and pack, Skyler ran towards the driveway. He looked back only once to see the woman raising the shotgun. She stumbled as she brought it to her shoulder, giving Skyler the extra few seconds to sprint out of range. He heard the shot the same moment a hundred pellets exploded into the dry timber off to his right. The woman was slow to pump a second shell into the chamber.

Skyler dropped his pack. In one motion, he pulled his third and last arrow from the quiver and brought it up to the string. The woman was just bringing the sights back up to her eye when Skyler let his arrow fly. He'd aimed low. The arrow impaled her at the hip. Its force was enough to knock her over backwards. The shotgun discharged towards the sky. Skyler grabbed his pack again and continued running towards the gate.

Chapter 24

They stood frozen in the garden at the sound of the first shot. It was well off to the southwest. Seconds later, they heard a second blast. Neither shot had the resounding crack of a rifle. They listened a little while longer before resuming work. James thought about Skyler. He'd been gone just two days this time and there was no knowing where he might be. He finally said quietly to Lara, "I hope the boy's OK."

James saw Skyler running towards them before he saw the blood. But as Skyler got closer, the blood that covered his chest became evident. There was so much blood, too much blood for it to be all his own. The boy ran up the trail. James pulled the pistol from his pocket, scanned the field from where Skyler had come, and waited anxiously for Skyler to come closer. The boy looked more than scared, he looked horrified, yet no one was pursuing him. His pace finally slowed as he made the last few steps and fought to get his breath. Sweat dripped from his scalp. Lara dropped her rake to search for the wound that had dyed his shirt crimson.

"Where are you hurt?" she asked.

Skyler, gasping for air, couldn't answer. He just nodded his head. Tears and sweat ran down his cheeks. An involuntary gasp for air allowed him to utter, "I'm OK."

They both wanted to throw questions at him, but knew better. If there was danger coming their way, Skyler would have alerted them first. They just needed to wait and hear. His gasps became shorter and further apart. Finally, he dropped his pack and peeled off his shirt. His skin had the look of a sunburn from the blood staining.

"I came across some people," he drew in a breath. "They were horrible. And they tried to shoot me."

"Why?" asked James.

"They wanted me. They were cooking meat. I don't think it was bird or animal." Tears ran down his cheeks.

Lara held the back of her hand against her mouth. The thought sickened her and she tried to put it out of her mind. She picked up Skyler's pack and joined James in putting a hand to Skyler's shoulder as they walked him up to the house.

Lara immediately set some pond water to heating, using the kerosene stove instead of the fire, since the warm September days made a fire unbearable. There was no question that they could afford to use some of the precious fuel in this case. Skyler washed the blood from his body with a small rag dipped into the warm water.

Once clean, calm and safe, Skyler gave the details of what had taken place. When he reached the part about the second man landing the blow to his head, he started crying again. "They were not good people."

"Were there only three?" asked James.

"Don't know. That's why I ran. But that's all I saw." He led James to his room and pointed to the map from his bedroom door, then showed them where the house was. Then he marked the new location with a black circle. Skyler explained that all the stars marked the location of friendly survivors.

James opened the glass cover on the nonworking gas fireplace. He reached in behind the ceramic logs and withdrew a bundle wrapped in dark canvas. He untied a string, allowing the bundle to spread out. The parcel was filled with aluminum arrows. James picked out five arrows, two with broad heads and three with target tips. There were maybe twenty arrows remaining when he placed the bundle back behind the logs.

Later that evening, the three sat out on the deck as James read from a book. Skyler tried to focus on his words, but the scene from earlier played over and over in his head. He shuddered when he thought about what would have happened if he'd missed the man's throat with the arrow. He was pretty sure that the two men were dead. The woman's wound was in no way fatal—unless it became infected, which could be possible if she was alone and had no way to tend to it. For a brief moment, Skyler worried that perhaps she'd been forced to live like that. But then he remembered her malicious grins, how she shot at him with such intention. She wanted him dead as much as the two men did.

Skyler stayed close to the house for the next few days. He kept the binoculars close by so he could periodically scan the end of Douglas Road a little over a half mile away, from where he half expected to see someone walking their way, someone angry about what he'd done. The farm was just a mile up the road on the other side of the hill.

Each morning of the three days back with James and Lara, Skyler walked down to the pond with the crossbow. But he was nervous every time he was away from the house. The slightest noise made him jumpy. Worse, the ducks weren't moving about on such warm summer days and he came home empty handed. He remembered the duck he'd left in the tall grass outside the farm, the one he brought as a gift of good will. Both would be rotting by now. He didn't care. He never wanted to go back up that road again.

On the fourth day, Skyler slept late. The fatigue of the last few days had finally caught up to him. When he came out of his bedroom, he found that Lara had left him an oatmeal cake on the counter. They were a favorite, a mix of oatmeal and carrot, shaped into a patty and fried. As he ate his cake, he wandered out onto the deck and looked out to the garden. Lara was pulling up carrots while James was hefting a bushel of beets toward the stairs. The harvest had begun. Skyler turned and saw a duck lying on the table, an indication that James had been to the pond earlier that morning.

James paused midway up the stairs when he saw Skyler. "How's it going?"

"Better, I didn't dream about them last night."

James continued up the stairs and set the bushel on the deck. He pulled up a chair and a bucket half filled with pond water and set to working on the beets.

"Would you mind if I went up to see Brandy today?" he asked James.

"No, I don't mind. You know you're free to do what you want. We just appreciate you keeping tabs with us to keep our worrying to a minimum." James smiled almost apologetically at Skyler, as if from a father to his mature son over whom he no longer has influence.

"Thanks, I'll only be gone a little while. I just want to make sure she's alright."

James nodded, and using a kitchen knife, he cut the greens off a beet bulb and tossed the bulb into the bucket to soak. The greens, worth saving, went into a large cooking pot. Then he picked up another beet. In silence, Skyler grabbed a knife and helped until the bushel was empty.

A short time later, Skyler left the house and walked towards Main Street. He took the direct route by walking up Church Road. He felt safe enough as long as he listened for sounds that didn't belong. He looked at his quiver and wondered if he should carry more than five arrows. What would have happened the other day had he only carried two arrows instead of three? He tried to think about something else, but every thought led back to those few moments just four days ago.

Before long, he'd arrived at the barricade and walked around it. Somewhere past the opening, there was always a sentry, a "listening post" tended by both men and women. For all their welcoming of him and even wanting him part of their "family," Skyler still didn't know where they hid the sentry, but it didn't concern him. He knew that the fewer people who knew about the sentry, the better.

He turned down the street of houses, which still, and intentionally, looked like a ghost town in order to keep strangers from thinking they were doing well. Petar came out holding a rifle and instantly Skyler was on the alert. The sentry usually only had his weapons on hand when a stranger came through.

Petar's expression told Skyler that something was wrong. "What happened?"

"The soldier boys came back yesterday morning. We heard them approaching so we all hid. But Scott had been across the road reworking the water system. He didn't know they were here."

"Is he alright?"

"He's been better." Petar's countenance was grim. "He walked right in and they surrounded him." Petar turned from grim to angry. "They beat on him for almost fifteen minutes, and all we could do was watch. What else could we do?" Petar shook his head in disgust. "When they finished, they pinned a note to his chest before leaving him lying there." He reached into his pocket and withdrew a piece of folded paper with blood stains on it. He passed it over to Skyler.

The note read, "We'll be back in four weeks. If there isn't 400 pounds of canned foods waiting by the logs, we'll burn this place to the ground."

Skyler handed the note back, angered by the news and the note. "Where's Scott now?"

"He's resting. Nothing was broken except his nose and some ribs, but he's bruised and sore all over. He's missing a few teeth, too."

"Can I see him?"

"Sure, follow me."

Since Skyler had so far declined their invitations to join their small community permanently, he had never been shown which house they lived in. But this time Petar led him down the street, around the corner, and to one of the few remaining houses with the roof still intact, its windows still boarded as with many of the other houses, partial or otherwise. Skyler was shocked by the amount of debris and garbage that filled its yard—and the neighboring yards, but then realized that the disarray contributed to the place looking uninhabited. Petar led him along a cluttered trail through the garbage.

The front door, or where one would expect to find a front door, was covered by a large sheet of plywood. When Skyler and Petar got closer, though, Skyler saw small hinges attached to the plywood. To get to the door, you simply swung the plywood outward. Inside, the living room was as dark as any cave, and they passed four sofas that doubled as beds.

Stumbling their way through the dark, Skyler felt bad for his friends. But as they approached the back half of the house, he realized that his concern was unwarranted. Here it was stunningly different. Light poured in through large windows. A large dining room table was surrounded by eleven chairs. Everything was neat and tidy. The kitchen appeared functional. Skyler saw a drop of water fall from the faucet.

Petar turned down a short hall and pushed open a partially closed door. It was a large bedroom with four twin-size beds. Scott was sitting up in one of the beds. Brandy sat on a chair at his side holding a straw in a tall glass to his lips. His left eye was swollen shut, and a gash above the eyebrow had been sewn closed. Stitches also held his upper lip together. Skyler saw dark bruises around his neck.

"Hey, teacher, I just heard. I wanted to say hello," said Skyler.

Scott opened his mouth to speak, revealing the gap where his teeth had been. "Not too pretty, am I?" Scott mustered a chuckle.

Skyler was caught off guard by the physical damage Scott had suffered and faltered, not knowing what to say.

Brandy broke the silence. "Skyler, you're going to have to be more careful. Those soldiers mean business."

"Don't worry," Skyler said. "I've quit traveling the main roads during the day. And I'm always cautious." Internally, though, he thought of the disreputable people he'd encountered recently. "I haven't seen the soldiers that much this summer."

"It's harvest time Skyler," Petar pointed out. "We're afraid we are going to see them more often between now and winter." The mood in the room was thoughtful and dark.

"I know that. And we just have to figure a way to deal with them. But that reminds me. Lara is canning tonight, and I promised her I'd help. I'm sorry, Scott. Sorry to you all. But I need to get back."

Petar's face brightened at this. "Can Brandy go with you and help? We haven't begun canning yet, and it would be helpful if she had a sense of it before we began. Do you think Lara could show her?"

Skyler only paused for a second, and this just to look at Brandy with a big smile, before saying, "Sure, she could be a lot of help." Then he asked, "But don't you have others who know how to can?"

"We do, but that's the problem. The only one who knows how to can food is Lydia, Brent's wife. And Brent's out looking for a new place now, even as we speak; after the soldier's came, Lydia insisted they move immediately, so there's no time for her to show any of us."

Thinking about his recent encounter, Skyler said, "I sure hope they find a good place, because there are a lot worse dangers out there. I've seen them." Maybe in the morning, Skyler thought, he would tell Brent about what happened, but not now. Instead, Skyler said his goodbyes to Scott and Petar as Brandy left to collect a few things into a pack. After they passed the barricade, Skyler and Brandy took the trail through the fields. It was a little slower this way, but there was no benefit in taking chances out on the road.

Looking around her with a smile of appreciation, Brandy said, "I haven't been outside of our neighborhood since last fall."

"Why not?"

"Petar thought it to be too dangerous. I'm surprised he even suggested that I go with you."

Brandy said this lightly, but both she and Skyler understood Petar's thinking; both recognized the danger they were up against with the soldiers. And with Brent and his family leaving, only eight remained, one in no condition to fight or run for several days. If they did get burned out, Brandy would have somewhere to go.

They walked side by side, talking about whatever came to mind. As they crested a small rise, Skyler spotted his house off in the distance and pointed it out to Brandy.

"You live so close to the main road. Don't the soldiers harass you?"

"Oh, they've shown up a couple of times. James does all the talking. So far they haven't gotten angry with us." He didn't mention the time they found their door kicked open.

They arrived at the house to find James in the back yard digging a pit. Lara was cutting carrots into small chunks, and Skyler explained why Brandy was there. Lara nodded, as if it was just a matter of fact, and smiled at the young girl. Skyler got knives for both him and Brandy, and they joined in to help with the carrots.

Lara talked as she cut. She explained the canning process to Brandy. Before them, there were a half dozen five-gallon buckets filled with beets, carrots and beet greens. Once these were cut up and washed once more, the small pieces would be stuffed into the Mason jars. Either salt or vinegar would be added to each jar depending on the vegetable. The jars would be topped off with water. Lids would be screwed on loosely and the jars would go into the large caldrons of boiling water. Once the water inside the jars boiled for at least ten minutes, they would remove them from the pot and tighten the lids down.

"As the insides cool, this forms a protective vacuum," Lara continued.

"Why can't you just put the vegetables in the jars and seal them?"

"Bacteria would grow and contaminate what's inside the jars. You'll get quite ill if you don't boil the contents first," Lara said. "Besides, boiling them also cooks the vegetables."

Brandy absorbed everything Lara told her. The three worked for two hours, finishing about half of the harvest. After his work in the pit, James lit a small fire in the pit to roast a duck. Over dinner, James explained that while the pit he'd been digging was great for roasting meat, it was specifically meant for the canning process. He would line it with bricks and, once the sun went down, build a fire within it to boil the large pots of water.

"Why after sunset?" Brandy asked.

"Best not to draw too much attention with all the smoke; the depth of the pit should hide the flames. Besides, our inside stove won't get hot enough to bring the larger pots to a boil."

Brandy nodded, taking all the instruction and information in. Then she sighed with satisfaction, looking at her plate of food. "We don't get meat very often up on the hill, and we don't have rice."

"What do you eat?" asked Lara.

"Mostly vegetables and potatoes in a broth. The potatoes began rotting during the middle of last winter, so we cut off the bad parts and dried what was left. Dried potatoes kept us alive."

James hadn't realized about their limited diet until now and asked, "When you did have any meat, what kind did you get?"

"Actually," Brandy said with a smile, "the first time was the goose that Skyler brought us. We were all too afraid to venture out to find anything to hunt, and Petar didn't want us to waste bullets."

James raised his eyebrows and looked at Skyler. The boy had never mentioned shooting a goose. He smiled to himself when he saw Skyler avert his eyes and focus on Brandy. Although a goose dinner would have been nice, James wasn't angry. He was glad to know that the boy had at least put it to good use.

"Yeah, that was a nice sized goose," said James with a grin and a wink to Skyler. "What else did Skyler take up to your family?"

"Fish, ducks, and the occasional crow. Everything went into the soup. Everyone's been so grateful for Skyler's help."

After dinner, Brandy and Skyler returned to stuffing vegetables into jars. The beet jars were filled with vinegar and a small amount of sugar, while a lightly salted brine was added to the carrots. The greens were boiled in just plain water. Lara methodically inspected lids and placed them on the jars. By ten o'clock, the fires were hot and they began placing the jars into large shallow galvanized washtubs James had found, each filled with water. They found that they could set twenty jars in each tub. It was after midnight before they pulled last of the jars from the boiling water and twisted their lids down tight.

Skyler saw that James looked more tired than he'd ever seen him. In private, James acknowledged he'd been up since the previous night. So Skyler volunteered that he and Brandy would do the watch that night. They would switch off every two hours, allowing the other to sleep. James accepted and was thankful for their offer, but said they first needed to hide their work. A fifth of the canned vegetables would go into the kitchen pantry—James expressed hope that the soldiers wouldn't take all of it when the time came—and the rest they shuttled downstairs to store inside the furnace.

Once they'd said goodnight to James and Lara, the night was uneventful for Skyler and Brandy. They sat in chairs scanning the moonlit fields, forgetting the plan of one sleeping while the other stayed watch. Instead, they talked about their past lives, their families, both the old ones and their current ones, the schools they went to, and the books they'd read. Dawn came sooner than they wanted and the magical night's spell was broken when they heard James and Lara move around inside the house. A few minutes later, smoke from the chimney filtered down towards them, telling that breakfast would soon be ready. Skyler hoped that Lara was going to make something special since they had a guest. He rose out of his chair, stretched his legs, and extended his hand towards Brandy to help her up and lead her inside. Before they reached the door, the air around them erupted with the sound of automatic weapons.

Chapter 25

Lyons's attitude had digressed to the point that the remainder of the squad feared what sort of mood they would need to suffer through each day. They'd stored away enough food to get them through the summer, but now those stocks were running thin, and Lyons was hungry—and nothing they had left would satisfy him. It was time to shake up the locals.

"First stop is that namby pamby group that thinks their wimpy barricade can keep us out," Lyons sneered. "Everyone, pack up to go 'shopping,' except you," Lyons pointed to one soldier, "you stay here and monitor the cameras." The Humvees flew up the hill, coming to an abrupt stop at the logs. Lyons motioned to one soldier to stay with the vehicles while he led the charge with the other five, commando style, around the barricade. They ran directly to the house that was obviously the only residence.

"What in the fuck is going on?" Lyons yelled when they found the place vacated. He was pissed more than the other four had ever seen him. "I'm gonna torch this whole goddamned place and then see where they're gonna hide." Lyons looked around then barked, "Carter, you and him—go back to the Humvee for a five-gallon Gerry can."

Lyons told the other men to scout out back and he went out to the street. In a few minutes he spotted Carter, but instead of just one man with him, he had two. Carter had the muzzle of his M-16 pressed against a civilian's back.

Lyons smiled at the new turn of events. "Carter, what have you found for us?"

"When we started up the street, this gentleman was walking towards us. It appears that he was unaware that he had visitors in town." Carter was smiling at his sergeant. All five soldiers now surrounded the man.

"What's your name?" demanded Lyons.

There was a pause, before the man mumbled, "Scott."

"Scott what? Do you have a last name or is it just Scott?"

Scott began to tremble. He finally answered, "Just Scott."

Lyons brought up the butt of his rifle so quickly that Scott had no chance of deflecting the blow. The plate on the end of the stock split his lip and knocked out four of his upper teeth. Scott fell to the ground in time to meet Lyons's boot with his right ribcage. He laid there gasping for a breath as blood poured from his mouth.

"I guess you can see that wasn't the answer I wanted to hear . . . Scott. Mind if I ask you a few more questions?" mocked Lyons.

The man curled into the fetal position. A stream of urine had escaped the large wet spot on his pants. No answer came from the broken mouth. Carter pushed the man with his foot so that he was lying on his back looking up at the five of them. He was still conscious.

"How many of you live here?" asked Lyons.

There was no response. Carter kicked the side of the man's head to remind him that he was expected to answer.

"Eleven. There are eleven of us." His words were barely discernable.

"And of those eleven, how many are women?" Every soldier had become attentive to this question. Carter raised his foot to plant another reminder when Scott answered.

"Two, just two."

"Thank you for cooperating. Carter, can you find me a pencil and paper please?" Lyons asked sarcastically.

Carter reached inside a cargo pocket and pulled out a small notebook and pen. He tore a page out and handed it to Lyons. The sergeant wrote something on the paper and when he was finished, he silently read it to himself and grinned.

"Now, Scott, it's important to me that your friends get this note." His sarcasm was obvious. "Just so you understand its importance, I think we should show you how we feel about trusting you with this task."

Lyons delivered the first kick to his neck, followed with another blow to his forehead with the rifle butt. Carter and the three others joined in. When they finished, the only sign that the man was still breathing was the slow escape of bubbles from his nose and mouth. Lyons jammed the note into the man's upper shirt pocket and all six stomped down the street and past the barricade.

The two Humvees descended the hill and returned to the refinery. As they entered the bunker, they found the seventh soldier sitting in front of the monitors. He stood as Lyons walked in ahead of the rest of the team.

"Did you see anything this morning, soldier?" Lyons asked.

"No sir, but I did turn the radio on. HQ has been trying to reach us. I answered their call and gave them our status."

Lyons was so stunned by this that he didn't move. He just stared at the soldier. Not knowing how to read Lyons's response, he continued. "The army is running the country. They want to rotate us out of here in a few days." He grinned as if he had just delivered good news.

Lyons's foot hit the man right at the belt buckle, sending him over the chair and across the floor. "Who in the fuck told you to turn on that goddamn radio?"

The soldier jumped up as if he might retaliate, but backed down when he saw the hate in his sergeant's eyes. He quickly uttered, "Sorry, sir."

Lyons wasn't through with him. "Sorry? Sorry? What do you suppose they'll think when we tell them that our CO is dead? How do we explain that? And what do you suppose they'll do to us when the locals tell the new soldiers how we treated them?"

The young soldier stared back at his sergeant, stolid, but near tears.

Lyons continued his banter. "The last time they'd heard from us, Alvorez was our CO and the only one they had contact with. Do you think they wouldn't notice that he's not here?" He kicked the chair across the room, breaking it into three pieces. "Do you know the punishment for killing an officer?"

The soldier knew the punishment but didn't answer only because he was afraid that Lyons's temper would escalate even further. The other men came into the room, keeping their eyes down, acting as if nothing caught their attention. Lyons finally turned and went back outside to think. On the day he had fired that bullet, killing Alvorez, he had decided that he wasn't going back to Fort Lewis ever again. He knew the score. If they all stood on trial, the men would protect themselves and rat him out.

Lyons became absorbed in thought. Too much was happening too fast. He went into the garage and bent down to grab a whiskey bottle. The box was empty. Tossing the cardboard aside, he opened the last case and stared at the empties. The empty bottles fell short of the amount that was vacant from the cases. Could it be one of his men? They were together almost twenty-four hours a day. He twisted the cap off the bottle, taking a long swig. The burn felt good. And what about that kid they'd seen a glimpse of on the monitors a few of months earlier? Leaving one soldier behind to watch the monitors was supposed to solve that mystery. But it hadn't. He couldn't' trust to leave anyone back any longer—look what that got him. He couldn't trust anyone. Period. Lyons went back inside the bunker and walked over to the desk. With his free hand, he tore the radio from the wires that connected it to the airwaves. Then he took a long draw from the whiskey bottle and stared at the radio in his hand. He carried it outside and walked across the drive towards the fence. With his left arm, he flung the radio over the fence into the dead brambles.

Five days passed without any sign of the army appearing on their doorstep. They were silent, edgy, and once again out of food— the first time in months. For the last five days they'd been living in fear of their future and of Lyons, so when Lyons got the men up before dawn and instructed them about his plan, they were ready. An early morning raid would be a welcome break from the monotony of waiting for Lyons to snap again. They donned their full armor. There was excitement in their banter. Lyons's plan was to hit two houses, and every man would be needed; they were all going. It was still dark when the two garage doors opened and the Humvees backed out.

The horizon to the east cast a red glow signaling that the sun was not far behind. Lyons parked his rig just across from the mouth of Church Road. The second Humvee settled in behind and shut off its engine. There was no reason to leave someone guarding their vehicles; no civilian would dare touch them. Instead of heading up Church, all seven walked single file down the long gravel driveway, weapons ready.

They made not a sound as they approached the house to the west of the stand of dead cedars. Lyons gripped the doorknob and gently gave it a twist. It was locked. Holding up three fingers, he counted down to zero. Two bodies slammed the door simultaneously, knocking it completely out of the door frame. The house was a split entry; two men went up and two down. Lyons stayed out front while the two remaining soldiers circled around the outside. Carter and the other, who sprinted upstairs, opened a bedroom and found an older woman, alone, huddled in her bed, holding the sheets to her neck. Carter kept his barrel pointed at her as his partner checked the other rooms and reached down to pull the covers from her body. It was flaccid, aged . . . She got up and ran into a bathroom, locking the door behind her. He smiled. She could wait.

The two soldiers circling the house arrived at the back just a few seconds apart, from opposite directions. One was met by a man with a rifle leveled at his chest; the man hesitated, and in that instant a volley of bullets danced across his back. He swung the barrel around as it discharged into the sky. Both soldiers opened up on him until he lay prone on the ground outside his back door.

When Lyons heard the automatic fire, he ran inside and was met by Carter.

"One target was outside and he's been silenced. There's an older woman. She's locked herself in a bathroom. Except for her, the upstairs is secure." Carter pointed down the hall.

Lyons strode down the hall to the closed door, sobs coming from the other side. "We don't have time for this shit," he shouted at Carter. He raised his M-16 and sprayed a burst of rounds through the hollow door. They heard her body slump to the floor.

In the sudden quiet, Lyons heard his two men downstairs, calling to him. "Sir, we've found something interesting!" Lyons arrived at the bottom of the stairs and stared in amazement. Military MRE's or 'meals ready to eat' half filled the one downstairs bedroom. Lyons looked at the boxes of meals stacked to the ceiling. What he wouldn't have given to have known about this last fall. The family room next to the bedroom contained several steel barrels with hoses leading into them. Water from the rain gutters was diverted into this room.

"Hmm. I'm impressed. This guy must have had some kind of government connection. Too bad he didn't think ahead enough to find a pretty woman."

Less than three minutes had elapsed since they'd knocked down the door. "Carter, take one man and move all the food and anything we can use outside, and then light this place up. Everyone else: follow me."

Furtively making their way through the dead cedars, they spread out around the structure. Two men reached the top of the stairs and found the door wide open. Lyons stayed down below waiting, listening for gunfire to erupt to indicate his men had encountered hostile occupants. He could hear the men as they methodically ran through the house. Finally one of his men appeared and flashed a hand signal signifying that the house was empty.

Lyons was pissed. He and his men hadn't been fast enough to get here before the occupants flew. "Damn it. I knew I should have split the team up," he growled under his breath. He ran up on the deck and scanned the surrounding fields. A flash of movement caught his attention. He pulled a small pair of binoculars from a cargo pocket and focused the glasses in that direction, only about a thousand feet away. At first he saw nothing. Then a man's head appeared above the tall grass. The man was staring back at him with binoculars. Two more heads poked up from the tall grass, then a fourth. "So," Lyons smiled to himself grimly, "there are four of you." Lyons wished that he'd brought the M-90.

Lyons watched as the man lowered his binoculars and stood; he was certain the man could see him. All four stood, then, and half ran, half stumbled through the tall grass. When they started to run, Lyons saw that two of the four had a distinctly different gait—women. He smiled.

"Shall I light this place up too?" Carter asked Lyons.

"No. Not yet. I want them to feel they can come back. But round up the food in the kayaks and take both Humvees back to base. I'm going to stay here and wait for them to return."

Chapter 26

At the sound of the sudden gunfire, Skyler and Brandy rushed inside from their overnight watch. They were close, too close. The shooting had to have come from Mike's house. James and Lara were already hurrying to gather a few supplies. "Come on! We've got to run," Skyler shouted, gripping his bow. The sounds of gunfire ended as abruptly as it had started and all four stood still. James turned on the radio and listened. Nothing. Within seconds, James was leading the other three down the stairs and towards the lower field. He held the nine millimeter out in front knowing that it could designate him as a target.

They ran with their heads down, silent, not looking back, hoping that they'd be far enough away before the soldiers got to their place and saw they were gone. There was just light enough to follow the trail. Once they were about three hundred yards away, James had everyone flatten out into the tall grass. They stayed silent, waiting for more gunshots or shouting.

He reached into the pack and found the binoculars. He rose and looked at their place.

"What do you see?" Lara whispered.

"Mike's place—" James paused with a hint of resignation, "they lit it on fire."

"What about ours . . ." Lara's question trailed off.

James refocused his gaze. "A very big soldier is standing on our deck with binoculars pointing right in our direction." James shoved the binoculars back into the pack and stood. "We need to keep moving. They know we're here." He looked grimly at his three wards and nodded assertively.

They continued south on roads still obstructed, impassable by the Humvees. Every hundred yards, James stopped and looked back. They weren't being pursued, but he could see that Mike's house was completely engulfed. It would be devastating if they torched his house too. They'd been quick to throw a few jars of canned food into their packs, enough to last them a couple days, but every means of survival was at that house. They'd left twenty-some jars of canned vegetables in the pantry. James was sure that those had been found by now, but he hoped they hadn't discovered the kayaks or, worse yet, the furnace drawer, with almost eighty jars. Before dropping down out of sight of the property, he halted their progress one last time. From this point, he could see the rear of the house and the field below it. The flames from Mike's house had spread to the line of dead cedars, but no further. Their house was still intact. James scanned the glasses up further and could see the steep grade of Church Road. He moved the glasses a little to the left and saw the rest of Main Street before it disappeared over the hill. As he watched, a tan colored Humvee entered his view and disappeared over the crest. Seconds later, the second Humvee followed.

"They're going back to the refinery!"

"Are you sure?" asked Lara.

"They just disappeared over the hill. I can only guess that's where they're going."

"And . . . our house?"

"It's fine; at least from here it looks OK. It wasn't torched, and the fire from Mike's hasn't spread"

Skyler looked at the fear on Brandy's face then looked to James. "What do we do now?"

James assessed the boy's demeanor. He showed such strength. "I want you to make a wide loop around and take Brandy back to her home. Lara and I will wait here a few hours. I'm not sure what we'll do, but we can't ever live in that house again." He paused before continuing with a determined sigh. "However, I need to go back. My bow and most of our arrows are still there. And all our winter clothes and other supplies—and food. I need to get as much as I can if the soldiers left anything."

Skyler asked, "Do you want me to come back to this point after I take Brandy home? Or meet you at the house to help?"

"No, stay up there tonight. We'll come find you when we figure out what we're going to do."

"James—?" Lara paused before she finished her question. "Do you *have* to go back? I mean, don't you still have one locker with food hidden?"

"Sure, I left a locker with some food, but I haven't seen it in months, and I have no idea if the food's still there or if someone found it. Besides, if it was still there, it's only enough to get one person through another winter." James set his jaw. "No, I have to get what I can from the house."

James gave Skyler a jar of carrots to take with him and Brandy, and the two youths bravely set out. Skyler had his bow and quiver but little else; there just wasn't time to pack anything, let alone grab much else.

Assuring himself that Skyler and Brandy would be alright, James led Lara down into the development where the coyote raised her pups. They inspected each partially standing structure for a possible place of shelter for the night. At an intersection they saw the mother coyote standing unalarmed as if she was waiting for another handout. James looked at her and shook his head as if to communicate that he had nothing for her this time. Her pups exited the den. James was surprised at their size; they were nearly full grown. They quickly withdrew around the corner at the sight of the humans. He and Lara would need to look in a different area.

Around noon, hunger, which had been blotted out by fear, crept into their bodies. They hadn't eaten anything since the previous night.

They stopped and opened a jar of pickled beets. The taste was weak because the vinegar and sugar had been diluted, but the nourishment was still good. They both had only three small chunks of beet.

"What about our old house on the other side of the hill?" Lara asked James.

"No, it isn't safe there anymore." James had never told Lara about his final trip to pick up Skyler. It had been over four months since they left there in haste. The vividness of the human forearm in the man's backpack made James shudder internally. He also remembered how vulnerable he'd been, essentially pinned inside the house with the man outside able to stay hidden, his rifle aimed so accurately. Then he thought of how Skyler had killed two men in less than one day.

"Maybe we could move in with Brandy's family after all?" Lara suggested.

"I'm afraid that as long as the soldiers are around, their days are numbered too, especially after what Skyler told us happened to Scott. We need to somehow find a place that didn't get destroyed by the wind and is out of the reach of the soldiers. If we can find the right place, and it's not already inhabited, maybe we can bring the others with us to live there."

Lara nodded, then brightened. "Skyler's covered a larger area as he's been out hunting, maybe he has an idea where we should be looking."

"Maybe. I just don't know. For now, let's wait until after dark, then go back to the house to grab what we can. The ATV has gas in it. The box in the back has enough room for all those jars hidden in the furnace. We can load it up and drive to our friends on the hill to spend the night. It'll take us maybe five minutes to get there."

As dusk began to settle in, James and Lara worked their way back towards their house. They were both thirsty, having only time enough to grab one bottle of water, which was now gone, but neither complained. They didn't talk any further; they only listened and watched as the sky darkened.

James climbed the steep trail leading up to the back yard. Lara was to swing wide and wait in front of the garage for him. If she saw someone coming, though, James said she should bang her fist on the aluminum door and run. On his way to the back stairs, James had to pass the garden; even though it was dark, he could see that it was just as they had left it. Corn and tomatoes awaiting for their turn to be harvested. He ascended the stairs very slowly. He wasn't nervous; he was downright scared. As his eyes reached the level of the deck, he stopped and peered over the steps; no one waited there for him. He took the last step up onto the deck and quietly moved over to a wall. His pistol was out in front of him. He leaned over and peered into the southern facing window. It was too dark to make out the interior.

The front door still stood open, so he was able to enter silently. He looked about the large room. Nothing was any different than when they'd left except the pantry. Its doors were wide open and the shelves bare; all the jars of vegetables were gone. James found his bow hidden behind the curtain, as he had left it. He silently opened the fireplace and took the bundle of arrows out from behind the fake logs. He grabbed the tent and sleeping bags that Skyler was always so good about storing away when not being used. He had to put the pistol into his pocket so he could fill his arms, but he could carry no more and headed for the basement. He'd have to make at least one more trip upstairs for their winter clothes.

It was pitch black in the stairway and he could see little over the bundle of sleeping bags he carried in his arms, but James was used to climbing its steps in the dark. Without dropping any of his awkward burden, James reached out a free finger on his right hand to press the handle down and pull the door to the garage open. The stale air of the enclosed space filled his nostrils. He walked a little further before dropping the load onto the ground. It was just too dark to see anything. He needed to get a candle out of his pack so he could finish. James knew he should have had it handy when he'd entered the house.

Outside, Lara made it to the garage doors and waited. The wind was calm and there were no sounds except distant frogs. Soon, she heard noises inside the garage and she breathed a sigh of relief at the thought of James loading the ATV. She was anxious to get out of there. She waited and listened. A moment later, she heard the click of the garage door and the rush of it opening. She stepped forward. Then she stopped short, letting out a gasp of fright. Standing directly in front of her was the large soldier, his rifle leveled at her stomach.

With his free hand, the soldier raised a radio to his mouth and said, "Come get me."

Lara shook herself from her fear and was about to turn and run when, from the faint twilight of the night sky, she saw James, his unconscious body lying next to the ATV. Both kayaks sat empty on the floor next to him.

The soldier never took his eyes from her. He dropped the radio in his pocket and said, "Run and he dies."

Chapter 27

"Let's head up this road," Brandy pointed at Douglas. It was just over the hill where Skyler had the encounter that almost cost him his life. It hadn't been a full week since he'd used all of his arrows and barely escaped.

"No, I know a better way." He didn't want to explain his reasons, but added, "We need to travel due north to reach Church Road, not west, so crossing the fields is better."

They crossed the road and climbed over an old barbed wire fence that had once kept in livestock. Skyler led her on a northwest route. He wanted them to be completely out of sight from his place, which was evident by a column of smoke from Mike's house. Brandy had no difficulty keeping pace with him, and he appreciated that she seemed aware that he didn't want to talk. He wasn't thinking about her or her family. His mind was trying to solve the enormous problem that the existence of the soldiers posed to those he loved, to anyone in the area for that matter. He desperately wanted to put an end to their reign of terror. Surviving was hard enough without the threat of the armed military hanging over their heads.

Skyler had traveled this way before, so they moved swiftly, not needing to stop and make navigation choices. They had reached the crest of the hill at the top of Main Street, where Skyler wanted to cross, in less than an hour. The top of the hill was actually a short plateau; anyone crossing here couldn't be seen unless it was by someone also on the crest, which would be highly unlikely. Once they crossed, their new path would be due north, paralleling Church Road. The last section would be slower through the tangle of dead trees and fallen branches and limbs, but it would be safer. No vehicle could travel there.

Once they were clear of the road, Skyler put his hand on Brandy's arm and said, "When we get there, I want you to tell Petar to move Scott somewhere safer. Tell them to expect trouble."

"I thought you were staying with us?"

"I changed my mind. I need to go and make sure another family is safe." He hoped that she took his lie as the truth.

"What if James and Lara show up? What do I tell them?"

"Tell them I'm coming. I should be back by noon tomorrow. If you aren't there when I arrive—and you shouldn't wait for me if something happens—I'll assume you're all in hiding."

Brandy considered this, and blocked any thought of what "something" might mean. Instead she asked, "What if you don't show up by noon? Where are you going? Where should we look for you?"

Skyler understood that Brandy was hurt that he wouldn't share with her, but he couldn't reveal his plan so said, "It's safest if you don't know where I'm going. Don't worry—I'll stay off the roads and make it back by noon. I promise. It's better that you all focus on getting all your necessities together and be ready, and to move Scott."

By 10:30, they spotted the barricades off to their right. Skyler stopped and turned to Brandy, giving her a quick hug and reminding her of what to tell Petar. He took off in a jog back the way they'd come, looking back only once to make sure Brandy had kept going. He liked her. What he was about to do was for her and their future. The only way he was going to make their world safer was to even out the field of play.

Skyler fingered a key in his pocket and replayed in his mind the day he'd stolen it. After his close-call at the refinery, he had sworn to himself that he wouldn't go back. But the allure of that locked room, the one that looked like a vault, had called to him—he was sure it was where they stored their ammo, and without bullets, their guns would be useless.

On that day four weeks earlier, he had pulled himself under the fence a second time and approached the bunker. He hadn't seen the soldiers leave, so he wasn't sure if any had stayed behind. But the garage doors had been left open and both Humvees were gone. He placed his ear to the interior door but only heard the hum of the fluorescent lights. He had inched the door open until he was sure the room was vacant. Skyler had one motive: find the key to the closet door. First he had pulled open the drawers on the desk. No keys were to be found there. Then he searched the kitchen, looking for hooks inside the cupboards or hiding places underneath, and found nothing. Finally, he had pulled the door to their toilet open. It was still filled with garbage. He took a quick scan and was closing the door when he heard a metallic clink. He arched his head around the door to see that on the opposite side was a row of five hooks with several keys hanging from them.

Skyler scanned the options. Two were obviously spare keys for the Humvees. Any of the remaining eight keys could fit the door. He had grabbed the first one on the right and took it to the closet. It didn't fit. Movement caught the corner of his eye and caused him to jerk his head towards the monitors. Both Humvees were almost to the turn that led to the gate. He had to leave now. Skyler ran for the door, not taking the time to return the key or close the door behind him. He had bolted across the driveway and dived for the shallow depression under the fence. The gate was just starting to open and had obscured their vision. Skyler was able to escape.

A couple weeks later, Skyler approached the refinery again. This time, as he was about to crawl under the fence, a soldier came out of the bunker to pee. Skyler was in plain sight of him. He stayed still as a painting. If he moved, he was sure that the soldier would have seen him, but the chain link fencing provided some camouflage. The soldier casually went back inside. He hadn't been back there since that close encounter.

Today, after making it across Main Street, Skyler used his new route out to the ponds, a trail that would keep him out of the cameras' sights. His hope was that the soldiers would leave for a long enough period of time either that afternoon or in the morning. Skyler looked up to the sky, now thickening with clouds, and reminded himself that he could tough-out hunger, thirst or a cold, wet night if he had to. He just needed five minutes to try the remaining keys and get into that closet.

By noon, he had reached the entrance to the ponds; there he stepped off the gravel road and into the bushes. It would take him another thirty minutes to get in position. From his vantage point at the fence Skyler saw his first obstacle: the garage doors were closed. Every other time he'd been here, the doors were left open and the status of occupancy was obvious. But who knew if they were there or not? Maybe they were still on their rampage, wreaking havoc on other innocent people, but had closed the garage doors this time. Skyler dare not crawl under the fence and advance unless he was sure the place was vacant. He sat down and waited, grateful for the dry ground.

It wasn't even ten minutes before one of the soldiers stepped outside to pee. Through the open door, Skyler spotted at least three others inside. It was early afternoon and he convinced himself that they'd have a reason to leave again before long. The reality of the situation was that there was nothing he could do as long as they were inside and the garage doors were shut. He wondered how James and Lara were fairing.

Dusk came slowly. He was thirsty and hungry and becoming chilled from his inactivity. The only movement he saw was the periodic soldier coming out to pee. He couldn't really tell one from the other, but he realized that not once did he see the biggest soldier come out, the one James had spied through his binoculars. Where was the big man?

An hour later, both garage doors opened at the same time and Skyler sat alert, watching. Six soldiers ran out, moving as if on a mission. Skyler saw the last man through the interior door shut off the light. All climbed into a vehicle, three to each, and drove out of the garage. They weren't leaving anyone behind, Skyler saw. He anxiously waited for the Humvees to leave and at the same time worried where they were going. Could they be heading again for Brandy's people? Skyler put that thought out of his mind. Maybe it was just a night-time raid of some other farm, or it was a pre-arranged time for them to go get their seventh man. When both vehicles were through the doorways, the automatic doors came down. Skyler knew that there wasn't any way inside unless they'd left the front door unlocked. Within seconds, he'd cleared the gap under the fence, pushed his pack under and followed it through. He stood, looked about, and jogged towards the bunker.

He didn't have the nervousness that he had harbored during his last two times inside. He'd seen them leave. It would be highly unlikely that they would drive back in less than twenty minutes. Still, he hurried towards the door in hopes it was open. They'd locked it. Next he tried lifting all three garage doors to no avail. He hurriedly walked around behind the bunker, making a full circle of the place; it was a fortress. He finally remembered the key in his pocket and tried it in the door knob. It was not a match. If this key didn't fit the closet inside, Skyler thought, and it didn't fit the exterior door, what did it fit? He looked at his watch: ten minutes had passed since the soldiers left. Time was getting very short. He moved his head and eyes about to spot *anything* that would have a lock on it.

He went back to the large garage doors and inspected them again. There was no external hardware or locking devices. Then, in the door jamb, he saw a security pad with a keyhole. Each door had one, right at eye level. Skyler tried the key in the first tumbler. It fit but wouldn't turn. He ran to the next one. Not only did the key fit, but it turned. Its door opened. Skyler ran through the garage and jerked open the door to the soldiers' quarters.

Groping for the light switch, he found it just inside the door. The bright fluorescent lights were a shock for his eyes, but he adjusted quickly. He had to. He opened the toilet door and reached around, grabbing all the keys. Without hesitation, he took the one key from the bunch that was different than the rest and tried it on the locked closet door. It was a perfect match. He threw the rest of the keys onto the floor. It didn't matter; more significant things would reveal he'd been here.

The door opened up to a large closet with shelves. Toilet paper and books and other mundane items filled one shelf. On the rest were various pieces of ammunition and weaponry: replacement parts for the M-16s, two metal tubes marked with LAW, a large rifle case, and boxes and boxes of rifle cartridges. With satisfaction, Skyler thought to himself: the war is about to begin. He opened the top of his empty pack wide and started throwing the boxes in. By the time he had them all, his pack was too heavy to lift. He dragged it towards the door. He had to get his bag and himself under the fence as quickly as possible. He glanced at the monitors before going out the door. Still no sign of the soldiers returning.

Skyler crawled under the fence first and then pulled the pack through; it almost stuck, but the fence had flexed enough and he was able to pull it through. He dragged the pack to where he'd left his bow and quiver. This would suffice, he thought, and piled limbs and debris over the pack to sufficiently hide it. Skyler was about to take his bow and run when he thought about the other items in the storage room. It had been over twenty minutes since they'd left, yet there still was no sign of the soldiers returning. He ran back.

Once back inside the bunker, Skyler opened the store room and found the long rifle case. He quickly unsnapped its four clasps and saw inside a rifle unlike the ones the soldiers carried. It was long and equipped with a powerful scope. The foam inside the case had been shaped to fit exactly around the rifle and scope. A pocket near the barrel contained three cartridge clips. All three were full. Another pocket held a bipod. He closed and locked the case, then pulled it from the shelf. It dropped with a thud, but it was not too heavy for him to carry. He was about to leave when his eyes caught on the tubes. Lifting one, he read its label: "M-72 LAW" in block letters. To Skyler's untrained eye, it looked like some kind of small missile. The only external parts were a pair of sights and a trigger. He pulled one off the shelf with his free hand, assessing its weight. He could carry it and the rifle case, he thought. Turning around, Skyler made one last sweep with his eyes before shutting the closet door with his foot. He would keep the key to it. Skyler scanned the monitors before quickly kicking the remaining keys under the couches. He knew it would only delay them a bit, but he relished the thought of a soldier having to get down on his hands and knees to look for them. He exited through the garage, closing the door behind him. Back beyond the fence, Skyler was arranging his cache when he heard the gate begin to open. Out of instinct he ducked down as a Humvee pulled in front of the bunker. A garage door opened. Once inside the garage, three doors on the Humvee opened and three soldiers jumped out—one was the large man who had been missing earlier. As the garage door was closing Skyler continued to watch. He let out an agonized cry when he saw the big soldier reach inside and drag a body out of the back seat and drop it on the concrete floor. It was Lara.

Chapter 28

Skyler realized that he must to do something quickly, or someone close to him would die. He had to believe that Lara was still alive, and he struggled with the urge to crawl back under the fence and rescue her. He knew this was impossible. He could not succeed on his own. Where was James? Skyler thought frantically. Something must have happened to him. He would have never let them take Lara without a fight. What seemed like an eternity of decision-making actually only took him about two minutes. He needed help to get Lara back.

With his bow strung over his back, Skyler grabbed the rifle case in one hand and the missile in the other. The pack of rifle cartridges was hidden and the hole under the fence covered up. He retraced his steps to stay out of view and had only gone a few yards when he heard the sound of the second Humvee returning. He stopped to watch, in case James was with them. Four soldiers got out and slammed their doors shut. Once the bay was closed, the area was left in total darkness. Thick clouds fully obscured the moon, forcing him to use his sense of direction as his only guide through the black night. Yet he ran harder than he'd ever run before, disregarding the dead limbs that scraped and stabbed his cheeks and arms.

When he reached the gravel road, Skyler looked at his surroundings; his night vision had improved ever so slightly, and a hint of light filtered through the clouds; he could make out a sign post just a few feet away and was able to get his bearings. He hid both the case and the metal tube in the ditch, confident he'd be able to find them again, and took off running. Nothing slowed him now. The route from here to his house would have fewer obstacles. And his bow and quiver were like part of his body.

Skyler added up the facts as he ran. The big soldier had been missing all day, obviously left behind somewhere. The other soldiers' sudden departure from the bunker must have been because he'd radioed for them to retrieve him. Skyler's thoughts turned to James and Lara—James had talked about returning to the house to get their staples and clothes. Could the big man have anticipated that and waited there? How was Lara taken? And why not James? Skyler didn't like to think it, but a good reason he was not brought back to the bunker was that James might be dead. Skyler had to get to the house. With all seven soldiers at the bunker—even once they realized they'd been broken into—it should be safe to go back to the house. They'd not think of that, Skyler assured himself.

At some point, the rain began to fall. Skyler's mind was so busy that he hadn't noticed it at first. While it had been thirty-six hours since he'd last slept, and the last time he'd eaten had been over twenty-four hours ago, he maintained a steady pace across the fields. His fear overrode his exhaustion, and his knowledge of the path helped him to move without hesitation even as the trail got sloppy and his footing uncertain. As he ran, his plan took shape.

Skyler reached the road at the top of the hill and ran the last section on the asphalt. His bow was clenched in his left hand with one arrow in his right. He didn't think he'd need them, but any error in judgment—if he was killed or detained—could cost Lara her life. He turned onto their street and could see the silhouette of the big house looming ahead. It was too dark to make out any features until he was almost to the stairs. And then he saw that the nearest garage door was open. A dark shadow, visible in the opening, startled Skyler. Then he remembered what sat in that space. It was the ATV.

Skyler shouted, "James, where are you?" He waited only seconds before running through the garage and into the house. Total blackness covered everything but he knew his way about, even knew the number of stairs from the basement. When he reached the top floor, the drumming of heavy rain filled his ears, and there was no response to his call.

There was always a candle on the kitchen counter, Skyler remembered. He swept his arm across until he found it. The butane lighter rested near its base. He lit the candle and glanced around the dark room. The fireplace glass had been left open. Only James would have done that. He felt inside behind the logs; the arrows were gone. With the candle in his hand, Skyler did a quick sweep of all the rooms. No sign of his friend.

He ran out onto the deck, not caring about the downpour. His candle was snuffed out. Skyler tossed it back through the open doorway then faced the rain once again. He shouted for James as loud as he could three times, each time pausing to listen. He heard no response and had started back inside when the faintest noise reached him through the pounding wind and rain. Skyler stood still and shouted once more, "James?" He listened intently.

Again a noise just barely audible above the downpour. "Where is it coming from?" Skyler whispered to himself. "Where are you?" The sound seemed close, but the deck was empty. Skyler walked along the rail raking it with his fingers. He felt something block his hand, something soft and cold on the rail. Fingers, wrist, arm. "James?" Skyler leaned over the railing, following an extended, taut arm. James was tied to the outside of the deck rail, his arms splayed like a crucifix, his body pulling on the knots. Without light, Skyler felt around and found electrical cord attaching each wrist to the rail. Nothing else supported James' weight. Skyler felt for his face; tape was covering the man's eyes and mouth. His feet dangled six feet above the ground.

"Oh my god. James. I'm here. It's me. I'm going to get you down."

Skyler ran the rest of the way down the stairs to the open garage. He ran his hands across the wall until he felt the toolbox they kept on a shelf near the door. Dropping its weight on the floor, he opened its lid and felt for the wire cutters. He turned to go back and tripped over something large. His hands grasped the deck of one of the empty kayaks. "Damn, they took the food," he snarled under his breath. Skyler ran his hand along the boat until he found the eyelet screwed into the end. The rope was still attached and he slipped it free.

Skyler ascended the stairs three at a time. He worked quickly as he reached through the stays of the rail and tied the rope around James' waist. Then Skyler wrapped the rope around the top rail twice to create a belay. Standing behind James, he kept tension on the rope as he cut the wires that pinned James' arms to the rail. The sudden weight jerked the rope as it put tension on the belay. Skyler dropped the cutters and used both hands to feed the rope through the rail. James' body slowly descended to the ground. When he felt the weight come off the rope, Skyler ran back down the stairs.

The darkness surrendered a large bulk below the deck. Skyler felt for his friend who lay in complete exhaustion in the mud, and gently tugged at the tape covering James's mouth and eyes. James winced but did not complain and the two men embraced.

"Lara?" James let out in a short breath.

"Let's get you inside," Skyler said in a calm tone, ignoring the query.

After some coaxing, James was able to stand, but he was so weak, he couldn't ascend the stairs. Skyler had him crawl on all fours as he pushed and stabilized the older man from behind. After what seemed like an hour but was only minutes, they finally reached the deck. Skyler dragged his friend the rest of the way inside.

Skyler retrieved the candle he'd tossed back inside and, once lit, used it to find three more. With the available light, he looked at his friend. James's face had taken a beating, but both eyes were open.

Again James uttered, "Lara?"

"I know where she is," Skyler said flatly. "We'll get her back. But right now let's focus on getting you out of those wet clothes and warmed up."

James just nodded weakly. Skyler peeled the wet and blood-stained clothes from James's body, leaving him naked on the floor. He disappeared briefly before returning with an armload of blankets. He wrapped his friend up snugly then lit the stove. Skyler was worried about Lara and that by waiting for James to recover somewhat, it could make her situation worse. However, he also knew that he needed James' help and couldn't get her back without it. Skyler just hoped he'd be strong enough to travel by morning.

Skyler worked on starting a fire while James sat watching from one of the couches. Twenty minutes later, James was in a chair next to the stove, sipping a broth of warm sugar water. Every so often, he looked at Skyler as if he wanted to say something, but couldn't find the words. James felt his tender wrists and rotated them; he was able to move his hands. His face wounds would recover and the bruises from where he'd been kicked and beaten would diminish. He would be alright.

Skyler put another piece of wood in the stove and turned to James. "I want you to get some rest—try to sleep. I have to leave for a little while, but I'll be back within an hour." James nodded, and Skyler reached into the closet next to the entry and pulled out James's raincoat. It was on and buttoned in one sweeping motion before he stepped out the door.

Skyler unscrewed the cap on the ATV's gas tank and stuck his middle finger down its throat. He felt wetness at the end of his finger. There would be more than enough to get him up the hill. James had not let him drive the ATV, but had showed him the many buttons and levers and Skyler had paid close attention. It started on his first try. Fumbling around the handgrips, he found the light switch; the gauge lights lit up along with everything in the path of the vehicle's headlights. A few moments later he was driving up the wet glistening asphalt of Main Street doing twenty miles an hour.

True to his word, Skyler returned to James an hour later. James was warmed and somewhat recovered from his trauma, but still exhausted.

Skyler picked up a candle and went down to the basement. The doors to the furnace were still shut. He pulled open the panel on the giant flue and felt down inside. His hand connected with a jar, several jars. Skyler sighed in relief; they had not found this stash. Grabbing one jar, he inspected its contents by candlelight: carrots. "These would do," Skyler said to himself, and headed back upstairs.

James ate with as much relish as his bruised jaw would allow, and Skyler could see that his wounds were going to mend just fine. Skyler ate some of the carrots too, until the entire jar was empty.

"So where is she?" James's expression was utterly forlorn.

"They took her out to the refinery. She was in the bunker when I left."

James looked up in alarm. "We'll never get inside that fence. Besides, they took my bow and my guns."

"We won't need to get inside. They'll come out looking for me," said Skyler.

James gave him a questioning look, waiting for Skyler to add an explanation.

Skyler didn't elaborate but told James about finding the soldiers' ammunition closet and the rifle. This seemed to instill some energy into James, who rubbed his wrist below his right hand. The marks from the electrical cord were still visible. "Good thing my trigger finger works." It was almost midnight before they each took a couch and lay down. James wound his watch as he did every night and set the alarm for five in the morning.

Chapter 29

The big man was on top of her in a flash, knocking her to the ground. When she came to, her wrists had been tied behind her back and she was being hurled into the garage. She landed next to James. She looked at her friend, wanting so badly for him to turn his head and see her. Except for a slow rise of his chest, he remained unmoving. His hands were also tied. At least he's alive, Lara thought. The huge soldier stood before her, glowering and smug as he waited for whomever he'd radioed. Lara searched her mind for something to hope for. She found nothing.

Two Humvees arrived at that point and the occupants piled out like children at a theme park. With flashlights out, they stood in a semi-circle around their captives. One of the younger ones kicked at James so hard that it rolled him onto his back. Lara now saw the damage that the larger man had inflicted on James.

"Damn it, I said I'd cooperate if you didn't hurt him!" she yelled at the big man, a new found bravery overcoming her. When he stooped down close to her face, she saw his name tag.

"I said that I wouldn't hurt him," Lyons said coyly. "I made no promises about my men," He looked at his cohorts and chuckled.

"She looks more like a man than a woman. Have you checked her plumbing yet?" asked the soldier that had landed the kick.

"Not yet. I've had enough on my plate with this one," Lyons kicked at James's gut. "Let's get her in the back seat. It's time we showed her how real men live."

Two of the men grabbed Lara by her upper arms. She frantically kicked out at them, screaming. They dragged her towards the Humvee, her body writhing, her legs thrashing about wildly. She fought hard enough that one of the soldiers took a short length of rope and roughly tied up her ankles.

As they tossed her inside the Humvee, Lara choked in desperation and glanced back at the supine body of her friend. She was desperate to not lose sight of him. She saw Lyons say something to one of his men. The boy gleamed as if he'd just been rewarded by his leader. As Lyons turned towards the Humvee, Lara saw two soldiers grab James by the ankles. Together they pulled and dragged his limp body out of the garage and towards the stairs. Lyons's body suddenly filled the door frame, blocking her view. Two men jumped in the front and the engine started. She twisted around to get a glimpse past her captor. The men were dragging James up the staircase.

"What are you going to do with James?" she demanded of Lyons.

With no hesitation, the large man reached across and slapped her with his giant hand. Her face stung and she could taste blood on her lip. "From now on, you don't speak unless we tell you to." His hand dropped to her chest as he cupped a breast through her coat, "Not as much as I was hoping for." Lara winced at his touch but contained her protest, fearing that his wrath would return.

"I wouldn't count on your boyfriend coming to rescue you. He's going to be tied up for awhile," said the driver with a smirk.

Tears ran down her cheeks. Why hadn't they talked about the 'what ifs'? James never coached her on what to do should the worst happen. He'd been so unselfish, so caring, and so careful to keep bad things from her. Had she been able to cope with some of the bad, maybe they would not be in this predicament. Yet, her biggest fear was that Lyons would not keep his word about not hurting James if she went with him.

Lara watched out the window. Rain began to fall. A few droplets hit the window and were elongated by the wind. Darkness hid all landmarks. She had never traveled out this way before. There'd been no reason to. If she managed to escape, could she find her way back? Did she want to go back? Tears rolled down her cheeks.

The Humvee turned into a driveway and slowed as the gate opened. Her heart sank further when she saw the solid, tall security fencing in the beam of the headlights. As the Humvee pulled into the garage, Lara was startled by the bright electrical lights. Almost a year had passed since she'd seen anything brighter than candlelight inside a building. Lyons got out, then reached in to drag her out onto the floor. With both hands and feet tied, she banged her head on the concrete. The blow was enough to briefly disconnect her vision. Her eyes focused in time to see the large door closing behind the second Humvee that had pulled into the next stall. She wanted to ask what they had done with James, but didn't dare.

Before she had time to take in her surroundings, she was dragged by Lyons through a door and into a big room. A strong odor of stale smoke stung her nose. She turned her head at the sound of several heavy boots to find seven men surrounding her. Each man had his eyes fixed on her. They made jokes about who'd go first. She was in such terror and she searched all around her for somewhere to escape to. "Please don't let this be happening," she prayed.

She breathed a sigh of relief when the soldiers removed their body armor, dumped it in a big pile in a corner, and moved to a small table on which one man had dropped a stack of dark green packages. From pieces of their conversations, she learned that they were dinners taken from Mike's house. She realized she was starving, but no one offered her food or water. If they offered, she told herself, she would accept. She resolved that she would do everything she could to postpone her worst fear, and to survive.

"Would one of you assholes make a bed up in the arms room?" demanded Lyons. "And make sure you remove any weapons before we lock her in."

"Can we dress it up like the honeymoon suite?"

"One more remark like that and your helmet becomes her toilet," barked Lyons.

Lara watched the way Lyons was looking at the other men, his anger clearly building. She didn't relish the idea of being locked in a closet, but it was better than being next to him. His anger was untethered and came without warning. Yet no one left his meal to initiate the task. Lyons finally stood, walked over to a door and opened it. From her vantage, Lara could see it was filled with garbage. His gaze was locked on the back side of the door.

"Where in the fuck are the keys?"

Lara noticed a change in his voice, a hint of concern mixed with the anger. The room went completely silent. Everyone stopped eating. Lyons looked around the room. No one had an answer to his question. His face went from concerned to worry.

"Has any one of you been in the weapons closet today?"

One of soldiers spoke up, "Yes, sir, I had to reload my clip after we returned this morning."

"Were there any keys hanging in here then?"

"The whole usual bunch, sir."

Everything went quiet again. Lara could sense that something was terribly wrong. Lyons walked over to a different door and tried opening it. The knob turned in his hand but the door remained tight. Lara could see the outside casing of a deadbolt just above the knob.

Lyons turned to his men, "Somebody fetch me a crowbar. NOW!"

Two soldiers bolted for the door to the garage at the same time, almost tripping over one another. One returned with a large pry bar. He reached out with the heavy tool while trying to stay out of Lyons's reach. Lyons grabbed the bar and tried shoving the narrow tip between the steel door and its steel frame; the space was too small. He made several attempts along every edge of the door, but there was no way to get the tip in far enough to grab without it popping back out. With each attempt, his frustration grew. Finally he threw down the bar and turned towards the others.

"We might be fucked. This room was designed like a safe." He looked towards Lara. "Put her in the garage."

Carter grabbed her by an arm to lift her when Lyons held up a hand. "Wait a minute. Let's keep her in here. If the keys are gone, the garage could be opened from the outside."

Carter asked, "Do you think someone broke in again?"

"I *know* someone broke in." Lyons looked around the room. "Count up all your rounds. We need to know how many we have." He thought for a moment and added, "Take your M-16s off full-auto until we get this door open."

Lara, able to hear everything going on, understood that something out of their control had taken place; someone had somehow taken their keys, one of which was their only way into the closet that held their weapons and ammunition. She didn't know what was going to happen, but she was grateful for the simple fact that a female captive was no longer their focus. The new tension in the air made her feel safer. If she was going to be abused, it wouldn't be soon.

Lyons stooped down and brought his face close to hers. "Can you, little lady," he implored with a viciously sarcastic sneer, "perhaps share with me what's going on here? Do *you* know who's been visiting when we aren't around?"

Lara shook her head. She literally had no clue. Skyler fished somewhere out this way, but he was just a boy. And James had never said anything about going near the refinery. She shook her head again. Lyons raised a hand as if to strike her, but let it drop in disgust. Carter stood before him.

"Sarge, we have a hundred and fifteen rounds not counting your clips."

"That ain't shit," he growled. Then he blurted, "Fuck! Okay, I want someone to watch the monitors at all times tonight, no jacking around. Two men keep watch in the garage, only one sleeping at a time. Whoever has those keys might try to come in that way. And no one, not no one, is to step outside to pee. That door," he pointed at the one leading directly outside, "is to remain shut and locked at all times."

Lyons walked back over to re-inspect the locked door to the ammunitions. He stared at it for several seconds before returning to where Lara lay curled up on her side. Picking her up by an arm, he dragged her over to the bunk beds. Without saying anything, he lifted her with one hand onto an upper bunk, twisting her arm so tight she winced in pain.

The rest of the night was the longest of Lara's life. Throughout, she watched through half-closed eyes as men wandered between the bunks and the monitors, but it didn't seem that any of them slept. Her exhaustion took over and she dozed for short spurts. When awake, her thirst was intolerable, the room so stuffy and dry. She vowed that when the next soldier came within whispering range, she would ask for water. But then she remembered that her state of dehydration made it unnecessary for her to have to pee, something she really didn't want to deal with in this situation. From her bed, she could see some of the men at the table. Most of their talk was hushed, but gradually the isolated words she could hear, combined with the angry outbursts, revealed that they were planning some kind of retaliatory strike, but where and on whom?

Lara laid still and pretended that she slept. Finally, she heard Lyons mention the log barricade. Beneath closed eyelids, Lara envisioned Skyler, there along with Brandy and her family, up on the hill. She heard Lyons say that they would need plenty of gasoline. When were they planning on doing this? In the morning? They hadn't said, but their loud voices told her that they were excited about something. She wished that there was some way to warn Skyler and the others.

By this point, Lara could only surmise that they had passed through the darkest hours. It should be daylight soon if it wasn't already. Her guess was confirmed when all the men got up and began putting their armored vests back on, all except one, who stayed intent on watching the monitors. He was obviously going to be left behind to guard her and the bunker. She prayed that he would leave her alone.

She must have fallen asleep again, because a shout caused her to jerk her head up. The soldier watching the monitors saw something. All six jumped to the desk, straining to see over his shoulder. Several seconds passed as the soldier at the desk fiddled with a controller. He tried magnifying the image without luck. Frustrated, Lyons took the controller from the soldier and made his attempt to zoom in on the area of interest. Whatever it was must have moved within the focal range of the camera, because the soldier in the chair suddenly said, "Sarge, I think he's carrying your rifle."

Chapter 30

James opened his eyes to pure darkness. His mind was clear; he knew where he was and what he needed to do. The alarm on his wrist watch had not gone off yet, but it was close enough. He woke Skyler before gathering the few necessities they needed. They wouldn't be rebuilding the fire that morning; there wasn't time and no need. They had to be in position by first light. Skyler had said that there would be help. He hoped that the boy was correct.

James' wrists were still quite sore, making gripping anything painful; a couple of ribs felt cracked, and his face hurt from the beating. However, he made no excuses. It was imperative that they rescue Lara, and after that, they needed to end the terror brought on by the soldiers. As Lara had put it before, as long as they lived under their shadow, they were waiting to die. Today would be the reckoning, or they would die trying

James started up the ATV while Skyler climbed into the back. Skyler said it would be better to drive it until it ran out and leave it where it stopped, than to leave it at a house they might never return to. The single weapon between the two men was Skyler's bow and his five arrows. The soldiers had taken everything else. Hidden in his distant storage locker, James still had a pistol and some arrows, but there was no time to retrieve any of it. They were going to have to rely on the rifle hidden out by the ponds, and the soldiers' weakened firing power. They just had to outlive the guaranteed onslaught until the bullets were gone.

The ATV slipped through the darkness and over the hill as it headed west. The rain had quit sometime during the night. A few stars were visible between the remaining clouds. Even the moon came out to watch what was about to unfold. As planned, Petar and the others would be somewhere along this stretch, staying off the road, but close enough to hear the engine. Finally, enough moonlight filtered through the clouds for James to kill the lights. The wet road almost glowed with the lunar light reflecting off its surface. Skyler had warned James that there was a chance they could encounter the soldiers on the road—if they found their ammunition missing—and if that happened, they'd have to figure a way to run and hide; without the additional rifle and ammunition, Skyler and James had no chance.

They had traveled three quarters of the way when the engine sputtered. The sky was still dark but the horizon to the east was already showing the arrival of a new day. They rode it out until the small vehicle came to a complete stop. Their need to hurry did not weigh upon them. All the other players needed to be in place before they could proceed. James and Skyler walked the last mile to the cache, Skyler assuring James that the cameras couldn't image this section of road.

"How many others can we expect?"

Skyler looked at his friend, "Don't know for sure, Petar and maybe two others."

"So at best, it sounds like five against seven."

"No, I don't think they'll all be together. Once I show myself, they'll send two or three out looking for me. That's what they did before."

James stayed silent the rest of the way. That's what they did before? What had this kid been up to over the summer? But James kept his questions to himself and trusted Skyler's judgment. The boy had not let him down yet; twice before he'd even saved his life.

When they arrived at the gravel road, two dark figures with rifles stepped out from behind a sign. Instinctively, Skyler had his bow up and drawn. It wasn't until he heard Petar's voice that he lowered the arrow's tip. The man with him was one that James had not met during his only visit to the top of Church Road. Now he knew why. Despite the civilian clothing, James could tell that this man was obviously once a soldier and probably a lifer. His muscular face, stiff stance, and close-cropped haircut, three good indicators. The fact that Petar kept him hidden away made him their ace in the hole. Before they were reintroduced, a third figure stepped out. It was Brent.

"Brent, it's great to see you," Skyler's voice was youthfully bright. "I thought you moved away."

"Tried to, but couldn't find a place as safe as the one I left."

Peter smiled at Brent, "We were happy to welcome Brent and his wife back."

The third man was called John McBride. The moonlight on his scalp showed traces of silvery gray hair on his temples. Like Brent, he was formerly a marine and had been in Iraq during the same time as Brent. During the introductions he added, "I couldn't let Petar and Brent have all the fun."

Skyler looked about for the signpost that marked the position of his last stop here. He moved quickly down into a ditch and brought out two items: the rifle case and a dark metal tube. James took the case from him and opened it up.

Brent looked closely over James's shoulder at the rifle. "That's an M-90 sniper rifle. Where in the hell did you find that?"

James already had it outside the case and had rammed a clip into its base. Skyler looked up at Brent, "In their bunker."

John McBride reached out a hand towards Skyler. The boy placed the metal tube in the man's palm. "Do you know what you have here?" asked John.

"I think it's some kind of missile."

"You're partly right. It's actually a rocket-propelled grenade. The LAW on the side stands for Light Anti-tank Weapon. It's an unguided missile. I've used several of these in the Middle East."

Daylight was increasing by the minute, so Skyler led the group of men across the road and down into a field. He assured them that the camera couldn't see them, but that they were close to being within its field of view. They stopped about sixty yards north of the Douglas Road to reconnoiter. "When I step onto that road, they should be able to see me. Once I work my way back over here, they won't."

"What makes you think they'll come after you?" asked James.

"I'll be carrying that rifle," he took it from James. "They'll want it and this back." He held up the key to their arms locker.

The four men positioned themselves among the dead trees. The plan was that Skyler would come running through the open space between the four men. He expected a Humvee to chase him down into the field. A dip in the terrain stretched the width of the field. It marked a ditch that Skyler would need to jump across. The ditch was barely visible because of the late summer grass. Once Skyler jumped the ditch, the Humvee would be forced to stop. The soldiers would have to climb out if they wanted to catch him.

Once Skyler left the road, James would be the first one that Skyler would run past. The plan required that Skyler drop off the rifle so James would have a weapon. He needed to run past James without the soldiers noticing. That would be the difficult part of the operation.

With everyone in position, Skyler threw his bow over his back and rested the rifle on his shoulder. The sun was just peeking over the mountains to the east. It was now or never.

Chapter 31

"Where's this road?" asked Lyons.

"It's about a half mile north of here. Douglas Road. Only the last two hundred yards on this end is drivable," answered Carter.

"Can you reach this guy?"

"No problem. He's about two minutes from being in my hands."

"Take someone with you and if he runs, wound him. I want my gun, the key to this room, and I want him alive!"

Carter tapped another soldier, Baxter, on the shoulder to come with him. It was Baxter who had dropped the civilian with the rifle the previous morning, saving Carter the trouble. Carter often referred to Baxter as his wing man. Both men grabbed their weapons and ran into the garage.

Lyons looked back at the monitors. His stare intensified as the figure moved within the focal range. "It looks like a boy! Somebody drag that bitch over here."

Lara had been following the actions within the bunker with interest, but from her position she could not see the monitors. When Lyons said it was a boy, a wave of fear swept over her. Two soldiers grabbed her by the legs and upper arms, and pulled her off the bunk. She didn't resist. She wanted to see the monitor for herself. She needed to know. When they set her on her feet close to Lyons, he reached out his arm and grabbed the back of her neck. He directed her face like she was a puppet.

"Who in the fuck is this kid?"

Lara looked at the image closely. It was grainy and lacked the sharpness of a photograph, but there was no mistaking his shape and the bow slung over his back. However much she didn't—and yet did—want it to be him, it was Skyler. Her dry mouth had trouble forming words.

"Well, who is it?"

"I, uh, I don't know." Her lie came easily and somehow she must have sounded convincing, as Lyons didn't push it further. Either way, she was sure her affirmation or denial would bring no mercy from this man. She watched as Skyler boldly walked up the middle of the road. God, she thought, did he not have a clue as to where he was or what was about to happen? On another monitor, she watched a Humvee pass by at a high speed and disappear again. When she looked back at the first monitor, Skyler had started to run off the road into a field. She wanted to turn her head away, to block out what was certain to happen next. But she couldn't. Then Skyler disappeared from the camera's range. Next, the Humvee appeared on the monitor, near the point where Skyler disappeared from the screen; it turned off into the field and quickly disappeared from view as it raced after him.

"That should teach that little shit to sneak in here." He turned towards Lara, his sarcastic smile returned. "If you're good to me, maybe I'll let you watch what we do to him."

Tears erupted from her eyes and she nearly fainted. The two soldiers caught her weight but when they tried to let go, she would start to fall over. Her hunger, fear, exhaustion and mental torture had taken the last bit of physical strength from her. Lara's world had come apart in the last twenty-four hours and was about to get worse, and all the bad things took over her mind. Would she have to watch as James and Skyler were murdered? And then suffer the same fate, only worse, as it would likely not come until she'd been abused beyond belief. Lara turned her head away from the horrible man not wanting to see his face anymore.

"Toss her back on the bunk. I'll deal with her when I'm through with this kid."

The men dragged her back to the bunk, tossing her on a lower one this time. Lyons stayed focused on the monitor for several more minutes. He said nothing. His gaze was finally rewarded by movement on the screen. He stood as he exclaimed, "Here they come."

All five soldiers watched with the exact same stares as the Humvee disappeared from one screen and reappeared on another. Finally, just as it loomed large on the last monitor, it dropped from sight when it turned onto the road leading in to their compound. Lyons moved away from his chair and walked over to the door leading into the garage.

Two minutes passed before Lara heard the sound of a motor reeling the large door open. Were they going to force her to witness their savagery? She laid there not wanting to live anymore but couldn't keep from watching as Lyons's large body filled the door's framework. The other four fell in behind him trying to get a look.

Suddenly, gunfire erupted from within the garage. Lyons spun around and fought to remove himself from the doorway. The other four men went down like bowling pins as the big man pushed through them. Bullets stabbed at the pile of men. More bullets missed their marks and impacted the cinder block walls. As quickly as it had started, the shooting suddenly stopped. Lara, huddled on the bunk, brought her hands from where they had covered her ears and heard the Humvee exit the garage and drive away.

Chaos followed. All five men scrambled for their weapons. Two soldiers had taken bullets to their torsos but were protected by their armor. Lyons's leg was bleeding but he ignored it, a minor injury. He grabbed a rifle, shouting, "I want all four of you in that Humvee now! I want those bastards brought down!"

Lara watched through half-covered eyes: the four soldiers moved in rapid unison through the door. She heard the engine start seconds after they disappeared from her view. Then she followed Lyons's movements as he launched back to the monitors to watch the progress of the second vehicle. The patch of blood on his pant leg slowly grew. She watched him intently, but he didn't even seem to remember she was there. But someone knew she was here, she told herself in a moment of gladness, someone had tried to rescue her. Lyons continued to watch as the progress of the Humvees moved from one monitor to the other. Lara heard the big man bark remarks to no one about the chase. Suddenly his excitement became elevated and he turned to Lara.

"Hey. Those stupid friends of yours think they can make a stand against trained soldiers." He turned his focus again to the monitor. Suddenly Lara saw his expression change to horror. He pulled a radio from his belt and just as he brought it up to his mouth, he was jolted off balance. The bunker shook as if someone had hit the building with a large hammer. The big man pulled himself back up and held the radio near his face as he crouched over the scene on the monitor. Finally he stood his full height, dropped the radio to the floor, and began walking towards her.

Chapter 32

Skyler cut across the field towards the road. The grass was soaking wet from the previous night's rain and his pace was slowed with each step as his pant legs got heavier and heavier. But he kept moving. He stopped once more to look back before stepping onto the asphalt. The field behind him appeared vacant, just as it should. He was counting on someone watching the monitors. It was a necessary part of his plan. He knew that once they saw the long rifle, the lure, they wouldn't hesitate to come after him. It was the catalyst that would speed up the process of getting Lara back.

Skyler hadn't taken but forty steps on the road before he heard the distant roar of the engine almost a mile away. A wave of fear swept over him. He fought back the urge to run. Timing was everything. His plan relied on the men, in their Humvee, chasing him in and out of the camera's view, but ultimately out of it. So Skyler kept a normal pace, acting as if he was unaware that soldiers were on their way to intercept him, as if he was unaware of the cameras. It was all part of the show for whoever was watching the monitors.

When Skyler could finally see the vehicle, it was travelling faster than he'd expected, but it was obvious they'd seen him. He quickly altered his direction, left the road, and sprinted out across the field. As he ran past James' position, he tossed him the rifle without breaking stride. The roar of the Humvee's engine became even louder when the vehicle turned down Douglas. Seconds later, it left the asphalt to continue its pursuit through the field. Skyler ran for and leapt across the small ditch without slowing. His feet almost slipped out from under him as he landed on the wet grass. He heard the Humvee skid to a stop. The driver must have seen the depression in the terrain and knew the ditch would be too deep for the chassis. A door slammed shut; the Humvee had stopped right where he wanted it to. Skyler kept running, trusting that the others would protect him now. His life was in their hands.

He glanced once over his shoulder. A soldier with a rifle had dropped to his knee. He heard the loud blast of a shotgun and dove to the ground. But the shot wasn't directed at him. A second loud crack followed the blast. Skyler raised his head to look back at what had taken place. James stood up from behind a dead tree, the M-90 in his hands. He'd been positioned on the driver's side of the vehicle. At the edge of the ditch lay the crumpled form of a soldier. That had been from the first shot Skyler had heard. John McBride was walking towards that body. The barrel of his shotgun pointed at the unmoving mass. Even from this distance, Skyler could see only blood where the man's head should have been. Someone's aim was true. That soldier would not be harming anyone ever again.

James edged closer to the Humvee, rifle reloaded and pointed. The driver was still behind the wheel, but as he neared, James saw his head slumped forward, blood and bits of human tissue covering the dash, windows and roof of the cab. James had fired the second shot through the door's window. Skyler, observing all this from his closing distance, felt a twinge of pride. He knew how James felt about taking another's life and had worried that James might have hesitated. Had he not shot the driver so quickly, the driver could have radioed a warning back to the bunker.

"We need to hurry or they'll be suspicious!" called out Petar.

McBride immediately began undressing the soldier on the ground. James had already pulled the driver from his seat and was doing the same. Brent and John were chosen to don the uniforms and ride in the front. They quickly stripped down and dressed in the fatigues and body armor. Skyler saw the name patch on the shirt McBride had put on. That dead solider was Carter, one Skyler remembered coming face to face with but who he knew was not missing any buttons. The shirt that Brent wore read 'Baxter' above the pocket. Skyler quickly checked that uniform.

Before climbing into the Humvee, James took a hard look at the men who had come to help. They didn't really know him or Lara, and they'd been offered no promises of success or pay-back, or even food, yet they still came. He was aware that while his primary goal was to get Lara back, they all shared a common goal to end the threat of the soldiers. James took one last look at the two bodies lying in the field recognizing there was no other way to achieve that common goal, but hating that it had to come down to this.

Since they couldn't be sure how much detail the cameras could pick up, it was necessary that two people were in the front seats of the Humvee going back. McBride would do the driving; his experience handling the vehicle would keep any viewer from getting suspicious. It was important that they maintain a speed that would be expected of the returning vehicle. Not too slow and not too fast. Petar, James and Skyler would stay hidden behind the front seats. James was anxious to get going, fearing that they'd spent too much time in the field, and that the last five soldiers could be waiting in ambush. They drove in silence, each one alone with his own thoughts, but not a one could know what to expect until they were inside the gate.

Shortly after making the last turn, Skyler told McBride to stop the vehicle: the cameras were too high up to see anyone this close to the storage tanks, and he and James got out. The other three would continue on towards the bunker with the Humvee. They would need the element of surprise. Both front door windows had been shattered when James had shot the driver. Once the Humvee pulled up to the bunker, it wouldn't take someone long to get suspicious.

As the Humvee passed through the gate, Skyler and James ran close along the outside of the fence. Speed was essential if they were going to rescue Lara. Their goal was to position themselves in the dead thicket just across from the bunker's doors. James still carried the M-90 even though its powerful scope wasn't intended for close combat. He could have swapped it for Carter's M-16, but chose not to. Skyler had faith that his friend knew what he was doing.

They were close to the gap under the fence when the Humvee disappeared into the garage. Skyler led James further into the dead brush just before rifle-fire erupted from the garage. Who had seen whom first? James and Skyler instinctively flattened to the ground. James moved the rifle out in front of him and placed the scope to his right eye. At this range, a human head would fill the scope's view. Shooting a moving target would be nearly impossible. There was no sign of any soldiers outside the bunker. They heard maybe twenty shots before they saw the Humvee flying back out in reverse. It sped down the drive and back out through the gate. James and Skyler waited for the next move from the remaining soldiers; with hope there were fewer than the five he knew had remained behind or at least some werewounded.

Less than a minute passed before four soldiers ran out and jumped in the other Humvee. Even at this close range, James could see blood on some of their clothing. James held back from firing at them. Brent said he'd had a plan if they gave chase, and they trusted that Brent would keep those four from returning. Shooting at them now would have forced them to take shelter in the bunker, and that wouldn't help them get Lara back. The second Humvee quickly backed out and sped away in pursuit. There was only one soldier unaccounted for.

With the fence between them and the bunker, James kept his rifle aimed at the door. In truth, they didn't know if Lara was still alive or if she was even in the bunker. They only knew that there was one soldier who hadn't come out yet. Had the others killed or wounded him? If he was dead, why hadn't Lara come out—unless she wasn't there at all or, the unthinkable, dead? There were too many unanswered questions. Just then, they heard an explosion. It came from out by the main road. But they didn't just hear it; they felt it reverberate through the ground underneath them. Skyler looked at James hoping his friend had some knowledge of its source.

"Did the soldiers carry any rockets in their Humvees?" James asked Skyler, seeming as in-the-dark as his younger companion.

"I don't know."

"Christ, what do we do now? Can we afford to wait and see which Humvee returns?"

Skyler only needed a second to think. "No, we need to go in now." He stood and pulled the bow from his back. "Follow me. We're going under the fence."

They moved quickly. Skyler led him to the depression that he had filled with dead sticks and twigs. They feverishly cleared the gap and enlarged the opening. Within thirty seconds, Skyler was under the fence and waiting for his friend. James started by passing the rifle through first. The boy bent down to pick it up when he saw James's face change. He turned around to see the door of the bunker open. Skyler quickly stood and stepped in front of James. They both froze when they saw Lyons standing in the doorway. His large arm clenched tightly around Lara's neck. He held a pistol in his other hand with the barrel pressed against her skull. The only reason they knew she was alive was her eyes; they were moving back and forth, frantic and intensely afraid.

"So you're the little shit that's caused me all these problems!"

Skyler needed to stall. His bow was in his hand but his arrow undrawn. How could he shoot with Lyons using Lara's body as his shield? Her arms appeared to be tied behind her, and Skyler could see the rope around her ankles. He was sure that the big man had not seen James yet. "If you let her go," shouted Skyler, "we'll let you and your men leave."

"You'll let me leave? That's mighty nice of you!" Lyons said sarcastically. "What if I don't want to leave? In fact, how 'bout I trade her for you? I'd get much more pleasure killing you than her. And I know how valuable she is to you all."

Skyler didn't know what to say. He couldn't look to see if James was able to get into a position without being detected. He needed more time. Lara's small frame was a poor shield for such a large man. Could James get a shot at him without the risk of hitting Lara? Would he even attempt it? He finally said, "OK, if you let her go, you can have me."

"Then start walking over here boy."

Skyler knew the score, knew there wasn't going to be a trade. He still held his bow and marveled that the soldier hadn't demanded he drop it. Skyler moved closer towards the bunker and stopped. "There's something I need to know."

"Oh yeah? And what's that?"

"My mother was killed the day before the storm hit. I'm looking for the person that did it."

"Why in fuck are you asking me? Do I look like a psychic?" Lyons gave a malicious snort.

"She was wearing a long red coat the day she died. I found her lying in the street, her body frozen in the ice and snow. Next to her hand was a button from a uniform like yours."

"Boy, this is your lucky day. I remember her all too well. If she'd cooperated, I might have let her go!" He laughed again, almost as a dare.

At that second, a Humvee came racing back in through the gate. Everyone's attention was drawn to the sight and sound. Were these the soldiers or his friends? Running was not an option. Lyons pressed the pistol even harder against Lara's head, as if it afforded him more protection, and she cried out in anguish. Lyons kicked her quiet. A cloud of dust trailed behind the moving vehicle, and as soon as the driver saw the scene in front of the bunker, the Humvee skidded to a stop, dust engulfing the body of the huge vehicle. The rumble of the engine went silent. Through the windshield, Skyler couldn't tell who was inside. And while all eyes seemed to be on the Humvee, he desperately hoped James had kept his sights on Lyons. The driver's door opened and a lone soldier stepped out, staying behind the door. Finally, Skyler heard a familiar voice. It was McBride.

"There's more soldiers headed this way. We heard helicopters in the distance!"

All went silent, as if everyone listened to see if McBride was telling the truth. Skyler heard it too, there was a distant whup-whup-whup of rotor blades slicing through the air. Lyons's head jerked upwards. The noise seemed to Skyler to be coming from all directions, with perhaps more than one helicopter closing in on the refinery. However many, they were coming closer at a fast pace. He turned back towards Lyons. He would have thought that the man would have been glad to hear the sound of reinforcements, but by the look on his face, he wasn't. He'd lost that sarcastic grin and now had an expression filled with the weight of worry. The noise of the approaching engines, clearly more than one aircraft now, was becoming deafening.

McBride yelled to Skyler, "We need to leave NOW!"

Skyler couldn't budge. He was at the place he vowed to reach: standing in front of his mother's murderer. The hatred he felt for this man before him was unmeasureable. And what about Lara? Had they gone this far for nothing? No, he couldn't leave now, and he knew James wouldn't leave either. If this stand-off didn't end soon, they would all die.

A helicopter came into view and rapidly descended. It landed at the opening of the drive, completely blocking their access to the road. No sooner had its wheels touched the ground than soldiers in tan-colored fatigues were jumping out and running, weapons drawn. A smaller helicopter appeared over the tanks. It was an Apache gunship. It swung a wide arc as if it was sizing up the situation. The pilot kept its arsenal aimed at the area in front of the bunker. Lyons only briefly looked up. Why wasn't he waving them in, Skyler wondered? Two large double-rotor Chinooks appeared next and circled the refinery at a distance. They also appeared to be looking for a place to land. Skyler looked past the gate and could count at least ten soldiers coming their way. He saw McBride reach back inside the Humvee. The gate rolled shut before the soldiers could reach it. This would buy them a few minutes but not more than that. Skyler had to do something soon. It felt like ending this deadlock was all on his shoulders.

Lyons looked towards the Apache Helicopter and said, "It looks like you are standing between the army and that big tank of gasoline, gentleman. I wonder who's going to win this fight."

James glanced up at the tank. Was that why the military brought the two large Chinooks? James wondered. Was there still a supply of gasoline here? James, desperate just to end this stalemate and get Lara back, shook his head in scorn. It wasn't human life, it wasn't stopping bad men from getting worse, it all came down to the need for gasoline. The same thing that had brought civilization to its knees was now being sought by what remained of the military. Of course, James continued thinking this explained why the soldiers had been left here through the atrocious winter. Why else? James looked at the heavy chain link fencing that stretched from tank to tank and saw that it shielded the large tank in the center.

Skyler moved closer towards Lyons. He fit his arrow's nock onto the string as he walked. He needed to force Lyons into reacting, and was gratified when he saw Lyons register what Skyler was up to and swing his pistol towards the boy. Skyler dove to the side at the same second he heard the shot. He made a complete roll and landed on his feet, his arrow drawn before his feet were planted. The big man had released his grip and had dropped Lara. His right hand still held the pistol but for some reason he was unable to raise it. And then Skyler saw the reason: the distraction had given James the shot he needed. The single bullet had shattered the big man's right shoulder. Lara lay on the ground at his feet. Undaunted and only delayed for a moment, Lyons switched the pistol to his good hand and raised it towards the boy. Skyler released his arrow without the slightest remorse. Lyons was still raising his left arm when the arrow pierced his right eye and exited out the back of his skull. Almost instantly, the large man crumpled to the ground.

Skyler lowered his bow. The man that had taken his mother's life now lay dead. Skyler felt a raw sense of agony and relief. He knew why he'd killed Lyons, but why had Lyons killed his mother? She would never have committed any act worthy of such a punishment. McBride stepped close enough to the body to kick Lyons's weapon away. The once threatening soldier was no longer moving. He would not cause any more harm. Skyler and John simultaneously moved towards Lara, weak but seemingly unharmed. They untied her bonds. At that moment, James rushed up and pulled Lara into a hug. She flung both arms around his neck, then reached out to bring Skyler into the embrace.

"I hate to say this," interrupted McBride, "but we're toast unless we can do something that will make them leave!" He pointed at the helicopters.

The soldiers had halted at the gate and all ten rifles were directed in their direction. For now, the Humvee shielded them.

Skyler stood up and reached into his pocket. Pulling out a key, he ran inside the bunker. Seconds seemed like minutes before he reappeared with another metal tube.

McBride looked at the weapon as if it were a cruel joke. "We can't fight against them with one rocket."

"No, but we can get rid of what they want," shouted James, who understood Skyler's thinking. The gunship's noise was louder now that it had picked a stationary position, its large guns directed at the four people on the ground. James ran into the garage and came out with a long steel cable that had hooks on each end. He ran towards the Humvee and climbed into the driver's seat. The gunship shifted its position to follow him. The other three watched as James backed the vehicle up to the tightly woven steel net. James stepped out with the cable in hand.

"Get Lara under the fence and out of here!" he yelled as he ran towards the rear of the vehicle.

Skyler could see that he was going to try to pull the protective fence free. He nodded his approval and, with McBride, turned his attention to Lara. They got her to her feet and ran towards the gap under the fence. The gunship shifted its position again trying to decide on which target to follow. James connected the Humvee to the protective net with the cable before hopping into the driver's seat. All four tires spun as the machine lurched forward and the cable pulled tight. The steel netting stretched but did not give. James backed up a second time and repeated the process. Once again, the net stretched out but the sides stayed attached to the outside tanks.

The pilot of the gunship must have deduced what James was attempting, as the helicopter swung around and took aim on the vehicles cab. The same second the pilot depressed the trigger that fired the Gatling gun, James launched the Humvee in reverse. Large armor-piercing projectiles shattered the engine compartment. The Humvee stopped dead in its tracks.

James flew out the door as the gunship raked the entire vehicle with a barrage of heavy fire. The Humvee danced as it was pounded by the heavy bullets. The gunship's attack sparked small weapons fire from the soldiers lined up at the gate. They directed their bullets at James and McBride.

Skyler was on the opposite side of the fence pulling Lara through the opening when the bullets went zinging past his friends. He saw McBride run back to the bunker and pick up the rocket. As he led Lara into the forest of dead trees, he couldn't help but fear that they just saw James for the last time.

McBride grabbed the M-72 without stopping. Under a hail of bullets, he ran back across the drive towards the fence. A bullet impacted against the body armor he still wore, sending him rolling across the gravel. James ran toward him but McBride was back on his feet before he arrived.

"Get under the fence, now!" he shouted at James.

James dove into the depression. McBride curled down alongside him to shield him from the hail of bullets; he took two more to the back. The gunship swung around over the tanks and took aim at the two men. By now, the soldiers had broken through the gate and were less than sixty yards away. A burst of small explosions erupted around James and McBride. The Apache had fired on them. The bullets weren't aimed to kill, only to stop them from leaving.

McBride pushed the M-72 under the fence. He was going under next, regardless of the threat. James grabbed his arm and pulled him through just as the ground under the fence danced like boiling water. McBride grabbed the rocket, extended its barrel and stood to aim over the fence. The Apache no longer hovered over the tanks. It had descended and moved over the roof of the bunker. It was sitting stationary with its guns aimed directly at the two men. McBride didn't hesitate. He pulled the trigger. The rocket shot out of the tube, its vapor trail like a rope linking the two men to the Apache. A shot came from the Apache only a millisecond later but went astray when the machine was jerked to the side in an attempt to dodge the unguided missile. The rocket-propelled grenade missed the fuselage and impacted with the tail rotor, exploding it. The gunship spun out of control as it sprayed its bullets in a full spiral.

James and McBride stayed only long enough to see the rocket impact the tail. They ran through the thicket following Skyler and Lara's path. The un-aimed barrage of projectiles could be heard piercing the dead forest around them. Tree limbs, and even whole trunks, were falling like matchsticks. The barrage continued in an arc until they heard the distinctive sound of the projectiles meeting metal. The outer storage tanks took the first few hits. Then, one of the Apache's large blades connected with the steel netting, increasing the speed of the fuselage's rotation. In less than a second, the helicopter spun about facing away from its original target. As the Apache fell, the stream of projectiles continued in an upward circle through the steel netting and impacted the one full tank.

James and John stopped when they heard the helicopter crash against the roof of the bunker, pausing long enough to witness the flames form. The center tank had a string of holes that looked like a giant sewing machine ran a stitch up its side, but these holes bled fire, not thread. McBride grabbed James's arm to pull him from his trance. They ran as hard as they could through the thicket. A giant slow-motion whoosh signaled that the wall of the tank had burst open. A wave of burning gasoline swept over the protective berm. The Apache was still rolling off the bunker's roof as the wall of flames engulfed it. The soldiers trapped by the fence had nowhere to escape; they were hit by a tsunami of fire the same instant their helicopter was swallowed by the wave of burning gasoline. The sudden explosion of hot air nearly knocked the two men down. Dead trees snapped like toothpicks as heated wind preceded the liquid inferno. A wall of flame passed through the fence into the dead thicket, the flames intensified by the ignition of the dry timber. James and McBride could feel the heat growing behind them. They didn't stop running.

Neither man knew where they were going. They followed the signs left by Skyler and Lara. Broken limbs provided a gap that guided their way. James stopped to catch his breath and ask McBride one question: "What happened to Petar and Brent?"

"I don't know," panted John. "I had them get out when we saw the helicopters coming in, but I don't know if they got away in time."

As they ran, the gap between them and the flames increased. The roar of the fire dissipated as the fuel quickly burned off. They heard the distant rotor thunder as the big Chinooks headed back in the direction that they'd come. Securing and retrieving the gasoline had been their mission. With their objective now obliterated, they would return failures—that is if they had enough fuel to get them that far.

James's fatigue was now showing. McBride had to urge him to keep moving. They stumbled through an endless sea of deadwood not knowing where they'd come out. What seemed like an eternity was only a half hour before they finally fell out onto a gravel road.

James recognized this place. It was where they'd all met earlier that morning. He knew the way home from here.

James jerked to a halt as a soldier appeared out of nowhere. Even McBride was alarmed at the sight of the armor-clad man carrying an M-16. Having dropped their weapons at the fence, neither of them possessed any weapon to fight back with. Had they survived the fight only to have it end here?

Then Petar and Skyler stepped out from behind the large sign. The soldier raised his hand to lift his sunglasses. A sense of relief swept over them. It was Brent, and he had a grin as wide as the road. Lara edged out next, keeping both hands on the sign for support. She was so wobbly that James held up his hand for her to stay put. He raced over to embrace his friend. This is what they'd come together for. Lara was alive, and the soldiers were no longer a threat. The one-day war was over. It was time to start that long walk home.